THE SUMMER THAT RUINED EVERYTHING

S. T. BELL

This book is a work of fiction. The story, all names, characters, and incidents portrayed in this production are fictitious. No identification with actual persons (living or deceased), places, business establishments, or products is intended or should be inferred. Any actual businesses referred to are done without permission and for historical accuracy.

For Linda, so she'll stop saying, "You really should publish this."

Thanks for being my original and most loyal fan.

You must burn yourself in your own flame: how could you become new if you had not first become ashes!

— FREDERICH NIETZSCHE, *ALSO SPRACH ZARATHUSTRA*

JUNE 1963

CHAPTER 1

*C*al walked out past the high tide line. He kicked off his loafers, letting his feet sink into the moist, crumbly sand that had been smoothed by the ebbing waters. The ocean was calm, the tiny waves glittering under the near-full moon.

He wished it was quiet, so that he could hear the water lapping at the sand. It helped him think.

Instead, the gentle peace he sought was drowned out by the noise pouring out of the beachfront mansion behind him. His parents had complained throughout the afternoon and evening — polite dinner conversation for once impossible, for which Cal was actually grateful — about the music and raucous party noise next door.

Cal didn't think it was that bad from inside the house, but out here...sound traveled on the beach, and the party could probably be heard for a mile. Despite the fact that it had been going on all day, it didn't show signs of letting up.

He wondered if his father would follow through on his threats to call the police. Maybe he already had. Maybe any second, the noise would cut out as everyone left to go their own way into the Westerly night.

At least the music was decent. Cal recognized the song currently playing, mouthing the words. It was something he listened to at school, a band out of England with what his mother would call *unkempt* shaggy hair, that people were going crazy for. It would never be considered appropriate at home.

He closed his eyes and wished he were back at school. *Only three months of this prison*, he thought, and then he could be himself again. Or, as much himself as he could ever actually be, anyway.

"Hey."

Cal froze at the sound of the voice behind him.

"Hey, you." The voice came again, brash and intrusive.

He turned very slightly, trying to communicate that he wanted to be left alone. "Can I help you?" he asked.

"Turn around, would you? I'm not gonna talk to someone's back."

"You don't have to talk at all," Cal muttered, but he turned. A lean figure, cast into silhouette by the bright lights of the house behind him, stood about ten feet away. He had a bottle of something in one hand, dangling towards the sand. The other hand was twisting at a thread on the hooded sweater he was wearing. The bill of a baseball cap threw a shadow on his face.

"Fuck me, you're gorgeous," he said.

Cal blinked, and then looked around, relieved to see the beach was deserted but for them.

"You shouldn't say things like that," Cal said quietly.

"What, that you're gorgeous? Why? It's a fucking fact."

Again, Cal glanced around. The guy wasn't speaking softly, that was for sure. He felt his cheeks heat at the compliment, one that was nice to hear, even if it shouldn't be spoken out loud. He knew he was attractive: tall, blond, golden skin, symmetrical features. But it was rare that someone actually said it to him.

"Well...thanks," he said, keeping his voice pitched low. "But I'm not...I'm not—"

"Me neither. I can still think you're gorgeous, can't I?"

"Would you stop saying that?" Cal said, exasperation in his tone.

"I like that it makes you blush," the guy said, laughing. "Makes you adorable on top of being gorgeous."

"How did you know I was blushing? There's not enough light out here to see color." There wasn't even enough light to see the guy's face under his cap. All Cal could see was his thin frame, and the long fingers playing with the damned drawstring.

"Well, I didn't know, but I do now. Gorgeous." The guy snickered. "What's your name, Gorgeous? Or I could just keep calling you that."

"It's Calloway," said Cal. He glanced up at his darkened house, wondering if he could make a run for it.

"Calloway? Jesus Christ, that's a heavy name. I need two fucking hands to lift it off the ground. You got a nickname, Calloway?"

"People called me Cal when I was a kid, but that stopped when I went away to school."

"Why?"

"Nicknames are for kids."

"If you were in school, you were still a kid," the guy pointed out.

Cal stared at him a moment. "I haven't been a kid for a very long time," he said.

"That's sad, Cal. You should always be a kid, at least a little." The guy swung the bottle up to his mouth, tipped it

5

back, and then dropped it down again, the liquid sloshing inside. "How come you're not at the party, Cal?"

"Oh. I wasn't invited," Cal said.

"Everyone's invited."

"How do you know?"

"It's my party." The guy stepped forward, stuck his hand out, and tipped his head back, allowing the moonlight to suddenly illuminate his face. "I'm Jack."

Holy shit. He certainly was. The face that grinned up at him was the same face he gazed at for hours in the magazines he kept under the floorboard in his room at college, the ones he'd painfully tossed in the dumpster when he came home for the summer, because having them here — and leaving them there — was too much of a risk.

This was none other than Jack Francis, the movie star.

The guy had splashed onto the scene the previous summer and released three hit movies in a row. The studios loved him, the audiences loved him, and he was lined up for more. Cal had fallen head over heels with his dark curls and high cheekbones when he'd seen the first film last fall.

And now he was standing here with his hand outstretched, introducing himself as *Jack* and waiting for Cal to actually fucking touch him.

And he thinks you're gorgeous.

"Not a hand shaker?" he asked, waving his hand around.

"Sorry," Cal said. He reached out, fumbled the grip for a second, and finally got it right, shaking Jack's hand firmly. The guy's fingers were cool and slim in his giant palm.

"Why don't you come up now? There's plenty to drink. And other things, if you're interested." Jack took off his cap and shook his hair out. "Probably gonna go all night, so you're not too late."

Cal fastened on his eyes, which were gleaming in the

moonlight. The guy was definitely a little drunk, but seemed clear and coherent enough.

"I don't think so," he said. "But maybe another time."

"Oh. Sure. I mean, this party will probably last through the weekend, anyway. You could come tomorrow."

If Cal didn't know better, he'd think Jack sounded disappointed.

"Yeah, maybe," he said, knowing it would never happen. At school, sure, he'd party. Here...he couldn't risk it. "I should go in," he said, waving up towards his house.

"That where you live?" Jack asked.

Cal nodded.

"Cool, we're neighbors. Have a drink with me before you go, neighbor."

Jack held out the bottle. After a moment of hesitation, Cal took it. He tipped it back and took a long swallow. *Bourbon.* It burned its way down his throat and into his chest, and he coughed before handing it back.

"Thanks," he said.

Jack took a swallow of his own, and then grinned. "Now you *have* to come to one of my parties. Since we've practically kissed." He gestured at the bottle and wiggled his eyebrows.

Cal let out a short laugh, and then turned it into another cough.

"I have to go," he said. "It was nice to meet you."

He started to back away, and then turned and plowed up the beach.

"Nice to meet you too, Gorgeous," Jack called.

Cal blushed his way up the wooden staircase to the back lawn and got all the way into the house, where he leaned up against the back door, gasping for breath, before he realized.

He'd left his loafers in the sand.

CHAPTER 2

*I*n the morning, Cal crept down the servant's staircase, hoping to make it out the back door before anyone spotted him. He'd rescue his loafers from the approaching high tide, then go for a walk down the beach. If he timed it right, he could return mid-morning, con the housekeeper into feeding him brunch, and disappear until dinner.

It had been his goal from a young age to avoid as much interaction with his parents as he could manage. Sometimes he was successful, sometimes not.

Today, he was unsuccessful.

"Calloway." Judith Buchanan's voice rang out in the rear foyer, and he froze with his hand halfway to the doorknob. Holding in a sigh, he let his hand fall to his side and turned.

"Good morning, Mother." He pasted on a pleasant smile.

She squinted at him from the doorway into the kitchen. "Where are you going? Flora is serving breakfast."

"I was just...stepping outside for a minute," he said. "To check out the weather. It—"

"It's sunny. You can investigate further after our meal.

Come take your place." She waved him towards her, and he ducked his head and complied, edging past her into the kitchen.

Flora nodded at him from the stove, where she was flipping a pancake. An impressive stack rested on a plate beside her.

"Morning, Flora," he said. He swooped up next to her and kissed her on the cheek. Then he lifted the lid off a plate to the side and snatched a piece of bacon.

"Calloway, manners," his mother said. "And where are your shoes?"

Silently, he continued on to the dining room, munching on the bacon and wishing his mother didn't have the power to make him feel like a grade school kid again with just the tone of her voice. He wasn't that young, awkward, kid drowning in shame anymore. At nearly twenty-one, he was an adult. He had been living on his own — sort of — for years. He was going to graduate college next spring and enter the real world. He was Phi Beta Kappa and a Fulbright Scholar. He had made future business contacts at Harvard that would make his father proud if he'd pay attention long enough to be aware of them.

None of that erased the shame, it seemed. He wondered if anything ever would.

He hid a greasy hand behind his back as he circled the end of the table and took his seat, his back to the windows. He'd often wished, as a child, that he could sit facing the windows, be able to see the spectacular view of the ocean beyond, but instead he'd spent every meal of countless summer vacations forced to count the stripes on the wallpaper of the opposite wall. He'd never counted much higher than a hundred before his eyes had crossed and he'd lost his place, so it remained an unsolved mystery to this day.

His father looked up from his newspaper and frowned at Cal over his reading glasses.

"Good morning, Father," Cal said. He picked up his yellow linen napkin and shook it into his lap. Then he poured himself a cup of coffee and held up the blue, gold, and cream porcelain carafe. "Would you like a refill?"

"Yes, fine." Theodore Buchanan dropped his gaze back to the paper. "What are your plans for the day?"

Cal hated this part. Any meal with his parents inevitably included an interrogation: What was he doing? Was it productive? Who would he be with? Who were their parents? What business were they in?

He topped off his father's coffee and set the carafe back on its dish with a *clink*. "Not sure," he said. "I was thinking of getting some air, and then going into town."

His mother strode into the room, followed by Flora, who was carrying two platters. Judith settled into her chair opposite Theodore and snapped her napkin into her lap as Flora set the platters on the table and began to serve up pancakes and bacon.

"I'm having lunch with Alan Richardson at noon," Theodore said. He folded the paper and set it aside. "You can join me."

"A lunch?" Cal asked, soaking his pancakes with syrup. "What for?"

"Include Margie," Judith said. "And I'll join you as well."

"I will," Theodore said, ignoring Cal. "We'll go to the club."

Cal perked up. If they were going to the club, maybe they'd golf, and it wouldn't be a total waste of an afternoon.

"Margie will like that," Judith said. "I'll call her to confirm."

"I need to be there?" Cal asked again.

"Yes, that's the point. It's time for you to develop an

investment portfolio." Theodore smeared butter between his pancakes. "Your trust will be released in August, and you'll need a way to manage that money, make it work for you. You'll want Alan Richardson's firm to do it."

Right. The Trust.

He'd been looking forward to getting his hands on that money for a while. Money meant freedom. Of course, he'd just do whatever he was advised, since the trust wasn't bottomless, but it was a start. Something.

His parents began to discuss the morning news then, and Cal tuned them out, preferring to focus on his meal. When he'd polished off the last piece of bacon and drank the last drops of coffee, he dropped his napkin on his plate and rose from his chair.

They barely registered his *see you at lunch*, and he gratefully slipped away.

He bounded down the staircase to the beach, his feet slapping on the weathered wood. He jumped the last few steps onto the sand and landed with a *whumpf*.

The beach in front of the Buchanan estate, the private stretch that was theirs, was empty. Completely empty. Not a shoe in sight. Cal frowned. He was sure he'd left the loafers just above the high tide line. Tide hadn't yet reached its peak, so they should still be here. Unless—

Cal looked to the east. Fifty yards away, the beach was far less empty. A large group of people were lounging on towels and chairs. A transistor radio played rock and roll music that carried down the beach. Coolers of beverages and food were scattered haphazardly around. A handful of guys were throwing a football.

In the center of it all, sprawled on a mint green plastic lounger, was Jack.

Cal swallowed. Memories of their meeting the night before seemed almost like a dream. A fantasy he'd cooked up

11

while in his bed, his hand down his pants and his breath coming in gasps. That morning, while shaving, he'd decided that the meeting had happened, but he'd imagined the flirting. That part he'd exaggerated in his mind, a wish that would never —and should never — come true.

It seemed his conclusion was likely. At the moment, there were three women hanging off of Jack. He was kissing one in a pink bikini, one in green sat in his lap playing with his curls, while a third, in yellow, sat on the sand at his feet and rested her hand against his thigh. He certainly didn't look like the sort of person who would have been flirting with *Cal*.

Cal wasn't disappointed. It would be ridiculous to be disappointed in something he'd only imagined.

Jack broke the kiss with Pink and looked west, his gaze immediately falling on Cal. He grinned.

"Hey," he shouted, waving.

Cal hesitantly raised a hand and waved back.

"Come on over," Jack called, beckoning with a long, pale arm.

With a short pep talk to himself about not acting like an idiot this time, Cal loped across the sand. Jack watched him approach, still grinning.

Cal was imagining, surely, the way Jack scanned him from head to toe, his gaze lingering a moment on his tanned calves. More wishful thinking.

"Hi," he said, when he reached the group. Several people looked him over, but most ignored him entirely.

Jack whispered something to Pink, and she gracefully stood from his lap. She went to a cooler, pulled out a tall can of Gansett, and crossed to meet Cal. She handed him the can with a smile.

He smiled back, and then, as if it were pre-arranged, Green and Yellow got to their feet and the three girls ran for the ocean. Cal watched them go, and then turned back to Jack.

"Pull up a chair," Jack said, gesturing around.

"I shouldn't," Cal replied. The can of beer was cold in his hand, and he was tempted to drink it and soothe his dry throat. But it was barely nine in the morning.

"Who says?" Jack winked. "Come on, sit down a minute. You're gonna give me a sore neck if I have to keep looking all the fucking way up there."

After another moment's hesitation, Cal dragged a blue plastic chair over from a few feet away and took a seat. He'd stay a minute, like Jack had suggested. He stretched his legs out in front of him and dug his toes into the sand.

"Nice shorts," Jack said.

Cal pulled his heels back and tucked them under the chair. Jack snickered.

"If you're not going to drink that beer, bring it over here," he said.

"Oh. Yeah, sure." Cal extended his arm across the space between them, offering the sweating can.

He expected Jack to take it. Instead, Jack cracked it open, cupped his hands around Cal's, and guided the can up to his lips.

Cal sat, transfixed, as Jack's fingers pressed into his skin, as Jack's Adam's apple worked up and down, as a tiny drop of liquid spilled out the corner of his lips and trickled down his jaw and neck.

Then Jack tipped the can back down and released Cal's hand. He blinked once, his green eyes full of mischief.

"Sorry," he said. "I should have left some for you."

"That's okay," Cal said, his pulse skittering at the sense memory of Jack's hands on his. "It was yours anyhow."

Jack leaned back in his lounger and tipped his head up to the sun, closing his eyes. Cal stared at him, at the way his long limbs stretched across the chair, the way his nose curved just so, the pale expanses of his skin. It was hard to believe, but he was even more beautiful in person than in the magazines Cal had furtively purchased for the past year.

"How was the rest of your night?" Jack asked.

"Last night?" Cal asked, stumbling to catch up as he was pulled from his thoughts. "It was fine. I just went back home."

"Did the music keep you up?"

"No. My parents complained about it at dinner, but I couldn't really hear it from my room."

Jack pushed himself up on one elbow and twisted to look up at the Buchanan mansion. "Where's your room?" he asked.

"West side," Cal said. "Second floor, down at the end."

"Hmmm. So have you lived here all your life?"

"I don't live here," Cal said. "I mean...I'm just here during the summers. I'm at school during the year. Harvard."

Jack let out a low whistle. "Fancy. And smart."

Cal shrugged. He could tell Jack he'd have gotten in on his name alone, even if he weren't smart, but since he was, it wasn't worth it. Besides, from what he'd read in the articles he'd pored over, Jack hadn't gone to college, so he probably wasn't actually impressed.

"But you lived here when you were a kid?" Jack asked.

"Not for a long time. I've been in boarding school since I was twelve." Cal reached down and set the now empty can on the sand beside him. "What about you? What brings you to Rhode Island? Bored with the California beaches or something?"

Jack giggled, and it was a musical sound that had Cal unconsciously leaning forward.

"Mostly," Jack said. "I had a break from shooting this summer and needed to get out of L.A. for a minute. My agent found this place. It's rented through August, in case I decide to stay that long."

Cal's heart sank at the idea that Jack would get bored and leave Westerly, hightail it back to the glitz and glamor of Los Angeles. It was likely, though. He himself was constantly bored here, longing to get back to school for three entire months.

He felt like an opportunity was slipping through his fingers. An opportunity for what, he wasn't sure...but he wanted a chance to find out.

"What do you think? Of the area?" Cal asked.

"I've only been here a couple of days," Jack said, "but from where I'm sitting, it looks promising."

He smiled at Cal, and Cal's pulse began to dance out a rapid two-step again. Okay, Jack was flirting again. Right? Or was Cal imagining this, too?

In his time at Exeter and Harvard, Cal had gotten fairly good at cracking the code of flirting with other men. You had to be careful, not be too obvious. Start slow, move forward in tiny increments. The risks and consequences of being wrong were too high.

Jack was not starting slow...but maybe it was different in Hollywood.

Cal cleared his throat. "It's not so bad," he said. "A little boring, I guess. Stuffy. But the ocean is nice. And there are good restaurants."

"What do you do around here, anyway?" Jack asked.

"Mostly I do what it takes to avoid my parents," Cal said automatically.

Jack laughed, and Cal grinned at him, relaxing into his chair. He stretched his legs out again, letting the sun and the ocean breeze hit them.

"What are they like?" Jack asked.

"A little boring, I guess. Stuffy." Cal smirked, repeating his phrase from earlier, and Jack laughed again.

"They fit in well here, then," he said. "But what is there to do? Besides throw parties?"

"Go out to eat. Golf. Watch television. Go to the cinema. This," Cal said, gesturing around at the beach scene around them. "There are also the beach clubs. A lot of people our age hang out there. I'm usually there a lot, but I'm waiting for more of the summer people to arrive. Most should be in town by this weekend."

"What do the beach clubs have that this beach doesn't?" Jack asked.

"Food and beverage service," Cal said.

Jack pointed at the coolers.

"Service," Cal said, laughing. "People taking your orders and bringing you burgers and whatever."

"I have a cook," Jack said. "You want a burger? She can make you a burger."

"The beach is bigger, and less rocky. It has volleyball courts. Boats to take out. Lifeguards. Sometimes music. You know." Cal shrugged. "It's really just a place to gather."

"Maybe I'll check it out," Jack said.

"You have to be a member." Cal cringed slightly, anticipating the offense that Jack might take at that.

"So I'll become a member."

"You'd need a referral from a current member," Cal said. He cringed again. "And they're kind of stupid about it. Claim to be full sometimes."

"I have pretty good success getting into things," Jack said, a little dryly. "Do you ever get to bring a guest?"

"Sure," Cal said. Jack smiled, looking at him expectantly, and he clued in. "Oh. I could, um...you could come with me sometime. To see if you like it. And I could refer you."

"I'd love that, Cal," Jack said, his voice suddenly honey smooth and pitched a note lower. "It's nice of you to offer."

Cal blushed, and turned away to look out at the ocean,

hoping that he might just look heated from the sun. He heard Jack chuckle softly beside him.

They sat quietly for a time. The radio continued to pump out its tinny guitar riffs and vocals. Cal watched Jack's friends cavorting in the water, having chicken fights and riding the waves. The football game had moved into the water as well. He felt himself relaxing further. As much as he hated being trapped here every summer under his parents' judgmental scrutiny, he did like the ocean, and the way it smoothed out all the rough edges inside him.

Finally, after maybe a half hour, Jack spoke again, breaking the silence.

"So, Cal. You're coming to my party tonight, right?" He cocked his head to the side, his dark curls falling softly across his cheek. "Should be even better than last night."

"Oh, maybe," Cal said. The answer was no, of course not. He could probably sneak out after his parents had retired for the evening, but if word got back to them he'd been at a party like this...no, of course not.

He couldn't. Could he? He wanted to.

"Maybe isn't a yes," Jack said, his lower lip jutting into a tiny pout. "Come on, humor me."

"You seem like you've got a full guest list anyway," Cal said, gesturing around.

"Yeah, well. I know these losers already, I brought them with me from L.A. You're new and interesting." Jack slid his foot across the sand. Cal's breath caught as Jack's toe trailed along the top of his foot. "Besides...you seem to be lacking in shoes at the moment."

Cal's head snapped up from where he was staring at their feet. "I am. Did you take them?"

"For safekeeping," Jack said. "Wouldn't want just anyone to walk away with them."

"Can I have them back?"

"Come to the party tonight and we'll see what kind of deal we can make."

"If I come to the party, you'll return my shoes?" Cal asked.

Jack shrugged one shoulder and pursed his lips. "Guess you'll have to come over and find out."

He stood up from the chair.

"I don't suppose you're wearing a swimsuit under that," he said, flapping a hand in Cal's direction.

"No," Cal said. "I was going for a walk. And I have to meet my parents and their friends at the country club for lunch and a round of golf in a while."

"Too bad." He swiveled on a heel and began to walk backwards toward the water. "Tonight. Come by anytime you hear music. Promise?"

"I…" Cal swallowed. *Fuck it.* "Yeah. I promise."

"Far out," Jack said, grinning broadly. "Can't wait."

Then he turned and ran for the water, his blue swim trunks hanging precariously from his narrow hips. Cal watched as he hit the surf with a splash. He shouted something, and the football sailed through the air. Jack caught it gracefully and then threw it back before wading up to his waist and then diving beneath an incoming wave.

When he popped up, slicking his curls back from his face, one of the girls maneuvered towards him and slung her arms around his neck.

Cal rose, and, with one last look over his shoulder, trudged back up the beach towards his house. He hoped he'd have the guts and the opportunity to fulfill his promise.

He wanted to see Jack again.

CHAPTER 3

*C*al was twelve years old and in his first year of boarding school when he realized he liked boys.

In retrospect, he had always known, but it wasn't until his dorm mates huddled around a contraband Playboy magazine one night, and he found he was more interested in being pressed up against Connor Clooney than he was in the centerfold spread of Diane Hunter, that he admitted it to himself.

Then it was this secret, this thing he pretended didn't exist. He knew he had to hide it, because of the way his father used the word *sissy*, the way his mother would then cross herself and whisper a prayer. He sat silently, staring into his soup during one Christmas dinner, as his mother spoke in false whispers of the son of one of the prominent families in town who had been sent to a "special camp" to be cured of his "madness."

The message was clear: being homosexual was an affliction, something to be ashamed of, to go to great lengths to be rid of, if you could.

Cal tried. He tried to like girls. When he started at Exeter, he decided that he would, no matter what it took. He pretended to enjoy participating in the ogling of the girls from the local high school. He hid magazines with centerfolds in easily discoverable locations, like his desk drawer. He went to the mixers and talked to the girls and tried to find their perfume alluring and their shapes desirable.

But in the dark, he was forced to admit to himself that it wasn't working. He liked boys, and that was that.

It was during his sophomore year that he learned he might not be the only one — at his school, or even in his class. James Grenville was assigned as his lab partner in chemistry. James turned out to be fun, a good conversationalist, smart...and he was adorable, thin with dark hair and large brown eyes.

Cal began to look forward to chemistry above all other classes, and he wasn't stupid: it was because of James. Then one night, while they were holed up in James' room working on a lab report on atomic mass, Cal looked up from his notebook and realized James was staring at him. A few seconds later, he was kissing his first boy, and knew without a doubt that this was worth keeping secret, because he never wanted to give it up.

He made a decision that day. He was going to be the most perfect student and son he could be. He'd follow all the rules, as best he could. He'd do exactly what was expected in every single area...except this one. He hoped that if everything he did was beyond reproach and exactly what everyone else wanted, he could successfully have this one thing for himself.

And no one would need to look close enough to find out.

The rest of his time at Exeter was for furtive exploration. By the time he moved into his dorm at Harvard, he had become an expert at the cautious dance of flirtation, at dating without dating, at having "cover" relationships with girls he could be with in public and take home to his parents.

He'd fancied himself in love a time or two, but nothing seemed to last, and he'd come home for his final summer without any attachments of the heart and prepared for three months of celibacy. It was simply too much of a risk to expose himself so close to home.

THAT EVENING, for the second time that day, Cal snuck down the servants' stairs to the back door. This time, the house was dark and silent. His parents had retired to their rooms after dinner, and he had as well, claiming a headache. Now, it was time to fulfill the promise he'd made earlier. He opened the back door, slipped out quickly, and shut it behind him.

Clutching a bottle of scotch that he'd pilfered from the overstocked liquor cabinet to his chest, Cal leaned up against the door and breathed a sigh of relief. Then he took off across the back lawn, down the stairs to the beach, and cast to Jack's house. Towards the music and the light.

His stomach flipped, knowing he was taking a risk. But it was worth this small thing to see Jack again.

It wasn't that Cal wasn't allowed to go to parties. He was an adult, after all, and could do what he chose. Mostly. His parents wouldn't be upset that he was going out at night, or even that he was helping himself to a bottle of single malt. It was more that this type of party, one that didn't involve acceptable people with acceptable parents, that was loud and maybe wild, that didn't end at a respectable hour, this type of party would draw criticism from Judith and Theodore Buchanan.

He kept to the rock line, where the sand wasn't as deep, to

21

avoid getting it in his shoes. A stiff breeze swept in off the ocean, ruffling his shirt sleeves and hair. From the smell of it, they were in for some rain.

When he reached the stairs up to Jack's lawn, he hesitated. Should he be going up the back like this, or should he have gone around to the front? That would have taken a lot longer, though it would have been more appropriate, and when the Winstons lived here, that's what he would have done. After a minute, however, he began to climb the stairs. Jack hadn't seemed terribly formal.

As he reached the top of the beach stairs and stepped onto the back lawn, his nerves kicked into high gear. They'd simmered the entire time he'd dressed — in tan slacks, a navy blue Oxford shirt, and brown leather shoes, an outfit that took far too long to select — as he'd styled his hair, as he'd left his house. But now was another matter entirely. Each step towards the house, which was brightly lit against the night sky, made his heart beat a little faster and his breath hitch. He could see people moving around in a room to the left. Was Jack one of them?

The back deck wasn't empty, as it had appeared from a distance. Cal came to a halt at the top of the stone steps, realizing that he was intruding on something. A guy and a girl were tangled up on a wooden lounger just to his left, and they were doing more than just kissing. They'd been obscured by shadows on his way up, but now that he was close...

The girl lifted her head. "Hey," she said.

Cal averted his eyes and cleared his throat. "Hi," he said. "I'm just — sorry, I didn't —"

"You were on the beach this morning, right?" she asked. She pushed up, untangled herself from the guy, straightened her blouse, and got to her feet. The guy made a sound of protest, and she ignored him. "You were talking to Jack."

"Yes," Cal said. Now that he had a better look, he recognized her as the girl in the yellow bikini.

She held out her hand, bracelets jingling up her arm. "I'm Penny."

"Calloway," he replied, shaking her hand.

She hummed. "You're cute, Calloway. How do you know Jack?" she asked.

"I don't. I mean, we met last night." Cal gestured behind him. "I was out for a walk. I live next door. He invited me?"

"Neato. A local. He keeps talking about embracing the locals. Come on in, I'll help you find him."

"Penny…" The guy on the lounger lifted his head.

"I'll be back in a minute, don't flip your wig," she said, rolling her eyes.

She bounced across the patio to the back door, and, with one last apologetic shrug towards the guy, Cal followed.

"That was Grant. Don't worry about him, he's just annoying," she said, grabbing Cal's sleeve and pulling him into the brightly lit house. She pitched her voice higher over the music, which was louder inside. "Last I saw Jack, he was in the kitchen."

Cal let himself be dragged around the corner and into the kitchen. Cans and bottles littered the counters, along with several open bags of potato chips, but aside from one guy who seemed to be passed out in the breakfast nook, the room was empty.

She shrugged. "Okay, maybe the rec room then. You want a beer?"

"Sure," Cal agreed. His nerves were still vibrating under his skin. A drink would help.

She pulled a can of Gansett out of the fridge and handed it to him, and then they moved through the kitchen to the dining room, out across the foyer, and through a large parlor. He was vaguely familiar with the house, since its previous owners had been friends with his parents, but it had been a while since he'd been inside.

The parlor looked like any other formal sitting room he'd seen in any of these beach houses, except for one thing: the stereo and massive speakers set up on and around the coffee table. It was deafening in here, and Cal couldn't help but wince slightly.

Penny noticed. "Too loud?" she shouted. He shook his head, but she dashed over to the stereo, fiddled with some knobs, and the volume decreased several notches, to something more reasonable. He was relieved, knowing the chance of the party being broken up by the cops had just diminished by about half. Penny sighed. "I told Jack he should rent a bunch of smaller systems instead of one big one — put them all over the house, you know — but he's a dummy sometimes."

"My parents have been complaining," Cal said. "Someone might call the cops if you guys keep blasting the music like that with all the windows open."

Her eyes lit up. "Fun," she said, with a giggle. "Come on."

Cal took a moment to digest the idea that having the cops called on you could be fun. He cracked open his beer and took a sip, and then followed her through a set of doors and into a large room full of people.

"There he is," she said, pointing. Cal scanned the area she was indicating and spotted Jack. He was leaning across a pool table, lining up a shot.

Cal's eyes naturally fell to his ass, which was on full display in a pair of snug jeans. His white tee was just as snug, revealing his trim waist and hips. Cal took another gulp of beer to wet his suddenly dry mouth.

Jack drew his cue back and then took his shot. It was good, and when the 8-ball spun into the left corner pocket, he stood up straight and whooped.

"Suck on that, G," he said to the guy on the other side of the table. Then he turned, spotted Cal, and his smirk turned into a full-blown grin.

Cal waved, and Jack tossed his cue onto the table and bounded over.

"You came," he said, laying a hand on Cal's chest.

Then, in a move that had Cal freezing in surprise, he leaned up and kissed the air beside Cal's cheek. Before Cal could process the way it felt to have Jack's cheek sliding against his, he repeated the process on the other side and then rocked back on his heels.

"He likes to pretend he's European," Penny explained from beside him, clearly picking up on Cal's surprise.

"I am European," Jack said. "Well...half."

"What's the other half?" Cal asked.

Jack leaned in close, and Cal could smell sunscreen, salt water, and cigarettes. "Pure New York Jew," he said in a stage whisper. His eyes landed on the bottle of scotch Cal was holding in his non-beer hand. "Hey, that for me?"

"Oh. Yeah," Cal said.

"That's nice of you. You didn't have to."

"Never show up to someone's house empty-handed," Cal said. "That's the rule."

Jack laughed. "Good rule." He took the bottle and examined it, let out a low whistle. "You don't skimp, Harvard, I'll give you that."

Then he grabbed Cal's hand and walked backward, pulling Cal with him.

"Do you play pool?" he asked.

"Yeah, I do," Cal said.

"I just won a game, so the table's mine." Jack detoured to a wet bar, released Cal's hand, and set the scotch on a shelf before continuing on to the pool table. "But if you don't wanna play, I'll give it up."

"I'll play," Cal said. He hesitated. "I should warn you, though, I'm —"

"Jack, you got a light?" someone called from a sofa to their left.

Jack dug into his pocket and tossed a slim silver zippo across the room, where it was caught handily.

"Don't klepto that," he called back. "It was a gift from Marlon."

"Brando?" Cal asked automatically. Jack merely winked at him and pulled him to the pool table, where they both picked up a cue and Jack began to rack the balls.

"You want to break?" he asked.

"Sure," said Cal. He looked around the room, at the dozen or so people moving around. "All these people came with you from Los Angeles?"

"Yup." Jack removed the triangle and hung it in its place.

"Are they here the whole summer?"

Jack shrugged. "Probably not. Some of them, maybe. Go ahead."

Cal set the cue ball on the felt and lined up his shot. He drew the cue back and then let it fly. The three and six thunked into the pockets. He glanced up and smiled.

"Guess I'm solids," he said.

Jack raised one eyebrow. "Smooth." Then he set his cue aside and folded his arms across his chest. "What else you got?"

Cal played pool frequently in Cambridge, and he was good. He toyed briefly with the idea of easing up a bit, but the desire to show off in front of Jack won out. He ran the table for a while, sinking three more balls before he missed a trick shot.

He backed away from the table and let Jack take his turn. Jack was good, too, sinking three balls of his own, but Cal cleaned up on his next turn.

Jack bowed his head in respect, then popped back up, tossing his curls out of his eyes. "As winner, you call next game. You want me again, or…"

"I want you," Cal said immediately. Jack grinned, and Cal's stomach clenched, realizing the double entendre he'd just made. He swerved, trying to soften the statement. "I mean...I'll give you a second chance. Maybe it'll go better now that you know what you're up against."

Jack tilted his head to the side, his green eyes sparkling. "Now that I know there's more to you than just a pretty face, you mean?"

"I'll rack, you break this time," Cal said, ducking his head to hide his blush.

They were well matched, and played several games in a row. Cal continued to edge Jack out, but just barely, because he found himself distracted. The first time Jack crossed behind him and trailed a finger along his shoulder blades, he jumped.

"Something wrong?" Jack asked.

"No, nothing," Cal sputtered.

When Jack decided he needed to take a shot from exactly where Cal was standing, he slid up beside Cal and nudged him with his hip. Cal couldn't resist standing his ground for a moment, letting Jack press up against him, all lean and wiry, before ceding the space. Jack shot him a knowing look.

Cal found himself enjoying the over the top flirtation. No one in the room seemed to notice or care what they were doing, and it was freeing for Cal to express interest in someone in a more open manner than he was used to. He felt seen, and in a good way.

Never mind the fact that the guy who was showing interest in him was Jack fucking Francis. That would likely give him a heart attack if he thought too hard about it.

But then a few of Jack's friends wandered over to watch,

and Jack introduced Cal around. He met Greg, whose glossy hair Jack affectionately ruffled; Joey, who walked up behind Jack, wrapped his arms around Jack's waist, and rested his chin on Jack's shoulder; and Scott, who returned Jack's lighter by slipping it right into his pocket.

Cal watched it all, participating in the lighthearted conversation around him. Remembering what he'd seen on the beach that morning as well, he couldn't help but wonder if Jack was this comfortable and physical with *everyone*. Maybe Cal wasn't a special target at all, and this is just how the guy acted.

After a while, Jack hung his cue on the wall.

"Okay, I'm willing to concede that you are the better player," Jack said. "Just a little better."

"Lots of practice," Cal said, shrugging.

"I need some air. Want to join me, or do you want to keep playing?"

"I can — I'll join you. If you aren't sick of me," Cal said.

Jack laughed, his eyes bright. "Not yet, I'll let you know."

Cal handed his cue off to a waiting Greg and followed Jack over to the bar. Jack snagged the bottle of scotch Cal had brought, along with two glasses. He handed them off to Cal and then tucked a finger in Cal's left front belt loop, turned, and led Cal through the house to the back patio.

It was empty now — Penny and Grant must have taken their activities elsewhere — and shadowy, since the moon was fully behind clouds. Jack let go of Cal and flopped onto the patio sofa.

"Have a seat," he said.

Cal sank onto the cushion beside Jack, not touching, but within sliding distance. He set the scotch and glasses on the coffee table. "You should close your windows. It's going to rain," he said.

"Yeah?" Jack peered out at the ocean. "How can you tell? Just because of the clouds?"

"The way the air feels heavy, like it's already soaking up the moisture. And the way it smells. Petrichor."

Jack swiveled his head and squinted at Cal. "Petra-what?"

"Petrichor. It's the way the air smells before it rains. It's like...earthy and wet and kind of charged." Cal shrugged.

"Okay, Harvard," Jack said with a giggle. "That's my word for today. *Petrichor*. Think up another good one to teach me tomorrow."

Cal's heart sank. He was being insufferable again. People told him that all the time, heaving sighs and rolling their eyes and telling him to stop trying to show everyone how smart he was. He never meant to. He just...read a lot, and remembered things he thought were interesting, and wanted to share that with others.

"I didn't mean to be a know-it-all," Cal said, fidgeting in his seat. "Sometimes I—"

"You weren't," said Jack. "You're smart, that's neat. Don't be ashamed of it."

"I'm not trying to show off," Cal said. "Or make you feel like...I know people get annoyed with me. For saying stupid shit like that."

"Cal." Jack laid a hand on Cal's forearm, rubbed gently. "I'm not annoyed. I like knowing what Petra- what was it again?"

"Petrichor."

"Petrichor. I like knowing what that is. I promise."

In the semi-darkness, Cal could just make out Jack's smile. And he could hear the sincerity in his voice.

They sat quietly for a few minutes, Jack's hand still resting lightly on Cal's wrist. The music from inside the house was more muted than it had been when Cal arrived, and he felt a calm settle over him. That shouldn't be, not when he was actually contemplating making a move on Jack Francis. He should be on edge. Instead, he was relaxed.

Then Jack dug a hand into his pocket and drew out the lighter and a slim cigarette. He flicked the lighter and then held the flame to one end of the cigarette, rotating it slowly between his fingers, before puffing gently on it to stoke the ember. He took a drag, blowing the smoke up into the air in a steady stream, and then held it toward Cal.

"You interested?" he asked.

Cal smelled the telltale hint of skunk in the air. It wasn't a cigarette, it was a joint.

"Oh," he said. "Um…"

Jack paused, his eyes going wide. "Have you never smoked pot before? I figured, you're in college…"

Cal hadn't. It was part of the *every area but* that he'd determined should be conducted within the rules. So he'd always declined.

He shrugged. "I'm just careful," he said, trying to explain. "With things that could risk…my education, or my future, or that would bring my parents scrutiny down on me more than it already is."

"Hey, it's fine," Jack said. "If you want to smoke this with me, you can, but it's not a requirement."

Cal hesitated. He wasn't at school at the moment. They were on private property, property that didn't belong to his parents. Parents who didn't even know he was over here. The risk really was minimal. If there was any time to try it, maybe now was that time. He'd been so good for so long.

And he suddenly wanted to share something with Jack, on this patio in the dark.

"Maybe I'd like to," he said, finally. "If you're offering."

"I am," Jack said. "You ever smoke cigarettes?"

"Occasionally," Cal replied.

"So it's just like that. Except maybe don't take as hard of a pull. And when you inhale, hold it in for an extra second before letting it out." Jack held out the joint between slim fingers, and Cal took it gingerly.

The tip was moist from being in Jack's mouth, and Cal savored the moment when his lips wrapped around the end. He took a healthy drag, inhaling the slightly acrid smoke. He tried to hold it in the way Jack had advised, but he could feel a cough building, so he breathed it out and watched the smoke swirl into the air around him.

They passed the joint back and forth for a few minutes before Jack pinched out the end and stuffed it back in his pocket.

"This shit's pretty strong," he said in explanation. "You're a decently big guy, but I don't want you to overdo it your first time out. How do you feel?"

"Fine?" Cal shrugged. "I'm not really feeling any different."

"You will," said Jack. He snagged the scotch, popped off the top, and poured two healthy helpings in the glasses. He handed one to Cal. "You do drink, right? You had that beer when you first came in."

"Yeah. I guess technically that's breaking the rules, too, since I'm not twenty-one yet, but...it's a more acceptable rule to break." Cal rolled his eyes. "Fuck, I sound like the biggest asshole."

"You don't," said Jack. "You sound like someone who's spent a lot of time knowing people are watching you, and you've learned to play their game."

Cal turned and stared at Jack. "Yes," he said. "Yes. It's just easier. Safer. You know?"

"Sure I know. I work in fucking Hollywood." Jack raised his glass. "Anyway, cheers to...knowing which rules to break and when to break them."

Cal clinked his glass against Jack's, and then settled back

against the sofa cushion and took a sip. Thunder rumbled softly in the distance. Out of habit, Cal began to count. *One Mississippi, two Mississippi, three Mississippi...*

He got to seven Mississippis before lightning flashed.

"Still a ways off," he murmured.

They sat in silence for a while, silence that was far too comfortable for having just met. Cal listened to the thunder growing gradually louder, watched the lightning follow more quickly. He felt the warmth of the scotch in his belly, and the alcohol was blurring the edges of his sensation, making everything feel softer. Like he was drifting.

"How do you feel now?" Jack asked. It seemed like his voice floated over to Cal through a gossamer fog, and Cal had to grasp at the words, pluck them out of the air and force them to attach to his brain.

"Goo-ood," Cal said, elongating the vowel sound. He said it again. "Goooood."

Jack snickered beside him. "Nice."

There was a thought in Cal's brain, just out of his reach. What was it?

"That's the pot," Jack said.

Yes; that was it. That was the answer Cal needed. This was what it felt like to smoke pot.

"It's...nice," he said.

"Yeah, it is," Jack agreed.

Cal liked this. He liked sitting here, in the dark, beside a guy who made his insides all shivery. He liked not being home, not caring if his parents would approve. He liked the way the smoking made him feel, relaxed and stress-free, and he wondered what else he'd missed out on by following all the rules.

"I've measured out my life with coffee spoons," he said.

"You've what?"

Jack's voice was hushed, and Cal realized he must have

whispered. That felt appropriate, as though he were sharing a precious bit of information.

"I've tried so hard to be...boring. Only remarkable in ways that would be acceptable to them. To everyone. And for what?" Cal turned to Jack, leaned forward. "They don't really approve of me. I'm never good enough, no matter how perfect I am. And if they knew, if they knew about...it would all be over in an instant."

"Knew about what?" Jack asked, leaning in as well, so their faces were mere inches apart.

"Knew about me. That I'm—"

The door opened, and two people spilled out onto the patio in an explosion of giggles. Cal jolted back in his seat and shifted a few inches away from Jack, his heart pounding.

"There you are," one of the girls said. It was the one who'd been wearing pink that morning. The other girl was new, Cal had seen her inside dancing in a corner, but they hadn't been introduced.

"You found me," Jack said, grinning broadly. The girl collapsed onto his lap in a heap and kissed him on the cheek. "Cal, this is Ginny. And that's J.C. This is Cal, he lives next door and has a great vocabulary."

"Hi, Cal," Ginny said.

J.C. took a seat between Cal and Jack. "Nice to meet you," she said.

Ginny poked Jack in the chest. "Where's that joint I rolled?" she asked. "I did the work, I should get some reward."

Jack dug into his pocket and pulled out the half-smoked cylinder and the lighter. "Here you go," he said. "Sorry we started without you."

In a moment, the joint was lit again, and they passed it around. Cal tried to ignore the sinking feeling he was experiencing in his chest.

The girls chattered about plans for the next day — something about shopping and dinner — as the thunder got louder up above. Cal felt the tiny prickle of a first raindrop, and then a second. The third was bigger, splattering right on top of his head.

He turned to Jack to say something about getting back inside, and gaped. Ginny had her hands on either side of Jack's face and was kissing him like she hadn't seen him in years. Jack gripped her waist, and didn't seem to be opposed to the activity.

"They tend to do that," J.C. said. "It's kind of annoying."

"Oh," was all Cal could say in response. He was beginning to feel sick.

"You wanna?"

"What?" Cal blinked and tried to focus on the girl.

"Make out. You wanna? You're adorable." She was grinning at him, a pretty, expectant smile.

Cal swallowed hard. Then he shook his head. "I shouldn't," he said.

She shrugged. "That's too bad."

He felt hot, and itchy, and like he needed to move, *now*, or else something bad was going to happen. He got to his feet.

"I have to go," he said. He realized he was still holding his empty scotch glass. He shoved it at J.C. "Here. It was nice to meet you."

Then he turned and moved towards the steps.

"Wait — Cal —" he heard Jack call.

Cal stopped, turned just his head. He couldn't really see Jack, just out of the corner of his eye. That was better.

"You're going?" Jack asked.

"Yeah. I have to get home. Thanks for inviting me." He hesitated. "It's raining. You should go inside. And close the windows."

Then he descended the stairs and crossed the lawn in

giant strides. By the time he reached the beach, it was raining in full, and by the time he made it back to his door, he was soaked.

Thunder crashed, and lightning cracked overhead. He snuck back into the house, wanting nothing more than to crawl into bed and blot it all out.

He'd been wrong about Jack, and that fucking sucked.

CHAPTER 4

*N*aked.

Cal woke the next morning with a clearer head than he would have expected and only one moment of confusion: *why am I naked?*

He looked around his bedroom, blinking sleep out of his eyes. The light coming in the windows was grey and muted, and as he oriented himself to consciousness he realized it was still raining, the patter of the raindrops a white noise around him.

His clothes from the previous day were tossed haphazardly across the chair in the corner, and his shoes were on the opposite side of the room, against the wall. The events of the night before flooded back in a rush, and he winced at the memory, the pit in his stomach growing larger.

When he'd entered his room, he'd kicked the shoes off impatiently, then discarded his clothes and crawled under the sheets without bothering to turn on the light and find his pajamas. He'd stubbornly squeezed his eyes shut until he finally fell asleep. Had he tracked mud through the house while coming in? He hoped not. It would just mean there'd be questions, and he didn't have answers.

He rubbed his hands across his face and gave himself a pep talk. He hadn't lost anything, he reasoned, because Jack was never his to begin with. It had all been in his head, the way he thought Jack was flirting with him and indicating interest.

Cal recalled what Jack had said on the beach — *you're new and interesting* — and what Penny had said the night before — *he keeps talking about embracing the locals* — and saw how he'd misinterpreted the situation.

Jack wasn't interested in him. Jack had a girlfriend. Jack flirted with everyone, was affectionate with everyone. He was just open, and friendly, and not hung up on things like whether it was acceptable for two men to be touching so much.

Cal was a novelty to Jack, that was all. It was his own damned fault that he'd read more into it than was actually there. He could blame it on his magazine fantasies and on getting a little star struck.

None of this made him feel any better, but at least he knew, rationally, that he was thinking straight again.

But what now? He couldn't just go back over there, not after the way he'd embarrassed himself. He pulled the covers over his face as if to hide from the memory. It was the pot, it must have been. He'd just kept talking, telling Jack things he had no business sharing with a stranger. For fuck's sake, he'd nearly—

Cal sat straight up in bed, his heart pounding. *He'd nearly told Jack he was homosexual.* But he hadn't. He'd stopped...right? He searched his memory for the moment. Yes, just before he'd been about to say it, the girls had interrupted. Thank god. He couldn't believe he'd been about to *out himself* to Jack Francis.

He'd never said the words aloud before. To anyone, not even himself.

With a frustrated huff, he threw the covers back and climbed out of bed. He just needed to put it behind him and move on. It didn't matter how bad he felt...that wouldn't change anything, so he just had to live with it.

He didn't feel up to facing his parents at breakfast, so he slipped down to steal some food and return to his room before they arrived. When he reached the kitchen, Flora was pulling fresh blueberry muffins out of the oven.

"Those smell incredible," he said. "Morning."

"Good morning," Flora said. "Will you eat two or three?"

He smiled. After years working for the Buchanans, she knew that when he arrived early he was looking to escape. "Two is fine. And maybe—"

She set a frying pan on the stove. "Bacon coming right up. Get yourself a glass of orange juice. Coffee will be ready in a minute."

"Thanks, Flora," he said.

"Next time you sneak in during a rainstorm, take off your shoes inside the door and leave them in here," she said, shooting him a look.

He blushed. So he had tracked evidence in, and she'd taken care of it. "Thanks," he said again.

"So where were you off to?" she asked, as the bacon began to sizzle. "Somewhere fun, I hope."

He hesitated, and then sighed. "It was supposed to be. I went next door."

"Ah, to see the movie star," she said.

He blinked. "How do you know—"

"He hired a friend of mine for the summer. But word will be getting around quick enough. You know this town." She turned the bacon. "What's he like?"

"He's nice," Cal said. It was true, at least. "Very friendly. A little odd."

"Odd?"

"He isn't...he doesn't seem concerned with what people think. He just does things and says things and seems to be having a good time." Cal smiled. "He laughs a lot."

"Good-looking gentleman, from what my friend tells me. And very polite." She winked, and turned off the burner. "Grab yourself a tray."

Cal went into the pantry to collect the item, and gave himself a second to breathe before he returned. Flora was sharp, and he'd wondered for a long time if she knew about him. He wasn't sure, but he thought she might suspect.

She didn't say anything more about Jack, or ask about his evening, as she set a plate with two muffins and four slices of bacon on the tray, along with the orange juice, a mug of coffee, and a dish of butter.

"Let the muffins cool another minute or two before cutting them open," she warned. "And bring everything back before—"

"Before the ants find it. Yes, ma'am." He leaned in and kissed her cheek as he took the tray. "Could you do me a favor and not mention about next door—"

"What would I mention? I know nothing," she said. "Go, before your mother decides to come down early to 'help' me again."

He smirked and skedaddled back up to his room.

BECAUSE HE'D SUCCESSFULLY AVOIDED breakfast, he decided to make an appearance at lunch. He could have gone out, but it was still pouring, and his summer friends were probably only just arriving. So he slid into his place at the table just as his father walked in.

The man was grinning, which was usually not a good thing.

He sat in his place and picked up his napkin, snapping it onto his lap. Then he took a sip from his water goblet and grinned at Cal.

"Guess who I was just on the phone with," Theodore said.

"Who?" asked Judith. She plucked a warm roll out of the bread basket and passed the basket to Cal. He selected a roll for himself and passed it along to his father.

"Joe Thornton." Theodore leaned back in his chair as Flora approached with the soup tureen.

"Oh? That's nice, how are they? Last time I saw Emily it must have been...was it as far back as Harvard-Yale last fall?"

"It was," Theodore said. "We spoke about what a good weekend that was for us all."

"Yes. I'm tasting the meal we had at the Oyster House just by thinking about it. Let's make sure to go back there this year."

"Agreed," Theodore replied. "That was quite the weekend, wasn't it, Calloway?"

Cal paused in blowing on his soup. "Yes, Sir. It was a nice weekend," he said.

His parents had come up to Cambridge for the annual Harvard-Yale football game. They didn't make a habit of visiting him at school, so whenever it happened it was an event. They'd stay at the Omni Parker House — *if it's good enough for a Kennedy, it's good enough for me*, Theodore was known to say to whomever would listen — make reservations at the finest and most prestigious restaurants, and stroll around campus pointing out locations fondly, since his father had attended Harvard while courting his mother.

Meanwhile, Cal would trail behind, trying to look and act the way the heir to Buchanan Industries should look and act.

"In any event," Theodore continued, "Joe and I were reminiscing about that weekend, as well as the trips we've taken together in the past, and he decided they're going to come out to visit this summer."

Cal carefully set his spoon down, and listened.

"That's wonderful," Judith said. "When are they coming?"

"They'll be here for Independence Day weekend and plan to stay a few weeks." He grinned again, this time directed at Cal. "I bet that will have you feeling more enthusiastic about the summer here."

Cal nodded. "Sure," he said, mustering a smile. "That'll be great."

If Joe and Emily Thornton were coming for a visit, that meant they'd be bringing Katherine. And that meant —

"I'm sure there will be some plans to be made," Judith said with a knowing smile. She reached over and patted Cal's hand, and he pushed his chair back and stood.

"That's great news," he said. "May I be excused? I need to—"

"Have a phone call you want to make?" Theodore chuckled, and waved his hand towards the door. "Go on, then."

Cal dropped his napkin on his chair, and Judith raised her hand.

"Oh, Calloway, your father and I will be out for the day tomorrow, to see the Harrisons, and we won't be back until late. Flora will leave meals for you, but I gave her the day off."

"Fine," he said. "I'll be fine. Don't worry about me."

Then he fled the room. The last thing he wanted was to make the phone call his father thought he was making, but he went into his father's study anyhow, to make it look like he was. He could hide in here until lunch was over, waiting for

41

the nausea to subside, just as easily as he could hide anywhere else.

~

ON SUNDAY, it was still raining. Theodore and Judith left after breakfast, anxious to get on the road for the day trip to Hartford before the new storm that seemed to be brewing unleashed itself. Cal watched them go with relief. If he was going to be cooped up in the house again, feeling depressed, he'd rather no one be around to see it.

He wandered from room to room for a while before settling in the den with a book. A couple of hours later, he was on the same page he'd started on and no closer to knowing what was on it. With a sigh, he set the book aside and went to make himself a sandwich.

After lunch, he was about to turn on the television, just to have some noise besides his thoughts to keep him company, when the back doorbell rang.

Cal frowned in the direction of the back door. Had one of his friends arrived early and decided to swing by without calling first? It seemed unlikely, especially coming to the back door. Who would be coming from the beach, in the pouring rain?

The bell rang again, and, with a shrug, he went to investigate. When he peered through the window, he froze.

Standing on the back patio, wearing a giant gray hooded sweater and yellow track pants, and hopping from sandaled foot to sandaled foot, was Jack.

What was Jack doing here?

Jack's face, partially hidden under the sodden hood, burst into a grin when Cal appeared in the window.

"Hey!" he shouted. "Open up."

Cal dumbfoundedly unlocked the door and twisted the handle. He took a deep breath before he pulled it open.

"Hi," he said. "What are you...I mean, hi."

Jack bounced on his toes. "I have a gift for you," he said. "That's the rule, right? Never show up to someone's house empty-handed?"

Cal realized Jack was holding his hands behind his back. The sweater was so bulky he'd missed that initially. "Oh. Um...yeah, the rule. But you don't have to—"

"Rules are rules." With a flourish, Jack produced Cal's loafers, the ones he'd left on the beach the other night. "For you."

"My shoes." Cal stared at them, and then at Jack, who was still grinning at him. He couldn't help the smile that crept across his face. "That's my gift?"

"Yup," Jack said, his lips popping on the *p*. "You left so fast the other night, I didn't have a chance to give them to you. Didn't want you to feel like I was holding them hostage forever, like some freak shoe hoarder."

Cal took the shoes, and shook his head. "I guess I forgot about them," he said. "Thanks for bringing them over. Especially in the rain."

"No problem," Jack said. "Gave me an excuse to leave the house. It's boring today, everyone keeps sleeping." He rolled his eyes.

"Do you...do you want to come in?" The question sent Cal's pulse racing. *Stupid, that was stupid,* he reminded himself. Jack had a girlfriend, no need to get so—

"Nah," Jack said, and Cal's heart sank. But then Jack gestured behind him. "I want you to come out with me instead."

"Out there? On the patio?" Cal looked around. Unlike the patio at Jack's house, Cal's back patio was covered. However, the wind still blew the rain sideways from time to time, so it wasn't exactly dry.

"No, down to the beach," Jack said. "Come for a walk."

Cal laughed. Jack was joking, surely. "It's raining," he said.

"Good observation, Harvard," Jack said. "What's your point? You never walked in the rain?"

"Sure I have. Just not on purpose," Cal said.

"Then you don't know what you're missing. Come on, put some shoes on, grab a sweater or something. Let's go." Jack cocked his head to the side. "Okay?"

Cal licked his lips. Maybe Jack wanted to be friends. A warmth bloomed in Cal's chest, and he smiled. He could do that. Even if it wasn't what he had thought...they could be friends.

"Okay," he said.

A few minutes later he was pulling up his own hood, locking the door behind him, and following Jack back across the soggy lawn to the beach stairs. They clattered down them side by side and then their feet slapped on the wet sand.

Jack turned west, and Cal fell into step beside him. The rain fell steadily, and even though it wasn't raining hard, it soaked his hood and shoulders in minutes so that the fabric clung to his skin. Every few minutes, the wind whipped around them, tossing the rain into his face. The sand was mushy and slippery beneath his feet.

Still, despite all of this, he grinned. It felt good to be outside, and the rain felt like it was washing away the mood he'd been living in for the past day and a half. Or maybe it was the guy beside him that was doing that.

He smiled at the way Jack was winding through the sand in no discernible pattern. Cal glanced over his shoulder and marveled at the difference in the tracks they left; his formed a clear straight line, while Jack's wove back and forth and looped around crazily.

They'd made it past two houses before Jack spoke up.

"So why did you leave?" he asked. "On Friday? You weren't having fun?"

He looked over at Cal, his green eyes wide and, to Cal's surprise, concerned.

"I was having fun," Cal said. "That was...you were...it was fun."

"Okay. Then what happened?"

"I was tired," Cal said feebly.

Jack frowned. "Are you sure? Because you seemed like you were mad." He shrugged. "I kind of wondered if I'd said something wrong, and if you'd slam the door in my face when I showed up today. If I did, I didn't mean to. I say a lot of shit and most of it is just...nothing."

"You didn't — I wasn't mad," Cal said. "I just...your girl-friend came out, and I didn't want to be in the way."

"My what?" Jack stopped walking, and when Cal turned around, his mouth was a round *O*.

"Your girlfriend. Ginny?" Cal shrugged.

Jack burst out laughing. He laughed so hard he doubled over, his arms clutched around his narrow waist, his dripping curls bouncing around his jerking head. Cal just stared at him.

After a minute, he took a breath and straightened up, then shook his head.

"*Cal*," he said, looking utterly delighted. "That's why you left? Ginny isn't — she's not —"

Then he was laughing again. Cal fidgeted, shuffling his feet in the sand and feeling cold. Was Jack saying that Ginny wasn't his girlfriend?

Suddenly, Jack sprang forward and smacked a hand against Cal's chest.

"You're too good to be true," he said, blinking up at Cal.

"I'm gonna have to pay my agent a bonus for picking the house next to yours."

He twisted his fingers in Cal's sleeve and began walking again. Cal followed along, letting himself be led further across the sand.

"So Ginny isn't…" Cal began.

"No, she isn't," Jack said. "God, imagine. She's just a friend."

"You were kissing her a lot," Cal pointed out.

"She was kissing me a lot," Jack said. "Right before we came out here, Ginny lost an audition because the casting director said she wasn't a convincing kisser. She took that hard and has been using me to practice." He snickered. "Me and everyone else. You're lucky she didn't lay one on you. Give her another day, she might."

"And you just let her?" Cal tried to wrap his mind around the idea of just kissing someone, at any time you wanted.

"Why not? Kissing is fun," Jack said. He shot a sideways glance at Cal. "Don't you think?"

"Sure, yeah," Cal said.

"So you really just left because you thought I was making out with a girlfriend?" Jack asked.

"I guess," Cal said. "I figured you'd moved on from hanging out with me and didn't want to overstay."

"You couldn't," Jack swung his arm, and since he was still holding Cal's sleeve, swung Cal's arm as well. "You're welcome whenever and however long you want. Okay?"

"Okay," Cal said. He looked down at where Jack was still gripping his sleeve. It was almost like Jack was holding his hand. Almost.

If Ginny wasn't Jack's girlfriend…maybe Cal hadn't been misreading Jack's flirting. His heart rate sped up. If only he had the guts to grab Jack's hand for real. If only he wasn't always worried about who might be looking out their window and see.

On impulse, he swiveled his wrist and pinched the edge of Jack's sleeve between his fingers. Jack stopped swinging his arm. Slowly, he slid his pinky down to stroke against Cal's wrist. Cal swallowed.

Then Jack let go and bounded in the opposite direction, headed east.

"Let's go back," he said. "It's wet."

"Well...it's raining," laughed Cal.

Jack turned and began to run, and after a second, Cal gave chase. They sprinted across the sand, leaving a spray of it behind them, and reached Cal's stairs gasping for breath.

"Am I..." Jack gulped air. "Am I coming up, or going back next door?"

"Come up," Cal said. "No one's home. My parents went to Hartford for the day. We won't be...it'll just be us."

He led the way up to the house and unlocked the door, ushering them both inside, where they stood, dripping on the wooden floor.

"Maybe this was a dumb idea," Jack said. "The walking in the rain. I have a lot of dumb ideas."

"No, it was...I liked it," Cal said. He peered at Jack in the dim entry. "You're shivering."

"I'm fine," Jack said, clearly shivering.

"You're not. We should put on dry clothes."

Jack glanced at the door. "I guess I could run home and change?"

Cal didn't want Jack to leave. Even with a promise to come back. He felt like there was some kind of charge in the air, and if Jack left, it might fizzle out.

"I can give you something. Wait here."

He kicked off his waterlogged shoes and took off for his

room, taking the back stairs two at a time. Once there, he quickly stripped off his soaked jeans, sweater, and tee, and replaced them with dry sweats. He grabbed a second set of sweats, snagged a couple of towels from the bathroom, and then ran back down.

Jack was waiting for him, alternating between hugging himself and holding his arms out to his sides. Cal handed him the clothes and one of the towels.

"They'll be big, but...the bathroom is just down there."

"Thanks," Jack said, flashing Cal a grin. He kicked off his own shoes and then gingerly made his way down the hall.

Cal quickly used the other towel to mop up the floor, then tossed it into the corner. He went into the kitchen and set up the tea kettle, pulling out mugs and tea bags and spoons and honey. By the time he heard Jack calling his name, the kettle was beginning to rattle.

"In here," Cal called. Jack rounded the corner a moment later, and Cal smiled.

He was swimming in the sweats. The neck hung low, and he was holding up the pants with his left hand.

Cal stared. He stared at the way the right shoulder sagged and the sleeves were bunched up and the legs were rolled at Jack's ankles. He stared at Jack's glistening curls that hung around his face. He stared at the way the guy's thin frame was still somehow visible under all that fabric.

Jack laughed self-consciously. "I look ridiculous."

"No," Cal said. He cleared his throat. "No, you…"

The kettle began to whistle, a piercing shriek that made them both jump. Cal fumbled with the knobs on the stove until it stopped. He grabbed a pot holder and busied himself pouring the water over the teabags.

"Do you like honey? Or I think there's lemon." He glanced over his shoulder.

"Honey is good," Jack said. "Thanks."

Cal finished preparing the tea, and when he turned around again, Jack was right behind him.

"Here." Cal handed Jack his mug. "Let's go into the den."

Jack followed him through the house, and they settled on the sofa in the den. Cal grabbed a couple of crocheted blankets and they threw them over their laps and sat clutching their steaming mugs, letting the warmth finally creep in.

"I feel like my grandmother," Cal said.

Jack giggled. "Is your grandmother six and a half feet of muscle?"

"No." Cal laughed. "She is tall, though. I think the word is 'patrician.'"

"Does she live here?" Jack asked.

"Newton," Cal said. "Just outside of Boston. My mother keeps trying to get her to move down here but she says she prefers civilized land."

"And this is not?"

"Golf clubs and beach shanties do not civilization make," Cal said, mimicking his grandmother's reedy tone. "I actually think she likes her card games and doesn't want to leave them."

Jack snickered. "What about your grandfather? What does he think?"

"He passed a few years ago," Cal said. "Which is why my mother would like her to move. But I check in on her every so often, and she seems fine to me."

"It's nice that you see your grandmother," Jack said. "I miss mine. I grew up with her living a few floors up in our apartment building."

"When did you lose her?" Cal asked.

"Oh, I didn't. She's still there, in the same apartment. But since I moved to L.A..." he shrugged.

"What are your parents like?"

They talked through the rest of the afternoon, the rumbling thunder a soundtrack to the meandering conversation. Cal asked Jack about Hollywood, and with a scrunch of his nose that made Cal's belly tingle, Jack talked about studios and contracts and directors and scripts.

"Is it hard to pretend to be different people all the time?" Cal asked.

"Not hard. I mean, it's a lot of work. But it's fun, and kind of freeing?" Jack replied. "I mean, have you ever wished you could just leave your whole life behind and be someone else for a while?"

Definitely, Cal thought.

Jack asked about college, and what Cal planned to do after he graduated.

"Work for the company," Cal said automatically.

"What company?"

"My family's company," Cal said. "Buchanan Industries."

"What will you do?"

"I'll —" Cal hesitated, and then laughed. "You know, I'm not even sure. I never thought to ask. I guess I'll find out when I get there."

Jack looked baffled by this, and Cal couldn't blame him.

When Jack's stomach let out a loud growl, Cal half expected him to say it was time to go. Instead, he said, "Got anything to eat around here?"

Cal heated up one of Flora's specialty casseroles for dinner, and they talked through bites of lamb and peas and potatoes, sipping on beer.

"Will your parents notice the beer is gone?" Jack asked, when Cal offered him one.

"Doubtful. Even if they do, they won't care," Cal said. "Or, if you want something stronger, they won't care about the liquor cabinet either."

"Beer is good," Jack said. He plucked the can out of Cal's hand and winked.

After dinner was cleaned up, they wandered back into the den. This time, when they sat, Cal noticed that Jack flopped onto the cushion directly next to his, significantly closing the gap that had been between them throughout the afternoon. Cal snapped on the television and they watched some mindless show for a while.

At one point, Cal turned to Jack to make a comment and saw that his eyes were closed, his lips were parted, and he was snoring gently. Cal smiled, pulled a blanket up over him, and turned back to the television.

Eventually, Cal fell asleep too. When he opened his eyes, the television was off, the sky outside was dark, and the lamp in the corner had been turned on. He turned and saw Jack, sitting cross-legged on the sofa, watching him, his eyes bottle-green in the glow of the lamp.

"Hey," Jack said, softly.

"Hey," Cal replied.

"We fell asleep."

"Yeah."

They watched each other quietly for a minute.

"Today was fun," Jack said. "I'm glad you weren't mad at me."

"I'm glad you came over. I like those shoes." Cal smirked.

Jack reached out and smacked Cal's shoulder lightly.

"Just the shoes?" he asked.

Cal's pulse picked up. He took a shallow breath.

"No," he said. "Not just the shoes."

Jack smiled. "Good. Cal—"

The sound of a car engine rumbled outside, and Cal sat up straight, letting the blanket fall to the floor.

"Fuck," he said. "My parents." He glanced back at Jack, eyes wide.

Jack stiffened. "Should I not be here?"

"Probably not. I'm sorry, it's not — it's only because—"

"It's okay." Jack got to his feet. "I get it."

The engine turned off, and Cal felt a chill run down his spine. It wasn't that his parents would suspect anything was going on, not really. But they'd no doubt disapprove of Cal hanging out with Jack at all. They might even forbid him from doing it again, and he'd rather avoid that complication.

He kind of wanted to keep Jack to himself, anyway. For now.

"Come on," he said. "They're coming in the front, you can go out the back."

Cal snapped off the light in the den, and they hurried down the hall.

"My clothes," Jack said, stuffing his feet into his sandals. "They're in the—"

"Got it," Cal replied. He dashed back to the bathroom and grabbed the still-wet things, then returned to the back door just as Jack was pulling it open.

"Thanks for dinner," Jack whispered.

"Thanks for the walk," Cal whispered back.

Cal could hear the front door opening, and he pushed Jack outside.

"I'll see you—" Cal began.

Suddenly, Jack tossed his things onto the patio. He leapt forward, and then his lips were on Cal's in a firm kiss. He lingered there a long moment, his hands on Cal's cheeks, before he jumped back and grabbed up his clothes again.

"Come by tomorrow, if you don't hate me," he whispered, and then ran off into the night.

Cal stumbled back across the threshold. He was dimly aware that his parents were moving around at the front of the house, and this alone spurred him to gently close the back door and then escape up the servants stairs to his room.

When he crawled into bed a few minutes later, he found himself wide awake, his heart pounding in his chest and adrenaline coursing through his veins.

He closed his eyes, but knew he was never going to be able to sleep.

CHAPTER 5

*I*t took Cal until after dinner on Monday to take Jack up on his whispered offer of the night before.

First, his mother had headed him off after breakfast and saddled him with a handful of errands. He'd been about to head out to the beach — the sunny weather having blessedly returned — in the hopes of running into Jack with his crew, but instead he found himself visiting various businesses downtown. He picked up altered clothing, delivered invitations, stopped for flowers...nothing he really minded, except that it was keeping him from doing the one thing that he really wanted to be doing.

Then, while he was grabbing a sandwich at Lou's, he ran into the Wallace twins. They'd arrived in town over the weekend, and were anxious to get back into the swing of the Westerly summer life. After some attempts at finding a way to decline, Cal had given up and agreed to join them at the club for an afternoon round of golf. He liked Sally and Richie Wallace, at least, and had been looking forward to spending time with them. If his mind hadn't been so focused on what had happened the night before, he'd have been more enthusiastic, but he didn't want to burn his bridges.

He'd decided to have dinner with his parents, so that he could mention he'd spent the afternoon with the Wallaces. It had the expected reaction: Judith decided to call Felicia Wallace to invite them over for dinner later in the week and Theodore mused that Richard Senior might be interested in some cigars he'd gotten his hands on.

Over dessert, Cal mentioned he might be going out. As expected, his parents assumed he was seeing the Wallaces again, which was going to come in handy. Theodore told him not to stay out too late and Judith told him to be quiet when coming in, and he was finally free to go see Jack.

This time, as he approached the back patio with a six pack of beer in his hands, laughter mixed with the music echoing across the lawn. The back patio was more lively than it had been on Friday — when he'd stumbled upon just Penny and Grant — and Cal hesitated. He hadn't expected there to be a party in full swing on a Monday night. Had more people arrived from Los Angeles?

He thought about turning around and going home, but the thought of not seeing Jack left him feeling empty and hollow, so he continued up the stone steps. A few people greeted him with a *hey* as he passed. In the dark, he couldn't quite make out faces, so he just smiled and nodded.

The back door opened easily, and he entered the house, not entirely sure where to go. Then one of the girls from Friday night — J.C., the pretty brunette who had offered to make out with him — wandered past. She stopped and grinned.

"Oh, hey," she said. "Cal, right?"

"Hi," he said. "That's right."

"Far out. Jack will be happy to see you."

She wandered away, leaving him to his own devices, but

he felt marginally better, and a little less nervous. Did that mean Jack had been talking about him?

He turned toward the kitchen, deciding to take the route Penny had led him last time. The kitchen was also livelier than it had been the other night, and he navigated around bodies to get to the fridge. He deposited the beer and then continued towards the living room and rec room.

The living room looked different. Furniture had been shoved to the side or removed and the rug rolled back, to create a large space in the center of the room. People were dancing, spinning and grooving to the fast beat pounding out of the massive speakers.

In the middle of it all was Jack.

Cal watched, captivated, as Jack wiggled and writhed, his feet moving in a complicated pattern on the wooden floor. He was dancing with Ginny, and he clutched her hand, spinning her around and pulling her close for a moment before bouncing away again.

A pang of longing reverberated in Cal's chest. He wished he could do *that*. Instead, he was standing off to the side, feeling suddenly too large and too awkward to be here.

The song ended, and another began, a slower song. He recognized this one, an Elvis number that had hit the charts last year. Something about falling in love. Ginny sidled up to Jack and wrapped her arms around his neck, and he looped his around her waist.

Now the pang in his chest was an ache, and it tightened around his lungs. No matter what Jack had said about not being in a relationship with Ginny, they looked awfully cozy.

Cal looked away from Jack. It didn't matter, he told himself. He had no claim to the guy, certainly not after one simple, stolen, two-second kiss.

He was thinking about going home, or at the very least going to a different room and finding some way to distract himself from the sight of Jack dancing with Ginny, when he realized something.

He recognized these other people. Some of them, anyhow. They lived in town. A wave of cold washed over him. These were townies, and they'd recognize him, too.

That meant he shouldn't be here. Or, if he stayed, he shouldn't flirt with Jack or make it look like they knew each other in any way other than very casually. It would be too easy for word to get back to his parents.

He glanced back over towards Jack just as Jack looked up, and their eyes met. The expression of surprise followed by pure joy that crossed Jack's face punched Cal in the gut, and he was grinning back before he could catch himself, all of his doubts dissolving in an instant.

Jack pulled away from Ginny and said something to her. Then she headed into the rec room and he was weaving through the dancers towards Cal. Cal stiffened at his approach. What was he going to do? How should Cal respond?

He didn't make a decision fast enough, and Jack slid up to him, running an affectionate hand down his arm and squeezing his fingers.

"Hi," Jack said. "You're here."

Cal pulled his hand away and took a tiny step backward. The flash of confusion on Jack's face had him regretting it instantly, but he just nodded.

"Yeah. I was...I didn't realize there'd be so many people here." He gestured at the crowd. "On a Monday."

Jack looked around and rolled his eyes. "Yeah, the guys wandered into town yesterday while I was with you and met some people and one thing led to another, I think. It grew a little more than we knew it would, but the more the merrier, right?"

"Sure." Cal cleared his throat. "I also kind of know some

of these people. And they know me, and my parents. Maybe I should..." He looked over his shoulder.

"Oh. *Oh.*" Understanding passed through Jack's eyes, and he nodded, relaxing once more. "Don't worry, we're solid. Wait here a minute."

He disappeared through the door to the rec room. Cal stood awkwardly against the wall, waiting and wishing he had a drink to at least make him look like he had something to do.

Eventually, Jack reappeared, this time with Ginny and J.C. in tow. To Cal's shock, J.C. went straight for him, throwing her arms around him and kissing him on the cheek.

"I'm your distraction for the evening," she said in his ear. "Lucky me."

"You're my what?" Cal asked.

"I'm your girl," J.C. murmured. "You can't keep your hands off me."

With that, she grabbed his hands, planted them on her ass, and laid her head against his chest.

Cal stiffened and shot a glance at Jack, who was holding onto Ginny in a similar manner and smirking.

"Problem solved," he said.

"Relax," J.C. said. "I do this all the time. I'm a pro."

Then she kissed him, and it all clicked into place. Jack had gotten them a buffer, so they could hang out and no one would suspect what was really going on. Or what might go on, if they got the chance. He could do this. He'd done it before.

Cal did his best to respond to the kiss, relying on all of his acting skills to pull it off. He was used to it, had been kissing girls and pretending to enjoy it since high school. Idly, he wondered about Jack's comment the day before — *kissing is fun* — and whether he was missing out by viewing this as an obligation rather than an opportunity, but it still felt like going through the motions rather than anything else.

When J.C. broke the kiss, he smoothed her hair back and smiled down at her. "Thanks," he said.

"Not too shabby a deal for me," she said with a smirk. "You're not a bad kisser."

They went back to the rec room to play darts. It was fun at first, but eventually Cal began to get antsy. J.C. was playing her part well, but it wasn't her Cal wanted to be wrapped around. He watched Jack, playing with Ginny's hair and chatting with other guests, and felt like a complete heel for wishing it were yesterday, so he could have Jack's attention solely on him again.

Eventually, they migrated outside to the back patio, grabbing drinks on the way. They found a sofa to settle on, Cal and Jack on the outside and the girls in the middle. J.C. nestled under Cal's arm, her hair tickling his cheek and her hand on his knee. They lit cigarettes and let the smoke swirl in a haze around them, creating an illusion of privacy.

Despite Cal's initial reservations, conversation came easily to the foursome. Cal found that both girls had a dry and acerbic sense of humor that was more than amusing, and he enjoyed listening to their commentary on the little beach town and its inhabitants. When he steered the topic to Hollywood, they had just as much to say.

Cal listened, exchanging amused looks with Jack. Occasionally, Jack would let the tips of his fingers brush lightly against Cal's, and a frisson would wash over Cal, his skin tingling.

As the night matured, things began to quiet down. Eventually, during a lull in the conversation, Jack smiled at Cal and then whispered something in Ginny's ear. Ginny stood and pulled Jack with her. He followed her into the house. Cal sat up, wondering if he should follow.

"Give them a few minutes," J.C. said, pushing Cal back onto the sofa.

"For what?" Cal asked.

She didn't answer. Instead, she finished her cigarette and smashed it out in an ashtray on the coffee table. Then she turned, swung a long leg over him, and straddled him, grinning. When she kissed him, it was with enthusiasm, threading her hands through his hair and pressing against him. He did his best to respond, but when she pulled away, she sighed.

"This really does nothing for you?" she asked, pouting slightly.

He glanced around wildly to see who might have heard her, but they were alone.

"Relax, there's no one here," she said.

"Then why the show?" he asked.

"Curiosity," she said. Then she shrugged. "Anyway, Cal, you're a good kisser, and a nice guy. Anytime you want me to play your girl just let me know. I won't even charge you."

"Charge me?"

She laughed. "I wasn't kidding before when I said I was a pro, I do it for guys back home all the time."

Cal's mind was spinning as she climbed off of him. She grabbed his hands and tugged him to his feet.

"Come on, gorgeous, show's not over yet." She winked and then led him back into the house. He followed, feeling a little dazed. When she started up the staircase to the second floor, he hesitated.

"Maybe I should go home," he said.

"Trust me, that's not what you want." She giggled, then leaned down and whispered, "Act like you can't wait to get me upstairs."

She turned and guided his hands to her hips. He followed her lead, and they wound their way up to the darkened second floor. She pulled him down the hall quickly, all the way to the eastern end and a closed door there. Before he knew what was happening, she had opened the door and shoved him through, closing it behind him with a giggle.

He stumbled into a set of narrow stairs in the dark. As he reached out and patted the walls around him and the ceiling that was just above his head, he realized where he was: this was the access to the house's widow's walk.

Carefully, ducking his head way down to avoid banging it on the low ceiling, he made his way up to the turn, and then through the open hatch at the top. Sitting in the center of the widow's walk, his back against the chimney encasement, his knees pulled up to his chest, and the bottle of scotch Cal had brought the other night in his hand, was Jack.

The moonlight illuminated his curls and his pale skin, giving them a bluish tinge. When he turned his head, it shone in his eyes as well.

"Hey," he said quietly.

"Hi," said Cal. He climbed the rest of the way to the roof and crossed to the center.

"Have a seat," Jack said.

Cal sank onto the gritty floor beside Jack and leaned up against the chimney. Jack passed him the bottle of scotch, and he took a drink, letting the liquor warm a pathway into his chest before handing it back.

"I have good taste," he said, gesturing at the scotch.

Jack smiled. "I think so."

"I'm surprised it's not empty," Cal said. "With so many people—"

"I took it and hid it in my room," Jack said.

"Why?"

"I don't know."

They looked out at the water. Someone had turned off the music in the house below, and now they could hear the waves breaking against the beach. It was one of Cal's favorite sounds, one he missed when he was away at school.

He realized he must have said something out loud when Jack spoke.

"Me too," Jack said, "Sometimes I think about buying a place on the ocean. In California."

"Why don't you?" Cal asked.

"Can't afford it yet. But even when I can...I don't know. Buying property feels so permanent."

"It can be," Cal said. "But it doesn't have to be. Look around. Most of the houses on this beach belong to people who don't live here year round."

"Seems like a waste, though," Jack said. "I mean...to have a place like this and not live in it."

"I agree," Cal said.

Jack passed the scotch again. They sat in silence, watching the moon glisten on the water.

"Things go okay with J.C.?" Jack asked, after a while.

"Sure," Cal said. He wasn't sure exactly what Jack was asking. "She was friendly."

Jack laughed, but his tone was serious. "She is a good friend. And a fox. Don't you think?"

Cal shrugged. "If you're into that sort of thing."

"Which you're not." Jack turned to face Cal, giving him a searching look.

Cal took another swallow of the scotch, and then set the bottle to the side. He returned Jack's look steadily. "I think you know I'm not."

A faint smile ghosted across Jack's face, and he shifted closer. An inch, maybe two. He slid his hand across the roof until it rested on Cal's, soft fingertips brushing lightly across Cal's knuckles. Cal's breath caught, as a shiver ran through him.

"I didn't think I was going to see you today," Jack said.

"I wanted to come by earlier," Cal said earnestly. "My mother — there were errands — and then some other things came up."

"I thought maybe I'd scared you away." When Jack looked up, his eyes didn't make it any farther than Cal's lips.

"No," Cal said. "You didn't. Scare me. Not at all."

"Well, okay then."

Jack closed his fingers firmly around Cal's and moved in quickly. Their mouths locked without effort, as though they'd done this a thousand times and not just the one half attempt in the dark.

Yes, Cal thought. Jack's lips were soft against his, more gentle and accommodating than he would have anticipated based on Jack's assertive and confident presence. The kiss was slow and tentative, as though Jack was seeking permission for more.

Cal granted it, lifting his hand to slide up into Jack's hair, threading his fingers into the soft curls so that he could control the angle of the kiss. He tilted his head to the left and parted his lips.

With a soft moan, Jack accepted the invitation, sliding his tongue against Cal's. That was all that was needed for the tone and tempo of the kiss to shift. Jack scrambled up onto his knees and then climbed on top of Cal, suddenly demanding.

Cal grabbed at Jack's hips, positioning him comfortably in place, and focused on Jack's mouth.

They kissed for a long time, alternating between forceful intensity and soft exploration. Cal reveled in the feeling of Jack atop him, in the way he took control and Cal could just ride the wave of sensation and desire. He felt safe in Jack's hands, content to let the guy take what he wanted without fear that it would be too much or too little.

The ease of it stunned him.

Eventually, Jack pulled away. He gazed down at Cal with a smile.

"Wow," he said.

Cal smiled back. "Yeah."

Jack traced his fingers along Cal's jaw. "From the first second I saw you in the moonlight, I was dying to know if you were into this."

"When did you know I was?" Cal asked. He thought he'd made it obvious that first time he'd come over, but maybe not.

"When you got upset that I was kissing Ginny," Jack said. "At least, I was pretty sure then. I thought it was possible before that, but then…" He shrugged.

"I have to be careful," Cal said. "This kind of thing, it's not...my family would disown me. I'd ruin my whole future, if anyone found out."

"Believe me, I know," Jack said. "I guess it's a little different for me. In Hollywood people kind of *know* about people, but everyone keeps quiet. I can't be officially public about it, but there are spaces where it's okay."

"It just can't get back to my parents," Cal said. "Or basically anyone I know here."

"Cal, I'm not going to tell anyone," Jack said. "I'm not that big of an asshole."

"I know. I guess I just needed to say it." Cal smoothed a hand down Jack's back. "So what now?"

"Now…" Jack glanced over at the open hatch that led into the house. "Now we go back downstairs and pretend we both got it on with the girls."

"Already?" Cal asked. He leaned forward and placed a small kiss on Jack's jaw.

Jack chuckled. "Yes, unfortunately. We should go before the girls get bored and go back to the party. They'll help us, but they're not saints."

He got to his feet, and held out a hand. Cal took it and let Jack pull him up. Then he grabbed the bottle of scotch and followed Jack to the stairs.

They crept back through the door to the second floor and closed it tightly behind them. Jack's room was all the way down at the western end of the house, and he knocked softly before opening the door.

Ginny and J.C. were sitting in the center of Jack's bed, giggling, a cloud of smoke over their heads. Cal looked around, at the piles of clothes draped over the chair in the corner, the empty beer cans on the desk, the stacks of paper on the nightstand. He suddenly felt like drinking in as many details about Jack as he could, just in case this was a dream, or a fluke, and he'd wake up in the morning and find that it had slipped through his fingers like a handful of dry sand.

"Hey, boys," Ginny said. "Did you have fun?"

"Wouldn't you like to know," Jack said. "Thanks for the help tonight."

"Sure," she said. "No sweat." She passed the joint to Jack, who took a hit and held it out to Cal.

Cal shook his head. "I better not," he said. "I should probably get home. My parents think I'm at the house of family friends, and I'm pushing the limits of how late I'd reasonably stay there."

"I'll walk you out," Jack said, nodding. He handed the joint to J.C. "You better not burn a hole in my bed," he warned, before cupping a hand on Cal's elbow and steering him out of the room.

Downstairs, the party had apparently reached a horizontal phase. The music had come back on, but it was turned on low to match the dimmed lights. The harmonies of the Beach Boys drifted over the bodies that were draped across the furniture. Cal raised his eyes at the couples that had formed, glancing at Jack in amusement.

Jack looked like he was trying not to laugh, and pushed Cal past the living room to the back of the house. They stumbled out the back door and onto the lawn before exploding into giggles.

"Must be something in the beer," Jack said.

"It's the music. It hypnotizes people," Cal countered.

"That must be it." Jack led the way across the lawn and down the beach stairs. When they reached the bottom, he smiled up at Cal. "I'm glad you came."

"Me too." Cal couldn't help reaching out and tugging at one of Jack's curls. "When can I — when will I see you again?"

"Whenever you want," Jack said. "Tomorrow. Come out to the beach."

"Okay," Cal said. "But when..." He caught himself, then shook his head and rubbed a hand on the back of his neck, feeling his cheeks heat at the assumptions he maybe shouldn't make. "Never mind."

"Oh." Jack laughed. "You want to know if I'm gonna kiss you again."

Cal chewed on his lower lip, then nodded. "Yeah."

Jack stepped close, pushing Cal up against the cliff wall in the shadows of the staircase, and latched firmly onto his mouth. His hands swept up Cal's chest to his shoulders and then back down to his hips, and Cal sighed at the touch, opening up instantly. He gripped Jack's hips, and then slid his hands around to Jack's ass, and Jack easily molded himself against Cal with a low growl of approval.

When Jack pulled away at last, he swiped a thumb across Cal's lips. "That soon enough for you?"

Cal groaned and let his head fall forward so his forehead rested against Jack's. "Yes."

"I plan to do that as often as possible," Jack said. "That's your fair warning."

"I can be all right with that," Cal said. "Okay. I should go."

Jack took a step backwards, letting Cal free. "Tomorrow?"

"Tomorrow," Cal confirmed. "I'll come out to the beach."

Jack grinned and began to back towards the staircase. "Night, Cal."

"Goodnight," Cal said.

Jack turned and dashed up the stairs, and Cal watched him disappear over the top before he made his way back to his own house.

He grinned all the way up the back lawn, as he opened the back door, as he quietly got ready for bed in the silent house.

Tomorrow. Cal could hardly wait.

CHAPTER 6

*C*al made a terrible mistake the next morning.

During breakfast, his father was talking about something going on at the office, and, thinking about the conversation he had had with Jack about exactly what he'd be doing at Buchanan Industries one day...he asked.

Theodore was thrilled, of course.

"I'm glad you're showing interest and initiative," he said, slapping his hand on his knee. "I think this summer is a great time to bring you in, let you get your feet wet, as it were."

Cal stammered out a feeble protest. "Oh. I didn't mean that I wanted to — I was just curious about how it might work, or what — I wasn't sure where I would start. I don't want to be in the way."

"Nonsense," Theodore said. "You won't be in the way. It's a good time to start learning the ropes. Next year will be here before you know it."

Cal swallowed back bile. He was well aware how quickly time was ticking by.

Before Cal knew what was happening, he was being

instructed to put on a suit and get back downstairs to go to the office with Theodore.

On his way out, he dashed over to Flora, who was alone in the kitchen, cleaning up breakfast.

"Can you get a message to your friend next door?" he asked in a low voice.

"To my friend? Of course," she said. "What shall I tell my friend?"

"Say that something came up, and that I'll be available later today."

She nodded, and he wrapped an arm around her in a brief hug.

"Thanks, Flora. I owe you."

With one last longing look towards the back door, he hurried out the front and to his waiting father.

The office was exactly as he remembered it: stuffy, boring, and full of old men. There were some younger ones, of course, but they were so annoyingly obsequious that Cal tried to pretend they didn't exist.

Theodore brought him around to re-introduce him to the important players. He did his best to give firm handshakes, make safe compliments, act like he knew something about anything. He was given a desk in an empty office and a stack of financial documents to read to "get up to speed on current projects." With a muffled sigh, he started plowing through them.

Two hours later, he knew more than he needed to know about the cash flow problems of a handful of factories in the Midwest, was no clearer on what he'd be expected to *do* when he started working there than before, and he was even more sure it would bore him to tears.

A secretary popped her head into the office shortly before lunch, her bobbed blonde hair curling up at the ends with a bounce that matched her step.

"Mr. Buchanan?" she said.

It took Cal a second to realize she was talking to him.

"Yes?" he asked.

"The other Mr. Buchanan would like to see you in his office. I can take you."

She waited for him to button up his jacket, and then led him up to a large corner office on the sixth floor. His father was sitting behind a large mahogany desk, and he was on the phone.

"We'll need those figures by Friday," he was saying. He looked up and waved Cal in, pointing to one of the wingback chairs facing the desk. Cal sat and waited for his father to finish the call.

When he did, he turned to Cal. "How did the morning go?"

Cal shrugged. "Fine."

His father was watching him carefully. "What did you think? Any opinions on what you read?"

"The companies seem to be in trouble."

"True," Theodore said. "The question is, any chance they can be profitable? Just your gut instinct, if you have one. Obviously, determining that for sure takes a lot more—"

"All of them except Ohio," Cal said.

Theodore blinked at him, and then frowned. "The one in Ohio has the most solid footing," he said. "Its debt is secured and it —" He stopped and shook his head, looking disappointed. "It takes time to really understand these things."

"The Ohio plant is going to be affected by pending federal environmental legislation," Cal said. "It won't happen immediately, but it's likely to end up costing the company a fortune eventually."

"That'll never pass," Theodore said, waving it away.

"Fred Donohue's father seems to think it will," Cal said. "I had dinner with him just before school ended and he was talking about it. It's got Republican support."

"Congressman Donohue told you that?" Theodore looked thoughtful. "All right. I'll put some associates on it. Thank you, that's a potentially valuable contribution."

Cal fidgeted in his chair, unused to the praise from his father, as mild as it was. He decided to take advantage of it.

"Would it be possible for me to head out?" he asked. "I sort of had plans today."

Theodore laughed. "All right, I'll let you get back to your friends. Have one last summer of freedom." He was relieved until Theodore added, "You can come in a couple of mornings a week to begin to get up to speed."

He buzzed his secretary to call a car to bring Cal back home, and Cal gratefully retreated from the place he least wanted to be.

An hour later, having changed out of his suit and into swim trunks and a tee-shirt, he threw a towel over his shoulder and bounded down the stairs towards the back door and the beach beyond.

His stomach churned with excitement. He'd done his best to put last night out of his mind all morning, because otherwise he wouldn't have been able to stand it. But on the ride back to the house, he'd gone over and over it, reliving the moments again and again until he was vibrating with anticipation.

The memory of the look on Jack's face right before they'd kissed, awash in moonlight and oddly determined, had haunted him all night long. He wanted to see that look again. Wanted Jack to take control like he'd done on the widow's walk, or when he'd pushed Cal up against the cliff wall.

Shivering at the idea, he reached for the doorknob.

Flora called out to stop him, coming through the doorway to the kitchen with a large basket in her arms.

71

"What's this?" he asked.

"Can't let you go over to that boy's place empty-handed," she said. "What would he think of your manners?"

She pushed the basket into his hands, and he lifted the lid to peek inside.

"Lunch?" He grinned. That's right, it was lunchtime. He'd completely forgotten about eating in his rush to get back to Jack.

"Go," she said. "He seemed anxious to see you when I called over this morning." She patted his hand. "Don't keep him waiting any longer."

"Thanks," Cal said. "Hey, if my mother asks—"

"She's out shopping. She went to Mystic for the day, won't be home until after dinner. Your father is going to the club after work. Maybe you have dinner plans too?" She winked.

"Maybe," Cal said, his spirits lifting further.

If his parents weren't around, then Cal didn't need to be, either. He could stay at Jack's all day. Would Jack even want him around that long? There was only one way to find out.

He made his way down to the shore, his nerves crackling. The ocean sparkled under the sun, waves crashing onto the sand. Gulls soared overhead, crying out as they looped over the sea. Cal squinted against the brightness and peered east.

There was a small group on Jack's beach, sprawled out on loungers and towels. A transistor radio was pumping out the ever-present music, and laughter floated across the sand. As he approached, Cal scanned the people, comforted that it seemed to be Jack's L.A. crew and not any of the locals from the night before.

Cal made his way through the spread towels, nodding his hellos, until he reached Jack's side. The guy was sprawled across a towel in the center of it all, one arm flung over his eyes and the other hand splayed on his stomach. Despite days of hanging out in the sun, his skin remained pale, and Cal resisted the urge to reach out and touch.

He set the picnic basket down and cleared his throat. Jack lifted his arm and blinked up blearily.

"Hi," Cal said. He couldn't help the grin that spread across his face. Jack lit up, coming awake immediately and pushing himself up on his elbows.

"Hi," Jack said. "Fucking hell, you're as tall as a New York skyscraper. Get down here."

Cal spread his towel out beside Jack's and sank onto it, pulling one knee up to his chest and tucking the other leg underneath him. Jack reached out and placed a single fingertip on Cal's knee. Cal stared at it, his pulse jumping at the simple touch, and then he raised his gaze to find Jack watching him with a sly smile. With every passing second, anticipation coiled in Cal's stomach.

Jack skimmed the finger down Cal's shin, and Cal swallowed. *Fuck.* If Jack could make him feel like this just by touching his knee...

"It's about time you got here," Jack said. "I was getting impatient."

"Sorry," Cal said. "I ended up having to go to my dad's office this morning. I got away as soon as I—"

"I'm kidding. Seriously, I'm just happy you came," Jack said. He squeezed Cal's knee, and then left his hand there, a warm, slight pressure that drew Cal's focus. "When do you turn into a pumpkin?"

"A what?"

"Like Cinderella. If you stay out past midnight—"

"Oh. Right. Like the movie." Cal laughed, remembering seeing the animated film while he was in high school. "Fan of Cinderella, are you? Was it the fairy godmother or the dress-making mice that drew you in?"

"I'm a fan of *movies*," Jack said. "So how long can I have

73

you today, before you run away from me like you keep doing?"

Cal glowed at Jack's phrasing — *how long can I have you* — and wanted to respond with *forever if you want me*. But instead, he just shrugged. He was about to find out how Jack felt about him staying *all day*.

"My parents are out for the day, past dinner. So they probably won't be looking for me until tomorrow."

Jack beamed. "Excellent."

He swiped his thumb across Cal's knee, then an inch along the inside of his thigh. Cal felt a tightening in his groin, and licked his lips. He blushed and his eyes darted around to see if anyone noticed.

Jack pointed at the picnic basket. "What's that?"

"Lunch," Cal said. "Flora — our housekeeper — sent it over. Never show up at someone's house—"

"Empty-handed. Right. I'm beginning to love that rule. And maybe your Flora, too. Is she the one who called me this morning?"

"Yeah, she was doing me a favor. Going to the office happened sort of suddenly, or else I would have called myself."

"What did she pack?"

"Let's see," said Cal. He pulled the basket over and flipped open the lid. "Sandwiches, fruit salad, potato chips. Enough for everyone."

Jack sat up and folded himself into a cross-legged position. "Far out. Lemme at it, I'm starving."

They dug into the pile of sandwiches, selecting what they wanted, took control of one of the bags of chips and a bowl of fruit, setting the food between them. Then Jack called for someone to bring him a couple of beers and pointed out the food to the others. The group descended, and the basket was empty in seconds.

Someone handed Cal a beer, and after a moment's hesitation, he cracked it open with a satisfying pop and hiss. Jack reached out and tapped his can against Cal's.

"Cheers," he said. "To new friends."

They drank, and Cal relished the taste of the crisp liquid. He wasn't used to drinking during the day, but there was something heady about it. Freeing.

He smiled, feeling the sun beat down on his face and listening to the music on the radio, letting all the tension of the morning slide out of him.

They talked easily through lunch, on subjects ranging from movies to baseball to politics. They argued good-naturedly about the superiority of New York City vs. Boston, and then Cal asked about Los Angeles.

"Do you not like it?" he asked. "You said you...I think you said you needed to get out, which is why you came here. Why did you need to get out?"

Jack, who had been lounging on his side, his head propped with one hand, sat up suddenly.

"That's a boring story," he said. "Let's go swimming, I'm hot." He jumped to his feet, reaching down to grab Cal's hand.

Cal let himself be pulled to his feet. He yanked his tee-shirt over his head and tossed it onto his towel. When he turned back towards Jack, the guy was staring at him.

"Holy shit," he muttered. His gaze flicked up from Cal's bare stomach to his eyes. "You're an Adonis."

Before Cal could react, Jack grabbed his hand and dragged him towards the ocean.

After several hours alternating between splashing in the waves and drying in the sun, Jack's crowd started migrating towards the house. Jack agreed that they could use a break from the sun, and Cal helped him gather up their things, stowing the beach chairs in the shed under the stairs.

"I should go home and change," Cal said, glancing over his shoulder.

"Why?" Jack asked, shoving the shed door closed with his shoulder.

"Because I'm sandy and coated in salt," Cal said. "I could use a shower and don't want to track stuff all over your house."

"I'm tracking stuff all over my house," Jack said. He peered at Cal, and then, with a glance around at the now-empty beach, he leaned in conspiratorially. "Here's the thing, Cal. You have a habit of going missing, through no fault of your own. If you go home, you might not come back."

Cal opened and closed his mouth, and then a smile crept across his face. He was still struggling with the idea that Jack truly cared whether he was around or not. The guy's proximity started his stomach dancing.

"I'll come back," Cal said. "Promise."

"Good," Jack said. "Because I haven't kissed you yet today."

He rose up on his toes and tipped his face up. Cal stilled, his heart giving a solid thud-thud as Jack's breath tickled Cal's lips.

"And I'm not going to do it now," Jack murmured. "Give you a reason to hurry."

He planted a hand flat on Cal's chest and pushed him away. Cal stumbled backwards, his breath coming out in a small explosion of air.

"Go," he said. "Don't get lost on your way back."

Then he winked and ran for the stairs, taking them two at a time as he bolted away. Cal watched him go, his head and heart spinning.

He practically sprinted up the stairs to his own back lawn, then barreled into the house. He dropped Flora's empty picnic basket in the kitchen and headed upstairs, where he showered in record time, then changed into shorts and a fresh tee-shirt. He took a few extra minutes to make sure his hair fell the way he wanted, slicking in a dab of pomade when a cowlick wouldn't cooperate with water alone.

Then he made the return trek to the house next door, excitement tightening his chest.

The back door opened easily and he stepped inside. The house was quieter than he'd seen it thus far. For once, there was no music blasting. He wandered through the house, walking softly to avoid disturbing a couple of people who seemed to be sleeping on the sofas in the living room. He followed the sound of voices and the clacking of billiard balls into the rec room, where he found a handful of people amidst a hovering cloud of smoke.

Greg, joint in hand, waved at him and smiled with bleary eyes. "Hey, Cal. Want to play?"

Cal scanned the space, looking for a lean figure and a mop of curly hair.

"Thanks, but maybe not right now," he said. "Have you seen—"

"He went upstairs," Joey said. "About twenty minutes ago. I think he's napping."

"Oh." Cal said. He felt suddenly deflated. Maybe Jack's enthusiasm for Cal to return had been a little exaggerated. Or maybe he'd just been wiped out from hours in the sun and fell asleep without meaning to. Cal tried to shake the disappointment off and decide what to do. Should he stay or go?

"You can go up if you want, he won't care," Greg said. "His room is down at the end of the hall. The big one."

"Right. If he's asleep, I can hang out here," Cal said, since he really didn't want to leave. "But I don't want to be in the way, so if you guys are sick of me, just say so."

"You're good," Joey said. "Grab a beer."

"Cal, there you are." Scott wandered in and plucked the joint from Greg's fingers. "Jack said to tell you he went up to shower but you should go on up when you get here."

He held out the joint in offering, but Cal shook his head. "Thanks but no thanks. I guess I'll go up then."

The guys turned their attention back to the pool table and the joint as Cal made his departure. He climbed the stairs, anticipation building again with each step.

He wasn't sure what it was about Jack that made him feel so inept. It's not like this was the first guy he'd ever been involved with. Cal knew he was good looking, and could be charming, and usually he could find ways to flirt, to take the lead, once he'd established mutual interest. This time, he found himself knocked off balance.

Maybe it was the way Jack seemed to dominate every space he was in. His self-assurance let Cal take a back seat, and while that was thrilling, he wasn't used to it.

Whatever the case, he had no idea what Jack would do next, or what his move should be. They'd kissed. Now he was going up to Jack's room, and he didn't know what to expect.

When he reached the room, he hesitated. The door was cracked open, but the room beyond appeared silent. Slowly, he raised his fist and rapped his knuckles lightly on the door frame.

"Come in," Jack called from inside.

Cal pushed the door open slowly. Jack was sprawled on his back on the bed, arms and legs stretched wide. He was wearing pale blue boxers and a white tee-shirt, and his wet curls spread across the pillow in a dark brown sunburst.

"Hey," Cal said. "Am I bothering you?"

"Of course not," Jack said. He raised his head for a second, smiling, before letting it fall back to the pillow. "I was waiting for you."

"Are you feeling okay?" Cal asked.

"I think I finally have a sunburn," Jack said, closing his eyes. "But I'm good. Are you going to stand there all day, or…"

Cal stepped further into the room. After a moment's hesitation, he closed the door behind him. He looked at the man lying on the bed several feet away, and suddenly wasn't going to be shy any longer. Jack had made it clear what he wanted. It was time for Cal to do the same.

He strode forward until he reached the bed and then climbed onto it, crawling up the mattress until he was even with Jack, hovering over him, his knees on either side of Jack's hips and his hands planted beside Jack's shoulders.

Jack's eyes fluttered open. "Hi," he said, his lips curving into a smile.

"I'm tired of waiting for you to kiss me," Cal said. "So I guess I have to do it myself."

He ducked his head and took Jack's lips with his own. If he'd been expecting a fight, he didn't get one. Jack opened to him immediately, coaxing his tongue inside with tiny, teasing licks. He slid a hand around the back of Cal's neck, holding him in place, and arched his back so that their chests brushed together briefly.

Cal happily ceded control and let himself be led. He let out a surprised grunt as Jack suddenly rolled them over, taking the top position and sweeping his palms up Cal's chest, skimming over his nipples and then cupping his jaw.

Trying to focus on what Jack was doing to both his mouth and his chest was overwhelming. Cal moaned softly, then gripped Jack's waist, pulling him down so he was laying flat atop Cal, their hips fitting together seamlessly. He cautiously laid a hand on Jack's ass, and when the touch wasn't rejected, he squeezed the firm muscle lightly.

Now Jack was the one who moaned.

The kissing and tentative exploration went on for a while, as the late afternoon sun began to sink in the sky. Jack was the one who finally broke the kiss. "That was boss," he said breathlessly. He sat back, settling his ass on Cal's abs, and began to trace loops and lines across his chest with a finger. He tilted his head to one side. "You've got really blue eyes. Like, ocean blue. They're pretty."

Heat rushed to Cal's cheeks, and Jack looked absolutely delighted. He slid a palm along Cal's left cheek.

"I love the way you blush. I was right about that, the first night." He snickered. "You know, I was a little drunk that night, and for a minute I thought maybe you'd come *from* the ocean, some mythic creature who'd offer me a deal: one epic night together in return for my soul."

"Would you have taken the deal?" Cal asked.

"I might have, the way you looked. Assuming I still have a soul left to bargain with." He leaned down and kissed Cal gently, then slid to the side, nestling himself against Cal. He draped an arm across Cal's stomach, a leg over his right thigh, and kissed his shoulder. "Sleepy," he murmured, closing his eyes.

Cal lay on his back, almost afraid to move. The long, lean lines of Jack's body pressed up against him. He could feel the guy's breath tickling his neck, and when he turned his head, he got a face full of shampoo-scented curls. He closed his eyes, took a deep breath, and let it out in a sigh that took with it every bit of tension in his body.

He felt himself drifting, dozing. It was okay. He could stay. He didn't have to be home at all, really. By the time his parents got back, they'd assume he was out, and would not expect to see him until the next morning. There was plenty of time.

Beside him, Jack sighed and snuggled closer. Cal smiled and let himself fall asleep, wondering if he was the one who'd made a bargain with his soul. It was the only way to explain his good fortune.

CHAPTER 7

*W*hen Cal woke up, the light in the room had changed to the warm glow of pre-sunset. He blinked, disoriented, and then Jack shifted in his arms, and the events of the afternoon came rushing back.

He looked at the man sleeping peacefully next to him with wonder. Jack's lashes rested against his pale cheeks, his pink lips were parted slightly, and his curls were spread across the pillow. He'd shifted in sleep so that his torso was resting on Cal's, and his right arm curled around Cal's waist.

This was the second time Cal had woken up with Jack. He could make a habit of this, if given the opportunity.

He traced a finger over Jack's brow, along his jaw, and then over the thin layer of uneven bristles on his upper lip. Jack smiled faintly and snuggled closer. Then his eyes fluttered open. They were cloudy for a moment, and then cleared.

"Hi," he said.

"Hi." Cal smoothed a hand down Jack's back, his fingers bumping over Jack's vertebrae.

"What time is it?" Jack lifted his head and peered around the room. His stomach rumbled against Cal's. "Did we miss dinner?"

"I don't know. I just woke up, too." Cal lifted his left arm and squinted at his watch. "It's almost seven."

"Just in time for dinner, then." Jack's stomach rumbled again, and Cal laughed.

"We slept for hours." Cal continued to run his fingers up and down Jack's back.

Jack hummed and stretched, his body elongating and contracting against Cal's side. "You're nice to sleep with," he murmured. "Cozy."

"Thanks," Cal said. "It's just because I'm big."

"No, that's not it." Jack wriggled his hips. "I move a lot in my sleep. Usually. Roll all over the bed and wake up tangled in the sheets. I drive people crazy. This time I didn't move at all." He pushed himself up and peered down at Cal. "You're better for my sleep than weed."

Cal snorted in surprise. "Glad to be of service."

Jack shifted to straddle Cal again. He began to trail his fingers up and down Cal's chest. "I want to touch you. Can I?"

"You *are* touching me," Cal pointed out.

"No, I want to—" Jack pushed his fingers up under the hem of Cal's shirt, where they danced along the skin of his abdomen. Cal gasped. "I want to *touch* you."

Cal's hips gave a tiny, involuntary thrust. "Yes, please," he said.

Jack grinned and licked his lips. Then his stomach whined loudly.

"Maybe dinner first."

Before Cal could protest, Jack hopped off of him and began rummaging through piles of clothing on the floor. Cal watched with interest as Jack tossed items around the room haphazardly. He'd never been allowed to just leave his things lying around. There was something oddly alluring about the idea of being able to throw something somewhere and not have someone following after you with a scolding finger.

An item landed on the bed, and Cal picked it up. Then he hastily dropped it.

"Jack?" he asked.

"Yeah?" Jack muttered an *aha* under his breath as he located a pair of jeans under a chair in the corner.

Cal poked at the silky, lacy blue fabric lying on the edge of the bed. "Something you want to tell me?"

Jack hopped to the side as he tugged the jeans on both legs at once. He paused and squinted at the camisole.

"Oh," he said. "That's not mine. That must be Ginny's."

Cal's stomach dropped. "Ginny's underwear is lying around your room?"

With one last hop, Jack yanked the jeans in place and then went on a hunt for shoes.

"She's probably looking for it. We should throw it in her room." He seemed completely unbothered, which increased Cal's discomfort.

He sat up and swung his legs over the side, flattening his feet on the worn floorboards. "I'm wondering...just because it seems...why is her underwear in your room?"

Jack stopped in his search and looked at Cal. He smiled. "You're concerned about this."

"No, I'm just...I thought you weren't...with Ginny..." Cal fiddled with a loose string on the edge of his shorts. *It doesn't matter,* he told himself.

Jack leaped across the room and tackled Cal, laying him flat across the bed and straddling his waist. He was grinning.

"You've got a hang-up about Ginny. Or is it any girl?" Jack

tilted his head to the side. "She sleeps in here sometimes. She probably pulled it off at night because she was hot."

Cal raised an eyebrow. "And you didn't notice?"

"No. It's not exactly weird. Ginny goes topless sometimes, so it wouldn't have been anything to remark about." He shook his head and laid a palm flat on Cal's chest. "I already told you that Ginny isn't my girlfriend."

"Right. You said that. But now she's sleeping naked in your bed—"

"Not naked. She was probably wearing underwear."

Cal stopped talking. It didn't matter. It didn't matter, because he had zero right to claim Jack, anyhow. They'd barely kissed. They certainly hadn't gone so far for him to feel reasonably possessive.

Even if he did.

Jack leaned down and kissed Cal lightly. "Ginny's not my girlfriend. She's my friend. We've known each other a long time. We share a place in LA, along with a few others." Another kiss. "Now, can we go get dinner, because I'm starving. And then I want to come back here and then *you* can be naked in my bed. If you want to be."

He trailed a finger across Cal's lower lip while biting his own, and Cal's mouth went dry.

"I...okay," Cal managed.

Jack jumped off again, this time pulling Cal with him. "Come on, let's go see if there's any food around here."

Cal let Jack pull him out of the room and towards the stairs.

On the first floor, a few people were milling around. Jack inquired about whereabouts, and they learned that a part of the group had gone out to dinner and everyone else awake had ordered pizza that was already gone.

"We should go out to dinner," Jack said. "And since you're here, you can take us somewhere good."

"Ah, yeah. I mean, okay. Just us?" As much as Cal liked the idea, it made him a little nervous to go out to dinner with Jack alone. It would look — and feel — like a date. And while Cal was fine with the latter, he needed to avoid the former, in case it got back to his parents.

Jack glanced at him, immediately picking up on his fears. "We can see if anyone wants to join. Want me to get the girls again?"

After a moment's hesitation, Cal nodded. Jack patted his cheek. "Give me two seconds."

It was more like seven minutes and two seconds, but eventually Jack reappeared with Ginny and J.C. in tow. Ginny was yawning.

"They were napping, too," Jack said. "And Ginny is hard to wake up."

She smacked him on the shoulder. "I am not. I just didn't see the point."

"Until he explained that you were taking us to dinner like a dear," J.C. said. She slipped her arm through Cal's and hung off of his elbow.

Ginny grinned sleepily and took up a spot on Cal's other arm. "Yes. So generous. Let's go."

Jack led the way to the front of the house, grabbing a set of rental car keys from a hook by the door. Once outside, J.C. let go of Cal and dashed down the steps.

"I'm driving," she shouted, climbing into a pale blue convertible without opening the door. She slid into the seat, somehow produced a mint green head scarf from out of her cleavage, and wrapped it around her hair. "Hey Cal, sit shotgun so you can tell me where to go."

Cal glanced at Jack, who was laughing. "Sit up front at your own risk," he said. "But find something to hold onto. J.C. is a terrible driver."

"Am not," J.C. shot back. She smiled sweetly at Cal and patted the seat next to her.

The drive into town wasn't long, but Jack was right. It wasn't that the girl was a bad driver, exactly. She handled the car expertly. It was more that she seemed to think things like stop signs and road markings and speed limits were merely suggestions. Subtly gripping the underside of the dashboard for stability, Cal directed them to an Italian spot he liked, and J.C. parked crookedly next to the curb.

They settled in a booth next to the window. A waiter in a white coat and black trousers brought a basket of warm, crusty garlic bread, and Jack ordered a bottle of the house Chianti for the table.

Ginny and J.C. began an intense discussion of what songs to select on the tabletop jukebox, spinning the metal dial to flip the pages back and forth. Jack dug a handful of dimes out of his pocket and deposited them on the table with a clatter, and Ginny grinned and kissed him on the cheek.

He turned his attention to the paper menu. "This says 'steamed Little Necks with drawn butter.' What is a 'Little Neck?'" Jack frowned. "Little neck of what?"

Cal grinned. "It's clams," he said.

"Clams have necks?" Jack's eyebrows shot up. "I guess if they do, they'd be little."

"It's a type of clam," Cal said, laughing. "They're really common around here."

"Are they good?"

"If you like clams, sure," Cal said.

Jack looked puzzled. "I don't know if I like clams. Let's try them."

The waiter returned with the wine, and they placed their orders. Jack poured the wine, the girls finished feeding dimes into the jukebox, and they settled into easy conversation.

When the clams arrived, Cal explained to Jack about the small bowl of hot water the waiter had placed in front of him beside the one with the butter.

"It's to wash the clams," Cal said.

Jack made a face. "They don't come pre-washed?"

"No, you have to...it's because of the sand. That might have still been in the shell. Here, watch." Cal picked up a clam shell, pulled out the meat, swished it in the water, then dipped it in the butter and popped it in his mouth. "See?"

Jack looked uncertain, but he followed suit. When he got to the washing part, he took his time, brushing at it with his fingers.

"What are you doing"? Cal asked. "Just..."

He reached out, took the clam from Jack's hand, shook the water off of it, then dipped it in the butter and held it out.

"Here. Try it," he said.

Jack opened his mouth, and Cal fed him the clam. Their eyes met for a brief second. A bolt of desire sliced through Cal as Jack's lips brushed his fingers, and he pulled his hand back, hiding it in the napkin in his lap. He looked away, hating that he was blushing.

"Okay, that's good," Jack said. Cal snuck a look back up and saw that his eyes were sparkling. "But honestly I think what's good is the delivery." He winked. "The butter, I mean."

They polished off the clams and then their dinners arrived. Cal was halfway through his chicken parmigiana, and laughing heartily at J.C.'s description of Jack trying to learn how to ride a horse for his role in *Burnt Horizon*, when he heard his name.

He turned to see the Wallace twins, along with Jay Ashford and Tom Benjamin, entering the restaurant. He froze.

It's fine, he reminded himself. *You're just having dinner.*

As if on cue, J.C. slid closer and rested a hand on the back of his neck, playing with his hair.

"Calloway," Richie called again, waving. Cal waved back and the group started over.

"Friends of yours?" Jack asked, watching them with interest.

"Yeah. Summer people. They don't live here year round, they just come for the summers."

"Like me?"

"No, not...well, sort of. But it's different." Cal put his napkin beside his plate and stood as his friends approached. "Good to see you," he said, extending his hand and shaking one, two, three. "Rich. Tom. Jay. Hi, Sally."

"Jay and Tom got in today," Richie said. "We rang the house this afternoon, but no one answered."

"I was on the beach," Cal said. He glanced over his shoulder, at where Jack and the girls were looking on patiently. "Hey, this is Jack, and that's Ginny, and—"

J.C. was at his side, snaking an arm around his waist. "I'm J.C.," she said, tossing her hair and flashing white teeth. "It's nice to meet friends of Calloway."

Gratefully, he draped an arm over her shoulder. "They rented the old Winston place next door for the season."

"What does J.C. stand for?" Jay asked.

"Just Cheeky." J.C. winked, and Jay laughed and exchanged a look with Cal. The look said, *she's a handful.* Cal just pulled her closer.

"Hold on, aren't you — you *are*," Sally said, pushing past her brother. "Calloway, this is Jack Francis. You're *Jack Francis.*"

"I know," Jack said, smirking. "You guys want to join us?"

Everyone agreed. They called the waiter over, and there was a flurry of activity before the newcomers were seated at a table pushed up against the end of the booth. Sally maneuvered herself into the chair closest to Jack and immediately began asking him questions. He seemed to enjoy the attention, his smile and laughter genuine.

Cal focused on the guys. He asked Jay and Tom about their plans for the summer and beyond. He answered questions about his parents, and mutual acquaintances from Harvard. J.C. put herself practically in Cal's lap, and joined in the conversation with an ease that Cal admired.

Another two bottles of wine appeared, and before long there was a lull of food coma and wine drowsiness. Cal idly thought about getting a gift for J.C., who seemed awfully interested in Richie Wallace but, to her extreme credit, continued to play her part.

Across the table, Ginny leaned into Jack, resting her head on his shoulder. At one point, he turned and kissed the top of her head. Cal watched them, wondering. Jack said they were close, but they seemed almost too close. He tried to stamp out the spark of jealousy that flared up when Jack stroked her arm.

Carefully, he slid a foot forward until it bumped up against Jack's. Jack shot a glance in his direction, but didn't otherwise react.

Then Cal felt a repeated pressure on top of his shoe, an answering *tap-tap-tap* and then a nudge.

"All right, I hate to cut the party short, but I think it's time to head back home," Jack said. "I think I got too much sun today."

Sally looked comically disappointed, but she quickly recovered. "I know what we'll do. We'll take you to Sea View tomorrow. As a big old Rhode Island welcome party."

"Sea View?" Jack asked.

"The beach club," Cal supplied.

"You'll love it," said Sally. "It's very posh."

"Oh, posh." Jack smirked. "Then I'm sure it's exactly my style."

Cal choked back a laugh. "So is that the plan?" he asked, eyeing Jack. "You interested in a day at the beach club?"

"Sure, I can dig it," Jack said.

Cal's friends stood and made room so Jack and his party could slide out of the booth. There were handshakes all around. Jack kissed Sally on the cheek, and she turned a shade of magenta Cal had never seen before.

Once back in the car — Cal driving this time, with Jack beside him and the girls in the back — Cal sighed.

"Do you really want to go to the beach club tomorrow?" he asked. "If you want to get out of it, I can make excuses."

"Are you going?" Jack asked.

"Yeah, I should," Cal said, pulling onto the road. "They'll expect me to."

"Then I want to go." Jack grinned at Cal, then slid over on the bench seat and laid a hand on Cal's thigh, where it sat, a light pressure that Cal knew was going to torture him. "And if Sally is going to be there, we don't even need to drag the girls."

"Oh no, you're not leaving us out," Ginny said. "J.C. wants to see what Richie looks like without a shirt and she will not be stymied."

"I'll be subtle about it, though," J.C. said.

"Hey," Cal said, "what *does* J.C. stand for, anyway?"

"Juicy Cherries," J.C. said.

Cal rolled his eyes, and tried not to let Jack's wandering hand distract him from driving.

Back at the house, Jack offered Ginny a hand out of the car.

"Thanks again, girls," he said. "For the cover."

"Our pleasure, honey," Ginny said. She kissed him on the

lips as she straightened up. "Any time we can get a free dinner…"

She glanced over and saw Cal watching, and smiled. As they headed in, with Jack in the lead, she sidled up to Cal.

"You've got nothing to worry about with me," she whispered.

"What?" Cal frowned.

"You're the shiny new toy, Cal," she said. "He's only got eyes for you right now."

"He does?"

She giggled. "He's been talking about you since the night you met, on the beach. He'll get distracted by someone eventually — he always does — but it won't be by me. I swear on my Chanel clutch."

She bounced up and kissed him on the cheek. Then she dashed away, grabbing J.C.'s hand and dragging her into the house, saying something about a dance party and leaving Cal staring after her, his insides churning with anticipation and confusion.

The music had already started pumping by the time Cal caught up with Jack in the kitchen. Jack was guzzling water from a glass. He refilled it under the tap and passed it to Cal, who drank it down.

"Please don't ask me to join the dance party," he said, setting the empty glass on the counter.

Jack smiled. "Okay. Let's go sit on the deck for a bit."

Cal followed him outside. Penny, the girl Cal had caught in action the first night he came to the house, was lounging on a sofa with Joey. They were passing a joint between them.

"Hey boys," Penny said. "How was dinner?"

Jack snagged the joint and took a hit. "Delicious," he said, the word choked off from holding in his breath. Then he blew out a steady stream of smoke. "Did you know clams have little necks?"

"Gross," Joey said, making a face.

Jack offered the joint to Cal, and Cal took it. He'd felt nice the other night, the first time he'd smoked, and now that he knew he could stay...with Jack...

He took a hit.

They settled on the sofa beside the others. It was a bit crowded, and after the joint made a second round, Jack leaned into Cal with a sigh. He took Cal's left hand in both of his and began to trace shapes and patterns on Cal's palm.

It felt so nice, Cal sank lower in the sofa and stretched his legs out in front of him.

"Tell me about summer people," Jack said, his voice going soft around the edges, like the bottom bits of a goose feather. "Why is it different from what I'm doing?"

"I don't know," Cal said. "Those guys, they...their families own houses up the beach. But they live elsewhere. Jay lives in Boston, and Tom in Hartford. Well, their families do, they're both at Yale right now."

"And I live in L.A." Jack took one more hit, but when he offered it, Cal shook his head. He was already feeling less substantial than a few minutes earlier. Jack passed the joint back to Joey and returned to play with Cal's hand.

"Right, but...Boston and Hartford are sort of close to here. And the Wallaces only live in Providence. But every summer they come and live in these giant houses that are empty for most of the year. I don't...I can't explain it." He stretched out his palm, giving Jack better access. "Then they kind of act like they own everything, like this place only exists when they're in it and isn't a functioning town year round. They treat townies like...servants sometimes."

"That's shitty. You're friends with these people?"

Cal shrugged. "Yes? They're not bad, really. They're nice people overall. It's just an attitude that they grew up with and have adopted and probably aren't even aware of."

"You could make them aware."

"I guess I could. I'm not sure it would make a difference. They'd probably laugh at me and think I was making a joke." Cal turned his head to find Jack watching him, his eyes shining in the moonlight, his mouth open slightly.

Without thinking, Cal leaned down and nipped at Jack's lower lip, sinking his teeth into it gently. Then he licked away the bite, tasting smoke and garlic. Unable to stop himself, he pressed his lips against Jack's.

The guy didn't seem to need any more encouragement. He kissed back, slowly, as if to draw the moment out. Cal parted his lips, and Jack advanced, sliding his tongue between them to tangle with Cal's.

It felt so good to kiss Jack. Cal had kissed plenty of people since that first sloppy dorm room experiment with James Grenville, but with Jack it was different. It wasn't just that Jack was an expert kisser — which we was — it was more that, from the very first, it had felt like they fit.

Jack shifted, his mouth breaking from Cal's long enough for him to climb into Cal's lap, straddling his thighs. Then he was back, his hands cupping Cal's jaw, pressing Cal into the sofa with a soft moan. Cal clutched at Jack's waist, then slid his hands down to squeeze Jack's ass. He lifted his hips, grinding up into the other man, and was rewarded with a shudder that made him smile around the kiss.

"Can you stay?" Jack whispered urgently. "Can you stay tonight?"

Could he? His parents were probably home at this point. Maybe in bed. They'd have assumed he was out with friends. He could probably sneak back in the morning before they woke up, or say he'd gone out for an early walk.

"Yes," Cal whispered back.

Jack slid off of his lap and Cal drew in a breath of ocean air and blinked. He'd forgotten they were out in the open, here on the deck. All he'd been able to focus on was Jack's mouth. He blushed, realizing that Penny and Joey were still curled up on the other end of the sofa, talking quietly as if they hadn't noticed what was going on two feet from them. Maybe they hadn't. Or maybe they had and didn't care.

The rush of freedom Cal felt in that moment would have knocked him over if he hadn't already been sitting down.

"Come with me," Jack said, extending a hand.

Cal looked up at him. His face was in shadow, the moon behind him a bright spot that made it difficult to see his features. All Cal could do was trust that Jack wanted this, wanted *him*, and leap.

He placed his hand in Jack's and let the man tug him to his feet. They entered the house, and Jack waved to a few of his friends crossing through the back hall. It wasn't even late. Maybe just past ten, about time for the never-ending party to pick up steam. But here he was, being led away from the crowd, *holding Jack's hand*, and it was absurdly obvious what was going on between them.

The weed must have dulled his panic responses, because instead of feeling like he needed to flee to a dark corner, he felt proud. That out of all of the people here, Jack had chosen him. Was interested in him.

For now, interrupted a little voice in the back of his head. He tried to ignore it, but it persisted. *A shiny new toy*, is what Ginny had called him. Jack would *get distracted by someone eventually*.

A surge of jealousy hit him, even though he knew it was stupid. This was not the thing to dwell on as he was literally climbing the stairs to Jack's room. He needed to enjoy the time he had, and not demand more than he deserved.

They reached the bedroom, and Jack shut the door behind them.

"Finally," he murmured. "Thanks for dinner, Cal. I was a

sure thing without it, but my stomach *is* the way to my heart."

Then he stepped close, pushing Cal up against the door, palms on his chest. He rose up and brushed their lips together.

"Can I touch you now?"

Without waiting for an answer, he skimmed his hands down to Cal's waist and then lower.

Cal gasped. "Fuck," he said, letting his head fall back against the door with a thud.

"Jesus Christ, you're a handful," Jack said with a giggle.

He grabbed Jack's shoulders and fastened his lips onto Jack's neck, sucking harder as Jack whined and arched against him. He began walking him backwards towards the bed, biting down on his collarbone and earning a tiny yelp.

Jack began to wriggle, and Cal realized he was trying to pull his tee-shirt over his head. He grabbed the end of it and yanked up, and after a moment of tugging, it was free. He tossed it on the floor and his hands immediately began to roam all over Jack's pale skin.

"God," Jack said, shivering under his touch, "your hands."

Jack let him explore for a minute, nipping and sucking and stroking wherever he could reach, before cool fingers were sneaking under the hem of Cal's own shirt. Then it was pushed up and Cal pulled it off impatiently, slinging it to the floor beside Jack's.

He was spun around and pushed onto the bed, and he scrambled his way up, Jack crawling after him, a predatory look in his eyes. A quaking desire washed over Cal. He was used to being the aggressor in matters of the bedroom. It was expected of him, since he was always the bigger one, and he didn't mind, but this... He didn't think anyone had ever looked at him quite like this before, and it was a heady feeling, being stalked.

"You're beautiful," Jack said, sitting back on his heels. He trailed a single finger down the center of Cal's chest. "I can't wait to taste every inch of you."

Cal's fists grabbed at the sheets. One of them closed over a softer fabric, and he lifted it off the bed.

The camisole. Ginny's camisole. He tried not to let what Ginny had said earlier come back into his mind, but there it was. He was a shiny new toy, and Jack would get distracted by someone else.

"What's the matter?" Jack asked, sensing a shift in the mood.

"So you're really not sleeping with Ginny?" Cal asked, holding up the camisole.

"We already had this conversation," Jack said, a tiny frown marring his features.

"Right. I'm sorry. You're so comfortable with her, like at dinner, it really looks like—"

"We're actors," Jack said. "And good friends. But also...we have slept together. We just aren't right now."

"Oh." Cal paused at that revelation. "Would you again?"

"If she offered at some point? Probably," Jack said. "I mean, I like girls too."

"What if she offered tomorrow?" Cal asked, hating himself with each word. "Or someone else did?"

Jack looked at Cal for a long minute. "Cal," he said carefully, "I don't do jealousy."

"What?"

"Jealousy isn't my thing. So as much as it would break my whole heart, if you're going to get jealous every time someone might catch my eye for a second, then—"

"I'm not jealous," Cal said, a cold fear snaking down his chest. He was going to mess this up before it had a chance to start, wasn't he? "I'm not — I won't—"

"I'm here for the summer," Jack said. "Just the summer.

Like you. And then I'll go back to L.A. and you'll go back to Harvard, and it'll be like...good memories — lots of them, I hope — that we can look back on."

A sense of unearned regret settled over Cal. Jack was right. He didn't know what he was getting so tense about, when this wasn't anything more than two men having a little fun for a while. He'd done it before, he'd do it again. For his whole life, most likely.

Dwelling on that would make him sad, so he shoved it aside.

"I know," he said. "I wasn't meaning to imply anything else."

Jack looked thoughtful. "What if I say that, as long as you and I are fooling around, I won't fool around with anyone else. Would that make it better?"

Cal nodded, and exhaled slowly.

"Okay then," Jack said. "While we're a thing, we're a thing. But if we do that, you have to promise me something."

"Promise what?" Cal asked.

"You can't get all jealous any time someone kisses me or I have my arm around someone or — whatever. I like to touch people. I like to be touched. I like to look and admire. But if I tell you there's nothing else, there's nothing else. You have to promise to trust me to be honest with you. I will tell you if I need to move on, you won't have to guess."

Cal swallowed. "Yes," he said. "I promise."

Jack smiled. "Good. Because I can't imagine wanting anyone else while I've got access to you, anyway," he said. "I'm going to kiss you now."

He climbed atop Cal then and made good on his word, sealing their agreement with a kiss that had Cal's toes curling. He reached for Jack, finding his waist and fumbling with the button on his jeans. Jack angled his hips up to give Cal better access, but continued his assault on Cal's mouth.

When the button finally gave way, Cal yanked the zipper down and then slid his hand inside.

"Umff," Jack moaned into Cal's mouth, thrusting himself against Cal's palm with short, jerky movements.

Then he rolled to the side, and fought with his jeans and boxers until he was able to kick them off the bed. They hit the floor with a *whumpf.*

"Now you," Jack said. He made quick work of Cal's shorts and his own boxers, sending them after the jeans. "Holy fuck," Jack breathed, gazing down at Cal with eyes wide.

Cal felt his cheeks and neck and — probably everything else — heat to a bright pink.

"I just want to — let me —" Jack scooted down the mattress. Then he dipped his head and Cal's breath stalled in his throat.

Everything went silvery and shimmery as they connected in this private space that was just for them. Again Cal wondered at being the prey for once, the one who wasn't in control, the one who wasn't calling the shots or making the moves. He surrendered to it, a willing passenger on a wild ride.

This man could give classes, Cal thought, his left hand dancing in Jack's curls. He wasn't going to last. He was already seeing stars at the edges of his vision, was already feeling everything tighten, already sensing that rush that was about to make it too late.

"I'm gonna — watch out," he managed, just before he exploded with a cry.

Jack pulled off, grinning like a satisfied cat, licking his lips and shaking his hair out of his face.

"Beautiful," Jack said, the word thick in his throat.

"Jesus," Cal breathed. "Thank you."

He closed his eyes and felt himself drifting in that hazy, post-orgasmic state. It might have had something to do with the weed as well, he realized. He felt Jack snuggle up beside him, sheets pulled over him, and forced his eyes open.

"You...I can take care of you," he said, the words slurring. He fought the drowsiness. "I want to…"

"Later," Jack whispered in his ear. "We've got all night."

"All night," Cal agreed. His eyes closed again. As he let the sleep take him under, he thought he heard one more thing, though he might have imagined it.

"We've got all summer," Jack whispered. "All summer."

CHAPTER 8

I'm *going to regret this.*

Cal knew it was risky, introducing Jack to the summer crowd. These were people he'd known all his life. Whose parents knew his parents. Word traveled fast in a small beach town like theirs, and all it would take was one wrong look, one accidental touch, one overheard comment, for all the carefully constructed dominos of his world to come crashing down around him.

He was already struggling to keep his hands to himself and his thoughts off of his face when it came to Jack, and it was downright terrifying to know he'd have to do it for an entire afternoon.

He watched his friends pull into the parking lot at the beach club, one right after the other, as if they'd coordinated a caravan. The Wallaces were in front in their blue Corvette, followed by Jay Ashford in his more sensible white Impala, and then Tom Benjamin in his cherry red Galaxie.

They turned into their parking spaces nearly in unison, like something out of a movie, honking and waving.

"So…" Jack said from beside him. "You're a member of a street gang, right? They're gonna spill out of those cars with knives and start a rumble with the Jets?"

Cal snickered. "Something like that," he said. He raised a hand and waved back at the arriving crowd.

And it was a crowd, or more of one than he had thought there would be. Tom had brought along his kid sister and a friend of hers, and they climbed out of the Galaxie, giggling and straightening their sleeveless crop tops and matching checkered shorts. Jay was joined by Brian Bridgewater and his sister Susie.

It seemed as though more of the summer people had landed.

"Calloway," Brian called. "Been a century. How's your portfolio?"

Cal rolled his eyes. "Better than yours."

"How's your portfolio?" Jack muttered under his breath. Cal glanced at him, and could tell he was suppressing a laugh.

Cal watched his lips curve, wishing he could trace them with his fingers. It was amazing that he still wanted to, that he still craved touching this man, after the night they'd had.

They'd woken up several times before dawn, falling together in easy, hushed exploration. Lips and tongues tangled and tasted, fingers skimmed over skin, they whispered and moaned in each other's ears as they learned each other from head to toe.

In the morning, Cal had woken Jack one last time before he had to leave, feasting on his mouth once more.

Then he'd snuck home, needing to get in before either of his parents awoke. He'd made it without incident and had lain in bed, reliving the hours that had passed with a dazed smile on his face.

Now, Jack looked up at him, and his expression softened. His eyes dropped to Cal's mouth, and Cal felt a thrill at the knowledge that — just maybe — Jack was remembering their night as well.

Stop, he cautioned himself. He cleared his throat and straightened up, resolutely tearing his eyes off of Jack and promising himself he'd keep it together. He had to.

The group gathered bags out of the trunks of the cars and made their way towards where Cal was standing with Jack, Ginny, and JC.

Cal shook hands with the guys and accepted kisses on the cheek from the girls. There was a flurry of *how have you beens* and *god I'm so glad it's finally summer* and *you look amazing.* Then Cal introduced Jack and the girls to the new additions. The women all eyed Jack, and he grinned at them, clearly enjoying the attention.

No jealousy, Cal reminded himself.

Still, even though he knew he was playing with fire, he couldn't help but place a firm hand on Jack's shoulder, gripping it tightly as if to stake his claim.

"Shall we go in and show the visitors what Sea View Beach Club has to offer?" he asked.

They headed into the clubhouse, checking in with the front desk and registering the guests for the day. Richie had called ahead and reserved a couple of cabanas, and the group collected lounge chairs and then exited the clubhouse onto the sand and headed towards their designated structures.

There was easy chatter as they set things up, laying out towels and unfolding lounge chairs onto the sand. The girls broke out the baby oil and began to lather themselves from head to toe. Ginny and J.C. joined the others and in no time were giggling and sharing wide-brimmed hats and stories.

Jack collapsed onto a sofa inside one of the cabanas, and winked at Cal before patting the cushion beside him. With a quick glance around to ensure that the others were busy, Cal accepted the invitation and lowered himself onto the sofa. The canvas cushion crackled underneath his weight.

He was careful to maintain a space between them, but his

skin rippled with nearness anyhow. Jack slid his foot to the right until it was just resting against Cal's. They exchanged a glance, and then Jack moved his foot away just as Richie entered the tent.

Careful, Cal reminded himself.

"I'm starving," Richie said, patting his stomach. "Let's get some food."

The rest of them agreed, and they raised the flag for the waitstaff. Within ten minutes, Richie had ordered burgers and fries for the group. He then settled into a chair near Jack.

"So what made you decide on Westerly for a summer vacation?" Richie asked.

Jack shrugged. "My agent set it up. I just needed to be somewhere that wasn't LA, and I wanted to be near the beach still, but somewhere kind of out of the way. He found this."

"We're so lucky that he did," Sally said, entering the tent and perching on the arm of Richie's chair. "That you ended up here. What's it like to be a movie star?"

"Amazing and a pain in the ass all at once," Jack said, flashing a set of white teeth.

"But will you need to go back to LA to film over the summer?" Sally asked. "Or are you here for the entire time?"

"I might need to go back for some reshoots," Jack said. "But I'm not scheduled to be on set again full time until September. In the meantime, I'm supposed to be reading scripts, but...I haven't really gotten around to doing much of that yet."

"Is that all the stacks of paper on your nightstand?" Cal asked, without thinking.

As soon as the words were out of his mouth, he wished he could swallow them back. How was he supposed to explain being in a position to notice what was on Jack's nightstand, of all places? *Fuck*, he was messing this up already.

But Jack was already answering. "On the desk, the floor, you've probably seen some on the deck and the kitchen counter. My agent has sent me boxes and I don't know how he expects me to read all of them."

"Are any of them good?" Sally asked.

Jack shrugged. "A few I've glanced at look promising. Some not." He rolled his eyes. "Unless a film about an alien who falls in love with a car sounds appealing to you."

"Are you up for the part of the car or the alien?" Cal asked.

Jack rolled his eyes. "Neither, smartass. I'm supposed to be reading for the car's owner, who the film is really about."

The conversation continued, and Cal slowly relaxed. It seemed like no one had noticed or thought it strange that he'd seen the scripts.

The food arrived, and they ate with gusto. J.C. dragged Richie into the ocean, and they were followed by some of the others. Jack seemed content to sit out on the sand with a beer, and Cal tried to decide if he should go into the ocean with the others, so as not to seem too glued to Jack's side.

Sally didn't seem to have such concerns, as she sprawled herself artfully on her towel and continued pestering Jack with questions. Cal tried not to be bothered by the way she kept touching Jack's arm or knee.

"You should let us take you out on the boat sometime," she said. "We try to take it out on most weekends, so if you're free you can join us."

Jack hummed noncommittally. Then he turned to Cal. "What about you? Do you have a boat?"

"Oh, the Buchanan yacht is amazing," Sally said, before Cal could answer. "Calloway, you haven't taken him out yet?"

"You have a yacht?" Jack asked, a corner of his lip quirking up. "I should have known."

"A small one," Cal said, blushing. "And it's my father's, not mine."

"It's so nice," Sally said. "Way better than our little thing." She stood up and peered down the beach, holding her hand over her eyes to block the sun and squinting. "You can almost see it from here, I think," she said.

"It's here?" Jack asked Cal.

"Yeah," Cal said. "Or rather, at the yacht club next door. It's easier because they'll maintain it for us as part of the slip fees."

"Will you show it to me?"

Cal fidgeted. Jack was watching him, a glint in his eye.

"Ooh, yes," Sally said, bouncing on her toes. "Let's show Jack the yacht."

"Sure, I guess," Cal said, with a shrug.

He got to his feet, and instinctively reached a hand down to help Jack up. The man squeezed his forearm and pulled himself to his feet.

They started off down the beach. Within a few seconds, however, Ginny came bounding up.

"Sally," she said, breathless. "Come on, you're coming with me."

"Why?" Sally asked.

"I need you. Girl stuff," Ginny said. She grabbed Sally's hand and started dragging her away, tossing a wink over her shoulder. Sally made a few noises of protest, but eventually gave in, leaving Cal standing next to Jack, bewildered.

"Let's go," Jack said, poking at Cal's bicep. "I want to see this impressive boat."

"Did you ask Ginn—" Cal began, trying to articulate his thoughts.

"No, but she's sharp. She sees us walking somewhere...she assumes we want to be alone if possible. I told you she'd help us."

With a roll of his eyes and a zing of anticipation in his stomach, Cal led Jack down the beach to the yacht club entrance. He checked in at security and signed Jack in as a guest, then they walked out to the slips and over to his parents' fifty-seven footer.

"There she is," he said, waving his hand with a flourish. "Home sweet boat."

Jack let out a low whistle. "She's a beauty." Then he glanced sideways at Cal and winked. "Or I'm guessing, since I know nothing about boats and have never been on a yacht."

"Never?" Cal asked.

"Nope." Jack squinted at the script scrawled across the white paint. "*Buchanan's Bounty?* That's the name?" he asked.

"Yeah, it's dumb, but my father likes his name — our name — on things," Cal said. He shoved his hair off of his forehead and laughed shortly. "Well...do you want to go aboard?"

Jack nodded eagerly. They made their way down the dock and, deciding to forgo the ramp, Cal stepped onto the gunnel. He unclipped the safety line, held onto the railing to make sure his footing was secure, and then extended a hand. Jack grabbed it and stepped aboard.

Cal showed him around, hyper-aware of Jack's slightly skeptical expression as he took in the kitchen, the luxury seating, and the fully stocked bar of the main cabin.

"It's a lot, I know," Cal said, trying to see it with virgin eyes. It was a nice setup, but also pretentious, with white leather and chrome everywhere. And who needed a full humidor on a boat?

"It's just...I've been sailing, and I kind of get that. It's fun and sort of freeing to be flying along on top of the water. But I don't get why you'd need to be on a boat if you're sitting in here on a leather sofa and smoking a cigar, with tinted windows around you. You can do that at home or at a restaurant. Isn't the point of being out on the water to be out on the water?" Jack frowned.

"Sure," said Cal. "But there's...come with me."

He began climbing the stairs to the deck on the bow, Jack following behind. At the top of the stairs, he stepped to the side, and heard Jack gasp behind him.

"Oh, okay," Jack said. "I get it. Here you can see the water, and not just through a window."

"There's also the aft deck, which is covered," Cal said.

Jack moved to the railing and peered out towards the ocean.

"So when you take this out, you go out there?" he asked, pointing.

"Yeah. But I don't take her out. It's mostly my dad, and mostly on weekends, and mostly he uses it for business and whatever and not so much pleasure. Takes associates and contacts and their wives or girlfriends out, wines and dines them." Cal shrugged. "I go along sometimes, but it can be boring. It's okay when it's the Wallaces or another family around here, because then my friends can go too. But the Wallaces have a Triton, and we usually go out on that if it's just us. It's easier."

Jack spun around and leaned back against the railing. "What's below deck?" he asked, his lips curving into a smirk.

Electricity began to crackle along Cal's skin at the look in Jack's eye. He cleared his throat. "I'll show you."

They went back down to the main cabin, and then Cal opened the door to the cabins below. He sidled down the narrow staircase, ducking to avoid hitting his head, and then headed directly into the first bedroom.

"Nice," Jack said, moving into the space and spinning around slowly, taking in the double bed, the teak built-ins, the narrow windows high on the wall. "Seems to have everything you'd need."

"There are two other bedrooms. One is almost exactly like this, but a little bigger — that's the master. Then there's one with bunk beds." Cal looked around. "Bathroom is through there."

Jack poked his head into the tiny bathroom. "Amazing," he said. "I haven't spent a lot of time on boats, so I never pictured there being so much space."

"Yeah, and this is built special because we're so tall..."

Cal trailed off as Jack twirled around once and then threw himself onto the bed with a *whoop.* He rolled onto his side and patted the mattress.

"Get over here. I've been thinking about nothing but touching you again since you crept out of my bed before dawn like a sexy ninja. By the way, you're awfully graceful for someone so...so...."

"Massive?" Cal laughed. "Thanks, I think." He hesitated, the rest of Jack's words registering. "So you had fun last night?"

"It was unreal," Jack said. He rolled onto his back and propped himself up on his elbows. "What are you waiting for? We've got a minute to ourselves, let's not waste it."

"Just hang on," Cal said. He crossed to the windows and drew the shades. It was highly unlikely his parents or maintenance would come aboard while they were here, or that someone would walk by on the dock, but.... *Better to be safe than sorry.* When he turned around, Jack was watching him, his eyes hooded.

"How long do you think we have?" Jack asked. "A half hour?"

"Probably," Cal said. "We can always say we stuck around to crack into the liquor cabinet, since I can't drink on the beach."

"Perfect," Jack said. He licked his lips and smiled.

The way the man was watching him left Cal almost

breathless, and he suddenly moved forward, feeling as if Jack was pulling on a string and drawing him in, inch by inch. When he reached the bed, he stretched out beside Jack, resting a hand on his chest.

They stared at each other for a moment. Cal let himself get lost in Jack's gaze, their surroundings fading away. All he could see and think about was the man beside him. He leaned in and placed a soft kiss on Jack's lips, drawing a soft sigh out of Jack before he returned the kiss.

With how anxious Jack had seemed to get started, and how limited they were on time, Cal expected it to be intense and urgent. Instead, Jack seemed content to kiss lazily, running his lips along Cal's neck and nibbling at his collarbone. Cal sank into the sensations, letting his hand roam down Jack's chest and stomach.

"Careful," Jack murmured, closing his eyes. "We don't have too much time."

Then his eyes flickered open, and he rolled Cal onto his back, straddling him and grinding their hips together. "I can't wait to fuck you," he whispered. "Or for *you* to — which are you? Top or bottom?"

"Either," Cal managed, moving his hips with Jack's easily. "*Fuck*...either."

He generally preferred to top, but with Jack...the idea of this man driving into him left him weak. That seemed to be the correct answer, because Jack grinned.

"Right on," Jack said, his eyes sparkling. "I knew we were compatible. I'm good with either, too." He dropped his torso onto Cal's and attacked his mouth again with relish.

After a while, he rolled to the side with a sigh and began to trace circles on Cal's chest with his fingers. "How many men have you had here?" he asked. "Ballpark."

"Here?" Cal asked, momentarily confused.

"On this boat. How many guys have you tempted with all the luxury?" Jack poked Cal's chest. "I'm just curious."

"None, actually," Cal said.

"None? Come on."

"None. I'm not with guys at all around here. Usually."

Jack stared at him. "Around here?"

"Westerly. Home. I only date at school. It's too risky here. Someone might find out, or tell my parents, and then—" Cal frowned and closed his eyes, the familiar lick of fear inside his chest. He shook his head. "It would be bad."

"Oh." Jack pursed his lips together. "But you're with me."

"Yeah."

"Why?"

"I guess I decided you were worth the risk." As soon as he said it, he knew it was true, and he surged up for another kiss, wanting to wipe away the uncharacteristically uncertain look on Jack's face.

It worked. When they broke apart, Jack was grinning again. "Was it my movie star good looks? My keen wit? My fascinating conversation style?"

"Yes, yes, and a little," Cal said, and Jack giggled. "We should probably head back."

"I suppose," Jack said.

They straightened the bed, raised the shades on the windows, and then shared one last kiss on the stairs before climbing back up to the main level. Cal jumped onto the dock and, just as he had on the way in, held out a hand for Jack.

When Jack's feet hit the deck, neither let go immediately, hanging on for a few extra seconds before releasing their grip and stepping apart.

"You hate all of this, don't you?" Jack asked, as they made their way back to the beach club. "All of this. What did Sally call it? Posh." He waved a hand around at the rows of boats, the swanky clubhouse with its outdoor deck full of coiffed loafer-wearing couples.

"No, I don't hate it. Sometimes I just don't feel like I fit, not really. Like it's an act I'm putting on, but it's not actually me." Cal was surprised as soon as the words were out of his mouth. He didn't think he'd ever articulated his thoughts on his life so clearly before.

"Yeah, I can see that," Jack murmured. He jumped off of the wooden walkway as soon as they had passed through the gate to the beach club and scuffed his feet in the sand. "Tell me about what's next for you. You finish Harvard, and then what?"

"Then I come back here and go to work for my father," said Cal.

"Right. And you don't know what you'll be doing."

"Well, I know what the company does. They buy and sell other companies. So I'll be working on that, I just don't know exactly where he'll put me. Maybe analysis." Cal sighed.

"You sound thrilled," said Jack.

"I mean, it's not what I would choose," Cal admitted. "But it is what it is."

"What would you choose?"

Cal stopped walking. Jack made it two steps further and turned.

"What's the matter?" he asked.

Cal shook his head and smiled. "No one has ever asked me that before."

Jack smiled back. "Well, I'm asking."

"I have no idea," Cal said.

"Hmmm." Jack cocked his head to the side. "Think about it and let me know what you come up with."

With a shrug, Cal started walking again. "What would be the point?"

"Humor me? Just in case," Jack said. "After all, you never know when something might be worth the risk."

Someone shouted Jack's name, and with one last glance at Cal, he bounded forward to meet Sally, who was waving from near the water. As Cal watched, Jack peeled his tee-shirt off and took off into the waves, laughing.

Cal waited another minute before his shirt joined Jack's in the sand.

CHAPTER 9

*I*t took two days for word to reach his parents.

Cal was almost surprised it had taken that long, but it seemed summer and a distraction in the form of planning their Independence Day celebrations — something Cal was trying not to think about — had kept his mother busy and out of the gossip loop for an extra day.

At dinner on Friday — just over a week after he had met Jack — she brought it up over rack of lamb with mint sauce.

"Felicia Wallace tells me that her daughter has been going on and on about our next door neighbor," she said. Her gaze focused on Cal, her blue eyes piercing. "She says that you introduced them."

Cal did his best not to choke on the bite he was in the middle of swallowing. He took a large sip from his water goblet and cleared his throat.

"Yes," he said. "We took a group from next door to Sea View a few days ago."

Theodore frowned. "I hadn't realized you'd met the neighbors," he said.

"Nor had I," said Judith. "Or that you'd been associating with them."

"Well." Cal carefully speared two roast carrots on his fork and brought them to his mouth, chewed and swallowed. "I ran into them on the beach. I knew you were having trouble with the noise, so I asked them to keep it down."

"That was considerate," Theodore said. "It has been quieter."

"I can still hear the music most nights," Judith said, her lips pursing. "But I suppose it's been better than at first, and doesn't go on all night."

Cal focused on his plate, hoping that was the end of the conversation. Unfortunately, his mother had other ideas.

"Felicia said they're from Los Angeles," Judith said, disdain clear in her tone. "The boy Sally seems to be enamored with is an actor."

"An actor, really." Theodore hummed. "Has he been in anything I've seen?"

"How should I know?" Judith replied. "Calloway, what do you know about this boy?"

Cal shrugged one shoulder, doing his best to appear like he didn't much care, and lied through his teeth. "Not much. He's an actor — popular — but I don't think you've seen any of his movies."

"Teen movies, I'd bet, if Sally Wallace is fond of him," Theodore said with a chuckle. "No doubt the type with all the beach scenes and dancing, like that Elvis Presley does."

It took a lot of control for Cal not to defend Jack's movies to his father, but he managed to set his fork aside and take another drink of water.

"They take drugs in Los Angeles," Judith said with a sigh. "There are probably drugs next door as we speak. I should warn Felicia. I'm surprised she's letting Sally associate with that crowd. I wonder if we should call Sheriff Lassiter and let him know."

"Let him know what?" Cal asked, his control snapping at his mother's suggestion. "They aren't like that. Jack and his friends are just people. They're here on vacation for the summer and are having a good time. They aren't a danger to anyone."

"Well, I'd prefer it if you didn't spend time over there, Calloway," Judith said. "You have a reputation to think of. Felicia Wallace may be willing to let her children run wild, but *you* are a Buchanan."

"As if I could forget it," Cal muttered.

"What was that?" Theodore asked.

"Nothing. May I be excused?" Cal set his napkin next to his plate.

Judith waved her hand at him in dismissal. "Please try to remember your appointment at the tailor tomorrow morning."

Cal made a face. More suits. Never a good sign.

"Have a good night, mother. Father." He turned on his heel and just barely managed not to stomp out of the room.

Upstairs, he closed his bedroom door, kicked off his shoes, and flopped onto his bed. He'd been hoping to avoid exactly what had just happened. Now he was technically forbidden from hanging out with Jack, and worse, his cover with the Wallaces was blown.

Damned Sally and her busy mouth and her unfortunate crush on his boyfriend.

Just as the thought swam through his brain, he regretted it. Jack wasn't his boyfriend. Except maybe he was. They weren't seeing anyone else, at least for now. It was temporary, and purely for fun, but still.

Boyfriend. Maybe.

He sighed. There was nothing to worry about with Sally,

not really. She'd get bored soon enough, and Jack had promised he wouldn't play around with anyone else. Cal wasn't jealous. There was no need to be.

Rolling onto his side, he stared out the window at the darkening sky. He wished he could go next door, but after the conversation at dinner, it would be best if he didn't, for tonight. He thought about sneaking down to his father's office and calling to let Jack know, but didn't want to risk it.

Jack would understand. He knew that Cal would come if he could. They'd spent the past two nights together, tangled in Jack's creaky bed, sweating into the sheets rather than move apart and create space between them.

Cal couldn't get enough of the man, couldn't seem to stop exploring every inch of his skin, getting acquainted with his muscles and movements, the way he breathed and moaned and whispered. And when they weren't kissing and stroking each other, but were talking...

...he couldn't get enough of that, either.

Jack had so many questions. Heavy, important questions. They'd progressed beyond simple likes and dislikes and amusements to things that made Cal's chest ache to even think about. *When was the last time Cal was happy? What made him feel inspired? What made him sad, helpless? How did he see himself? How did he want others to see him?*

These things he had never allowed himself to dwell on for long. Maybe a rumination at night while staring out at the ocean or walking the streets of Cambridge. But when Jack asked, he had to respond. He had to confront it all and pull the answers out of the darkest parts of himself and offer them to Jack, guts and all.

The fact that he wanted to, and wasn't afraid of what Jack would do with them, even though they'd only known each other a week...that in and of itself should worry him. It didn't.

Cal pictured Jack's moonlit face as he lay, his head resting on the pillow, his cheek smooshed up and the opposite side of his mouth curled into a playful smirk, and everything tightened. He wanted to *go*.

What if he did? What if he just got up, slipped into his shoes, walked downstairs past where his parents would be enjoying their after-dinner cocktail, and left? What if he didn't sneak, and when they asked him where he was going, he'd tell them the truth. That he was nearly twenty-one and not a child, and it was his reputation and therefore his decision who to "associate" with, not theirs.

He laughed bitterly, knowing it was merely a fantasy. If he did that, they'd be suspicious about why it was so important to him. They might look closer, too close. They might find out about him and then it would be all over.

No. Better to lay low for a few days, let them think he wasn't spending all his time next door, let them forget about the people from Los Angeles. Jack would understand.

God, he hoped Jack would understand.

By Sunday, Cal was going out of his mind. He'd had Richie, Tom, and Jay over for cards on Saturday night, which pleased his father. Theodore had poured them all bourbons and passed around cigars and asked about their futures.

It all sounded the same. Boring, dry, unoriginal. All three were joining their respective family businesses, which involved real estate or finance. All three had trust funds that had either recently been released or would later in the year, and Theodore spoke with all of them about investment portfolios.

Cal wanted to throw the bourbon in their faces and tell them to wake up. Ask them what they really wanted, the way

Jack had asked him. Ask them if they were truly excited at the prospect of putting on a suit and going to a sterile office for the rest of their lives.

Instead, he politely listened and agreed and feigned enthusiasm over the idea of blue chip stocks and club memberships. He pretended to be smug — even though it made him sick to his stomach — when Theodore mentioned Cal being lucky to have Katherine and inquired about the others' prospects for settling down and families.

He enjoyed the card game, but the rest of the evening left him cold and longing for the warmth and vibrancy of the house next door.

Now, he was going stir crazy. He'd stayed off the beach for two days, knowing that if he went out there he'd run into Jack. He considered going into town, but it held no appeal other than as a distraction. So he was holed up in the house, forced into conversations with his mother about the goings-on of her friends and the benefit luncheon she was organizing for her auxiliary club.

He'd managed to talk to Jack twice on the telephone. Jack was disappointed that Cal was staying away, but hadn't pressed him on it. He'd listened to and accepted Cal's explanation that Judith and Theodore had expressed displeasure in the idea of Cal spending time next door, as expected, and that Cal didn't want them becoming suspicious. Jack had seemed happy to hear from Cal each time, and Cal was praying that he wouldn't lose interest and move on.

When the rear doorbell rang just after six o'clock, Cal was reorganizing some books in the library before dinner. He looked up, listened, and when it seemed like his mother wasn't moving to answer it — she'd been in the kitchen last he saw her — he set a book down and made his way to the back hall.

The opened door revealed a grinning Jack. Cal gaped at

him. His stomach flipped at the sight and his pulse jumped, his hands itching to reach out and grab hold. Instead, he gripped the edge of the door tightly.

"What are you doing here?" he asked.

"I'm here to meet the neighbors," Jack said, his green eyes sparkling. "I've been a bit delinquent in that, so I thought it was time."

"To meet the—"

"Calloway?" Judith's voice rang out from the kitchen. "Who is it?"

Cal turned, unsure how to answer. He watched his mother appear in the doorway, his mind racing.

"I—this is—" he glanced back at Jack, who was wearing neat-looking, pressed trousers and a yellow Oxford shirt with the sleeves rolled up. He looked…

"Mrs. Buchanan?" Jack asked, as Judith came to the door. "I'm Jack Francis. I'm staying next door for the summer, and wanted to introduce myself."

"Hello," Judith said, a polite smile pasted on her face as her eyes took in Jack critically. "It's nice to meet you."

"Nice to meet you as well. I've admired your house from the beach. It's beautiful." Jack's smile was genuine and charming. "I've brought a small token to apologize if we've been a little loud. I'm not used to how sound carries on the ocean."

Cal realized that Jack had not shown up empty handed. He was holding out what looked like a pie from the bakery in town.

"It's not homemade," Jack said. "I can't really cook. But we had one of these at the house the other day and thought it was tremendous."

"Thank you," Judith said, accepting the gift. She hesitated, and then her manners won out. "Would you like to come in?"

"I'd love that, thank you," Jack said. Judith stepped aside, and Jack shot Cal a wink before crossing the threshold.

Judith laid a hand on Cal's shoulder. "Calloway, take our guest into the living room. I'll get your father. It's time for drinks anyhow."

She retreated into the kitchen, and Cal looked at Jack.

"What are you doing here?" he whispered.

Jack grinned and responded in a whisper. "I missed you. Figured if you were barricading yourself in here, I'd have to breach the wall."

"You missed me?" Cal smiled. His eyes dropped to Jack's lips.

Jack shrugged. "You didn't miss me?"

"Oh, I did." Cal reached out and grabbed Jack's hand. Their fingers tangled together for a brief moment, and something quieted inside Cal. "Come on, let's go to the living room."

He led Jack down the hall, releasing his hand but allowing their knuckles to brush as they walked.

"How've you been?" Cal asked.

"Okay. A little bored," Jack said. "My friends decided to take a trip up to Boston for a long weekend, so the house is pretty quiet."

"Why didn't you go?" Cal asked.

"I didn't feel like it," Jack said. "Thought I'd stay here, get some work done."

They reached the living room and stepped inside. Cal glanced down the hall and then, seeing it deserted, quickly dipped his head and pressed his lips to Jack's briefly. When he retreated, Jack was smiling.

"Look at you, taking a risk," Jack said. He poked Cal's stomach. "But you'd better watch yourself, because I'm hanging onto control by a thread as it is."

He turned and crossed to one of the sofas and settled onto it.

"You should sit over there," Jack suggested, pointing at the other sofa with a smirk.

Rather than listening, Cal moved to the drink cart to begin putting together his parents' pre-dinner cocktails. A scotch, neat, for his father, a Manhattan for his mother.

"Would you like a drink?" Cal asked Jack.

"If it won't make your parents judge me," Jack said. "I'm trying to make a good impression here."

Cal tossed a grin over his shoulder. "I'll have a scotch with my father," Cal said. "So you should be safe."

"Then I'll have the same."

Theodore and Judith entered as Cal was finishing pouring the drinks. Jack immediately got to his feet.

"This is Jack...Francis?" Judith confirmed. When Jack nodded, she continued. "He's in the Winston house for the summer."

Theodore reached out and shook Jack's hand firmly. "Good to meet you," he said. "You've been a topic of conversation around here."

"I have?" Jack asked. He accepted the drink Cal passed him with a quiet, "Thank you."

"Yes, we were wondering about you. And it seems you've made an impression on Calloway and some of his friends."

He accepted his own drink and passed Judith's to her, and then they settled on the sofa opposite Jack. Cal picked up his glass and, after a brief hesitation, took a place on Jack's sofa, being sure to leave a couple of feet between them.

Jack shot a smile at him. "Calloway has been great. He's helped us learn about the community, introduced us to people and places. He's been very hospitable."

It was odd hearing Jack use his full name, and Cal

smirked into his glass. The way Jack was making it sound, they barely knew each other.

"Glad to hear it," Theodore said. "Then you're settling in all right? How long are you planning to stay?"

"The summer," Jack said. "When we came out, we weren't sure, but now that I've seen this coastline and what a lovely community you have, I plan to stay until I need to be on set in September."

Cal's heart soared. This sounded more definite than Jack had been when they first met.

"Calloway said you were an actor," Judith said. "Do you enjoy that?"

"I do," Jack said. "It's all I've ever really wanted to do, and I'm lucky that — for now — they're letting me."

The clock on the wall chimed half past the hour, and Judith set her drink down and got to her feet, laying a hand on Theodore's shoulder. "I need to finish up dinner," she said. "It'll be about ten minutes."

"It smells wonderful," Jack said. "Is it roast chicken?"

"It is." Judith watched him for a moment. "Would you like to join us?"

"Only if it wouldn't be an imposition," Jack said.

Cal froze. An entire dinner with Jack *and* his parents?

"Not at all," Judith said. "I'll set another place. You boys finish your drinks and make your way to the dining room. Ten minutes."

Jack and Theodore chatted idly for another few minutes. Jack asked about the house, and Theodore's business, which pleased Theodore.

When they moved into the dining room, Cal leaned over and whispered in Jack's ear.

"Who are you?" he asked.

"An actor," Jack replied.

Dinner was surprisingly smooth. Jack was a pro at

managing the Buchanans, and he seemed to be winning at least Theodore over with his charm. He seemed genuinely interested in Theodore's talk about his business, asking all the right questions. He was polite to Judith and complimentary of the meal and the table. Cal relaxed and tried to enjoy having Jack around, since he knew it wouldn't last.

Over dessert — Judith had heated the blueberry pie Jack had brought — Jack spoke up.

"I'd love for Calloway to join me tonight," he said. "There is a special on broadcast television that I thought he might enjoy, and I just got a new chess board I'm looking forward to breaking in. That is, if you don't need him here."

"I think that would be fine," Theodore said. Judith didn't look as certain, but she didn't contradict her husband.

Theodore got to his feet, and Jack and Cal followed suit.

"You boys have a good evening," he said. "Judith, I'll be in my study if you'd like to join me for a cocktail."

"I'll be in after I clean up," she said.

"Thank you for dinner, Mrs. Buchanan," Jack said earnestly.

"You're welcome. Thank you for the pie, it was delicious." Judith stood as well. "Would you both help me bring the dishes into the kitchen?"

"Of course," Cal said.

They gathered the dishes and deposited them in the kitchen, and Judith shooed them out with a last farewell.

Cal could hardly believe his luck as he silently ushered Jack out the back door, down the patio steps, and across the lawn. They broke into laughter as they clattered down the steps to the beach, and once there he shoved Jack under the steps and against the cliff wall.

Jack looked up at him, his eyes glittering with amusement. "So, what did you think of my jailbreak?" he asked, giggling.

Then Cal was kissing him, pressing their bodies together with a desperation he hadn't known was simmering inside. He twisted his hands into Jack's hair, tugging at his curls, as he plunged his tongue inside Jack's mouth.

Jack responded by surging up against him, wrapping his arms around Cal's neck and hiking a leg up over his hip. They ground together until Cal pulled away, breathing hard.

"We should go inside," he said.

"Yeah," Jack agreed. "That was fucking painful, sitting across from you and not able to touch."

"You can touch all you want now," Cal said. "You've set it up so that I can stay the night, if you want me."

"Oh, I want you," Jack said. "You think I'm going to put on this—" he gestured at his preppy outfit "—and come over and play all proper for the fun of it? I had an ulterior motive."

He grabbed Cal's hand and tugged, and they were running across the sand and up the stairs to Jack's house. As soon as they made it inside the back door, Jack was on him again, hands roaming over his chest and stomach, lips sucking at his neck.

"Didn't you want to watch a movie? Where's your — where's your chess board?" Cal joked breathlessly.

"In the bedroom," Jack said. "If we look hard enough, we might find it between the sheets. Come on."

He pulled Cal through the empty house, leading him upstairs.

"There's really no one here but us?" Cal asked.

"It's really just us," Jack said. "Until tomorrow sometime. So you can be as loud as you want."

"Me?" Cal laughed. "I don't think I'm the one who has to work to keep quiet."

Jack grinned at him and entered the bedroom. "Let's see, shall we?" He immediately pulled his shirt off.

"Wait," said Cal, grabbing at his hands before he could unfasten his pants. "Let me."

With a smirk, Jack surrendered himself to Cal, who slowly unbuttoned the pants, slowly dragged the zipper down, and slowly slid his hands underneath the fabric to squeeze Jack's hips. Jack tried to wriggle out of them frantically, and Cal tightened his grip.

"What's the rush? We've got all night," he asked, bringing his hands up Jack's sides and back down, loving the way the man arched into his touch.

"The rush is that I've been deprived of you for two days. I'm no good at abstaining from things I like. I prefer indulging." As if to emphasize his point, Jack made quick work of Cal's shirt, wrestling him out of it and tossing it aside before leaning in and licking a stripe from his breast-bone to his neck.

"Everything in moderation, though, right?" Cal said, echoing his mother's favorite caution. "Exercising control over your desires shows character."

Jack snorted. "Fuck that. I believe in enjoying what makes you happy. As much as you fucking want. That's my character."

Cal finally slid Jack's pants over his hips and let them slide to the floor. He loved the idea of taking what he wanted, when he wanted it, and enjoying it. It just wasn't how he'd been raised. He'd been raised to be afraid of the very things that made him happy, since they were largely forbidden.

Like this. This was forbidden. He wasn't supposed to want this, and if he wanted it, he definitely wasn't supposed to take it. But he was sick of living like that, sick of feeling guilty for something he had no control over. Sick of feeling bad for wanting to be happy.

He shivered as Jack unfastened his pants and shoved them down. He stepped out of them.

"Yeah," Cal said. "Fuck that."

Jack pushed him backwards and onto the bed, crawling on top of him, pupils wide, licking his lips. Cal reveled in the way Jack seemed desperate to touch him. He still couldn't quite believe his luck, but he wasn't about to question it now.

He pulled Jack flush against him and went in for another kiss, lining up their hips and starting up a rhythm that was going to drive them crazy in no time. Jack let him drive for a while, whimpering into his mouth and letting his hands roam all over Cal's skin.

Then he propped himself up on his elbows and smiled.

"What?" Cal asked.

"Fucking finally," Jack said. "When I hung back and didn't go to Boston, this is how I imagined spending the weekend."

"You didn't go to Boston so you could stay here? With me," Cal said. His heart leapt and then sank. "And then I stayed away."

"It's okay," Jack said. "I got some reading in. I was behind on reviewing those scripts."

"I'm sorry," Cal said. "You should have said something. I'd have figured out a way."

"You're here now," Jack said, tracing a finger along Cal's brow. "I want to fuck you. Tonight. Now. Can I?"

Cal's mouth went dry, and his gut tightened. He nodded. "Yeah. Yes. Please."

Jack made a joyful sound and dove back in, kissing Cal roughly. Their teeth clacked together, and Jack cupped Cal's jaw, his fingers pressing into the joint with a possessive force. Then he climbed off and scrambled for the bedside table.

"Roll over," he called out as he rummaged in the drawer.

Cal obediently rolled onto his stomach, and Jack returned. He ran his hands over Cal's back and ass, humming with satisfaction. Then he began to drop kisses down Cal's spine, starting at the nape of his neck and trailing down to his tailbone.

"You sure you're good with this?" Jack asked. "If you'd rather, you can fuck me."

"I'm good," Cal said, sighing as Jack began to massage the muscles of his lower back.

Then everything was a haze of anticipation and revelation as Jack took control and Cal was able to let go and let himself be taken. His last few partners had preferred it the other way around, so it had been a while since Cal had done this. In the past, there had always been an anxiety, a low hum of insecurity and nerves, that came with being the one in the vulnerable position.

He felt none of that with Jack. Just a sense that this was exactly where he was supposed to be and exactly what he needed.

It was almost like they'd been doing this for ages. There was no fumbling for a rhythm, no need for adjustment, no awkward positioning. Jack fit inside him perfectly, and they moved together without missing a beat.

"God, you're beautiful," Jack murmured, running his hands all over Cal's back. "Every inch of you is perfect."

Cal whimpered at the compliment, and not long after that Cal was spilling all over the sheets with a shout. Jack sped up behind him and followed a minute later, and they collapsed onto the bed, breathing hard.

They lay there for long minutes. Cal loved the feel of Jack draped across his back, loved the weight pressing down on him as he breathed in deeply, loved the way Jack's fingers traced languidly along his arms.

He could happily stay here forever.

Jack seemed to have the same idea, because he didn't

appear to want to move. After a while, Cal felt himself dozing, drifting in and out of consciousness.

Eventually, Jack grunted and shifted, pulling out and sliding to the bed beside Cal. He curled against his side and kissed his shoulder.

"Doing okay?" he asked. "Was that—"

"It was incredible," Cal said. He rolled onto his side and pulled Jack into his chest. "Can we do it again?"

Jack grinned. "As much as we want, remember? Next time, you do me."

"Deal," Cal said. He stretched and grimaced.

"Sore?" Jack asked.

"Sticky," Cal replied.

"Shower," Jack said.

A few minutes later, they were jockeying for position in the shower, laughing as they soaped each other up and narrowly missed giving each other black eyes as they twisted around in the narrow space. Somehow, they managed.

When they returned to the bedroom, Cal picked up Jack's clothes and draped them across the chair.

"Where did you get these?" he asked. "I didn't know you owned threads like this."

"They're Greg's," Jack said. "But I might keep them. In case I need them again."

"You were great, by the way," Cal said. "I barely recognized you, but my father liked you."

"Not your mother?"

"She says you probably have drugs."

Jack laughed. "Well, I do have drugs. Speaking of...come outside with me, I wanna smoke a joint."

They donned pants and made their way out to the back patio. Jack set about rolling the joint, and Cal sat back and watched the orange rays of the setting sun play across ocean waves. After a minute, he picked up a stack of paper from the coffee table.

It was a script. He flipped through it idly, reading a few lines here and there.

"This something you're considering?" he asked.

Jack glanced over and shrugged. "Maybe. The part is decent. I'm not sure about the movie as a whole, though." He picked up the joint, swiveled around so his back was against the side of the sofa, and slung his legs across Cal's lap.

Cal continued to skim through the script as Jack lit up the joint. He snickered at one line of dialogue.

"What part's funny?" Jack asked.

Cal passed Jack the script, and Jack offered the joint to Cal. He took a hit while Jack glanced over the page and smiled.

"Oh, yeah. See? This character's decent. Do me a favor?"

"Sure," Cal said, passing the joint back.

"Read this scene with me?" Jack asked. "You can be the best friend. I keep coming back to this one, and I want to get a feel for it, see if it fits."

He scooted closer so they could both see the pages in the fading light.

It felt awkward at first, but after a couple of pages — and a couple more hits — Cal began to enjoy himself. They read more than the one scene, Jack flipping back and forth to find other bits to try. Eventually, when the light had faded too much to see any longer, he sat back and sighed with contentment.

"I think I like it," he said. "What do you think?"

"It's good," Cal said. "Funny in places, but...substantial, somehow. Like it seems to be saying something."

"Yeah, I think so too." Jack peered at Cal. "Hey, you were good. Have you ever acted before?"

"No, not really. A school thing here and there."

"What kind of school thing?"

Cal shrugged. "I was the Stage Manager in Our Town in high school."

Jack blinked at him. "Well, that's not nothing."

"It was just a school play." Cal fidgeted, playing with the cuffs of Jack's pants. "It's not like it was professional."

"Did you like it?" Jack asked.

Cal looked out at the horizon. The last hazy violet-grays were beginning to slide towards black. The moon hadn't risen, and soon it would be very dark.

Had he liked performing? Yes, he had. But it had never mattered. His parents had allowed the dalliance because his studies hadn't faltered, but that's all it was, in their eyes. So that's all it had been in his. Something to pass the time, nothing more.

"Yes," he said, finally. "I loved it."

Jack was quiet for another minute, and then he said, "Want to read more scripts with me?"

"Sure," Cal said.

"After I get you naked again," Jack said. "Priorities."

"Priorities," Cal agreed, laughing.

He was still laughing as Jack tackled him onto his back and kissed him until he was once again breathless.

CHAPTER 10

*F*or the next two weeks, Cal had a glimpse of a type of freedom that he'd never before tasted.

Even at school, although technically out from under his parents' roof, he always knew eyes were on him. The need to be careful, to watch every step, every word, every look, lest some acquaintance pass word home that *Calloway isn't behaving as a Buchanan should,* was ever present.

But somehow, right here in Westerly, something had changed. Jack's visit to dinner and the way he had expertly charmed Theodore paid immediate dividends. Suddenly, it was fine for him to spend time next door. It was fine to miss dinner in favor of going out on the town with the Los Angeles people. It was fine to back out of golf games, to skip a day trip to Hartford, to cut his hours short at the office.

When Judith once again expressed concern about negative influences, Theodore simply said, "Calloway's generation has a natural grasp of diversification in a way ours did not. They know the world is expanding, and they see the benefit in reaching across traditional divides to form relationships and increase opportunities. It's smart — sometimes the old methods fall short, and Calloway's way seems to be the future."

Not used to being called smart by his father, Cal had blushed and mumbled something about the untapped potential of new Hollywood wealth.

Of course, Theodore's permissive attitude didn't extend to Cal spending the night with Jack, so that was still done under a cloak of secrecy. Often, he'd simply sneak back in the morning, pretending to have gone for a run on the beach. Most days, the only person who caught him was Flora, since he made sure to come in with the sun rising over the ocean behind him. She'd merely wink, hand him a cup of coffee, and tell him to go change for breakfast.

Nights with Jack were like some kind of a dream, where true freedom reigned. He found that he could be authentic and genuine with Jack in a way he'd never been with anyone, not even himself. In the darkness, with fingers tracing delicate patterns on his chest and stomach, the man would ask him questions that he'd never before dared to contemplate. He discovered that there were things he wished for in the deep, secret parts of his soul.

Voicing them was often uncomfortable and always frightening, but Jack listened and validated and encouraged in such a way that, while wrapped safely in the cocoon of the bedclothes and the arms of his lover, Cal dared to imagine he could one day have a life he actually chose.

And Jack didn't only ask questions. He opened up as well, confessing to Cal the doubts that plagued him about his position in Hollywood and his worth in his field.

"It must be nice to just know what you're meant to do. To know what you're good at and just do it," Cal said one night. He was holding Jack's hand in his, playing with his fingers and bumping his thumb over Jack's knuckles.

Jack snorted beside him. "Is that what you think?" he asked. "That I'm completely sure of everything?"

"Aren't you?"

"God, no," Jack said. "I never know if I get a role because I'm good, or because I just look right, or because I'm popular right at this second and they all want to cash in."

"But when you get the role, you can prove you're good," Cal said.

"Sure. Right now. But what happens if people get bored with me? Or I misstep? Get a bad rep? Someone decides they don't like me for some reason and blacklists me?"

Cal was surprised at the note of uncertainty in Jack's voice. It was the first time he'd heard it, and it was unsettling.

Jack pushed himself up on one elbow and peered down at Cal, his curls tumbling over his face and sending it into inky shadow.

"Do you know why I'm here?" he asked.

"Here? In bed with me?" Cal searched for meaning in the darkness.

"No. Here, in Westerly, and not in L.A." Jack's voice was suddenly urgent, a whisper that seemed like air squeezed through a microscopic crevice.

"No. Why?" Cal asked, whispering as well.

"I got myself into some trouble. In L.A. So my agent booted me out of town while he sorted things out."

Cal was quiet for a moment, digesting that information. Jack had mentioned a few times that he had needed to get out of L.A., but Cal had assumed he had just meant he needed a break.

"Say something," Jack said, when the silence stretched out a little too long.

"What kind of trouble?" Cal asked. He wasn't entirely sure he wanted to know, but he had to ask.

"It doesn't matter. I didn't...it's not like I killed anyone or anything. More of a problem of perception than anything actually bad. But the point is, I don't really know what I'll be going *back* to. If I'll even have a career to return to at the end of the summer."

Jack sounded bitter, his normal upbeat and snarky tone erased in the wake of this revelation.

Instead of putting Cal off, however, the reversal had the opposite effect. Jack was making himself vulnerable, exposing something real, and the possibilities of what that could mean gave Cal the freedom to surge up, find Jack's lips, and kiss him thoroughly.

When he pulled away, Jack said, "What was that for?"

"Thank you for telling me," Cal said.

"Oh." Jack flopped back onto the pillow, and Cal rolled onto his side so that their faces were an inch apart. "Well. I was just…"

"You were sharing something that scares you. I'm glad you feel that I'm safe to do that with." Cal found Jack's hand again, clasped it tightly. "And I don't know how serious a problem this is, but I hope it works out. Because you are good, and you know you are, and they should want you for your talent."

Jack let out a soft sigh, and Cal could feel the tension leaving his body.

"Yeah. They should. And fuck them if they don't." He giggled. "Hey, if it turns out I'm done, I can just stay here. Or go back to Harvard with you. You can keep me in your dorm, tell everyone I'm your cousin visiting from France."

"Will I have to speak French with you? Because if so, I'd better learn it first."

"Oh, it's easy," Jack said, giggling some more. "Repeat after me: embrasse-moi."

"Embrasse-moi," Cal said, the strange words clunky on his tongue.

Then Jack was kissing him, and he forgot to wonder what he'd just said.

Cal relished his new circumstances until the end of June neared. Then one Saturday morning, over breakfast, his father brought up a subject Cal had been doing his best to pretend didn't exist at all, and reality hit him like a bucket of cold water.

"The Thorntons will be here on Wednesday," Theodore said, peering over his newspaper. "Is that right?"

Cal choked on his bacon. *Fuck.*

"Yes. I spoke with Emily yesterday. They'll be driving up from the Hamptons and plan to arrive early afternoon," Judith confirmed. She glanced at Cal. "Are you all right?"

"Yes," Cal said. He coughed once more, then cleared his throat. "Sorry."

"Drink some water," she instructed, before turning back to Theodore. "They'll stay through the twentieth. Have you arranged for the yacht to be stocked and staffed for Thursday?"

"No, I'll do that this week. Do you have preferences for the menu?"

"I think so," Judith said. "I'll write some things down for you."

"Very good. Calloway, you must be excited to see Katherine. Have the two of you talked about how you'll spend your time?" Theodore asked.

"No, sir, not yet," Cal said. "Maybe the club for an afternoon. She enjoys golf."

"I'm sure she'd like that," Judith said. "And perhaps you could take her up to Providence, see a show. Have dinner."

"Mmm. Maybe," Cal agreed. "We could all go."

"Oh, I'm sure the two of you will be anxious to be out of the range of prying eyes of your parents," Judith said, smiling knowingly. "After so much time apart."

Cal took a large bite of his western omelet in order to avoid a verbal comment. As his parents began discussing how else to entertain the Thorntons while in town — *we'll invite the Wallaces to brunch, Emily Thornton just loves Felicia Wallace...Joe would like a few rounds at the club and an afternoon in the cigar lounge* — he realized with a sinking sensation that, from Wednesday afternoon, he'd be occupied with Katherine and their parents for two and a half weeks.

Which meant he'd have to tell Jack he wouldn't be around.

Which meant he'd have to tell Jack about Katherine.

He pushed back from his chair, the omelet and coffee churning in his stomach.

"May I be excused?" he asked.

Judith waved a hand at him, continuing a debate with Theodore about whether the six of them should take a trip up to Boston for a weekend, and Cal fled.

ON MONDAY NIGHT, Cal went with Jack and a crew from the house out to the bowling alley. They paid for their rental shoes and balls and took up three lanes side by side, jostling each other and making bets on who'd embarrass themselves the most with the lowest score.

Cal ended up on a team with Jack, facing off against Scott and Greg. Halfway through their second game, the roller-skating waitstaff brought their burgers and more beer, and they took a break to chow down. Jack downed his beer and ordered a third, and by the time they returned to the game, his eyes were bright and his cheeks were tinged with pink.

Cal sat back on the wooden bench and took in the sights around him. The lights were bright overhead. The air smelled of burgers and fries. The music was loud, the noise from the balls hitting the pins was louder, and the atmosphere was one of general chaos.

It was time. He'd decided to tell Jack tonight, and thought it would be better to do it in a crowd. It made it more casual, minimized its importance. Put less pressure on Jack, and their relationship, by passing it off as less than a big deal than if he did it when they were alone.

He hoped.

He waited until Scott and Greg had turned to talk to Will and Graham in the next lane, and Jack was hefting his giant purple ball into the air.

"I need to let you know," Cal began. "My girlfriend's family is coming to stay with us for the holiday. So I won't be around much, starting Wednesday afternoon."

Jack paused mid-stride. He turned to look at Cal, the bowling ball dangling from two fingers.

"I'm sorry," he said, his brows furrowing, forming a tiny wrinkle on his forehead. "Your *what?*"

Cal cleared his throat. "My...uh...my girlfriend. Her family is coming to visit. They'll be here for a couple of weeks, and it's going to be hard for me to—"

Thunk. The ball hit the waxed floor and rolled to the side.

Jack frowned and shook his head. "Hang on. I'm still on the part where you're telling me — just now — that you have a girlfriend. What the fuck?"

Glancing to the right to make sure Scott and Greg were still occupied, Cal shifted in his seat.

"Yeah. I mean, it isn't really a big deal. I haven't seen her since we left school, or even talked to her. Once, I guess. But while they're here, I'm going to have to be—"

"Got it. You don't have to explain." Jack looked around, his eyes alighting on his friends, the crowd at the bar, the waitstaff zooming by, and huffed out an annoyed breath. "I'll be back in a minute."

He turned on his heel and strode towards the back hall between the lanes and the billiards room.

"Wait," Cal said, but Jack just shook his head and kept going, his shoulders hunching forward and his hands shoved in the pockets of his snug jeans.

Shit, that had been a mistake. He'd clearly miscalculated.

"Restroom," he said to Scott, by way of explanation, as he exited the lanes and hurried after Jack.

He found the man leaning against the tiled wall in the mint-green restroom, his face a stormcloud. When he spotted Cal pushing through the metal door, he grimaced. A few curls had escaped from the tie that held his hair in place at the base of his neck, springing around his temples and giving him a slightly wild look.

Neither of them said anything while a guy in a flowered polyester top shook water off his hands and wiped them on his hips. They waited until he'd left, and then Cal turned back to Jack.

"Hey—" he started, but Jack held up a hand and cut him off.

"You shouldn't have come after me," Jack said. "I told you I'd be back in a minute."

"Yeah, but you're upset." Cal decided to keep his distance, leaning up against the door.

"You just told me you have a fucking girlfriend," Jack said. "One you've conveniently never mentioned. What the hell am I supposed to be, if not upset?"

Cal swallowed, his heart beating faster than he'd like. "Are you jealous? I thought you didn't do jealousy. Right?"

Jack's face cleared, relaxing into a neutral expression. "I don't," he said firmly.

"Then why are you upset?" Cal asked. He held his breath, watching Jack's mouth twitch back into a frown.

"I don't...I feel like you've been lying to me," he said,

finally. "You've never said anything about having a girlfriend. We said that we weren't going to be with anyone else while — I just don't like being lied to."

"I wasn't — I didn't mean to lie," Cal said. He pushed his hair off his forehead, hated how much he was suddenly sweating. "I kind of forgot about her."

Jack's left eyebrow shot up. "You forgot? That you had a girlfriend?"

Cal flushed in embarrassment. "Yeah. She's kind of an old family friend. So she's always just sort of been there. I don't even know how we ended up — at some point we started dating, mainly to shut up our parents, I think? She's safe. But I've barely thought about her since I left school."

"Do you like her?" Jack asked quietly.

Cal shrugged. "I mean, she's all right. As someone to take places. I guess."

"But are you—" Jack shook his head, his escaped curls flying around. "Do you like her."

There was a long beat of silence, and Cal sighed.

"No," he said. "No, not like that. And I don't intend to break what we said about not seeing anyone else while we're together. It's just appearances. We've never even...she's just a girl I take around sometimes, to make our parents happy."

"Never?" Jack asked.

"We've kissed," Cal said. "That's all. I don't—" He couldn't help but make a face. "I'm not interested in her that way. You should know that."

He looked at Jack, silently begging him to understand. Katherine wasn't his choice, she was Theodore and Judith's choice. And since his own choices would be impossible, Katherine was the path of least resistance. He didn't really mind her, and it could certainly be worse.

Jack sighed. "Maybe I am a little jealous," he said. "Which is weird. I don't like it."

Cal's pulse jumped, his heart leaping at the idea that Jack was feeling possessive. He couldn't help that one corner of his lip turned up. Jack noticed.

"You do like it, though," Jack said, on a half laugh. "You like that I hate her already."

"Yeah," Cal admitted. "I do. If it makes you feel any better, I'd hate anyone who you...you know."

"It does make me feel better," Jack grinned. "So this girl—"

"Katherine," Cal said.

"Right, okay. Katherine and her stuck-up parents are coming to stay with you and your stuck-up parents, and all the stuck-up parents will be expecting you two to...what?"

Cal shrugged. "They'll expect us to be a couple. So I'll have to go to dinner and the club with them, and also take Katherine out. I think we're supposed to go up to Boston for a weekend, too. I've been avoiding the preparations, so I'm not totally sure of all the details."

"And while all this —" Jack waves his hand in the air and his lips curl in distaste, "—is going on, you won't be available to me."

"No," Cal said. "Maybe here and there, but not like it is now. They'll be expecting me to be Calloway Buchanan."

"So I'm supposed to just sit around? And hate the fact that you're cozied up to some pretend society girlfriend while I'm all by myself? Does she know you're—"

"No," Cal said quickly. "She doesn't know. Jack, I'm sorry. I fucked this up. I should have told you about her, but I didn't want to think about it so I put it out of my mind. And now it's here, and there's nothing I can do about it."

A flicker of something passed over Jack's face. "Yeah. I mean, we're just having some fun. You don't really owe me anything. And I can see how — if you don't really think of her as significant, you might not have thought it was important to mention."

Jack folded his arms across his chest and dropped his gaze to the floor, where he was scuffing his rented shoe on the tiles.

Cal cleared his throat, knowing he had to say what he was about to say, and hating it. "If you...I mean, I don't want to tell you what you can and can't do, so if you move on while I'm unavailable, I can't blame you."

Jack's head shot up. "Are you giving me permission to see other people?"

"Not permission," Cal said. "You don't need my permission. And I don't like it. I don't want it. But I'd understand."

Someone tried to open the door, and it thudded against Cal's back. He quickly stepped out of the way, muttering an apology to the guy who walked in and headed for a urinal. Jack glanced at Cal and started for the door, gesturing with his head for Cal to follow.

Out in the empty hall, Jack smoothed his curls back and tucked them into the tie, then turned to face Cal.

"Two weeks isn't so long," he said quietly. "I guess I could wait for you."

Cal's heart sped up. He took a step forward involuntarily, and stopped short just in time.

"If I could, I'd kiss you right now," he said, his voice pitched low so as not to carry away from them.

Jack smiled, an impish gleam in his eye. "I dare you. I double dog dare you."

Cal glanced around, and then, pulse racing, he surged forward and pressed his lips against Jack's once before taking a large step back.

Jack stared at him, eyes wide and lips parted. "I didn't think you'd do it," he said.

"Neither did I," Cal said with a shrug. "But it seemed worth the risk. For someone who'll wait for me."

"For two weeks," Jack said. "And if I hear about you giving

her anything other than a performative peck, all bets are off. Apparently I get jealous now, and since it's new, I can't predict how I'll react. Deal?"

"Deal," Cal said, laughing. "We should get back before they send a search party."

Jack turned, letting his fingers tangle with Cal's for the briefest of moments before heading down the hall and back to their game.

WHEN THE THORNTONS arrived on Wednesday afternoon, Cal was as ready as he was going to get. He'd spent the night before with Jack, as usual, and there was a frantic urgency to the way the man claimed him just before dawn.

"Sneak away at least once?" he had said, his lips skimming along Cal's collarbone. "Think you can manage?"

"It'll be tough, with all the extra people in the house," Cal had said with regret. "The guest rooms are near my bedroom — and one faces the beach — so it will be harder to come in and out without anyone noticing."

"Try. You don't have to warn me. If you see an opportunity, take it." Jack nibbled on Cal's jaw.

Cal had agreed with a simple, "Okay."

He knew he'd try. Jack was worth it. He just wasn't sure if he'd get the opportunity.

He and his parents came outside as the car pulled up to the house, lining the stone staircase like something out of a movie. Mr. Thornton exited the driver's side first, and then came around to open the passenger door for his wife and daughter. Mrs. Thornton slid into view with a nod for his parents, and then Katherine emerged, one hand on her yellow wide-brimmed hat and the other holding a powder blue clutch.

She peeked up at him and waved the clutch. He waved back.

Then he was shaking Mr. Thornton's hand, kissing Mrs. Thornton on the cheek, and Katherine threw her arms around his neck with a tiny squeal. He hugged her back, his arms wrapping around her tiny waist as she pressed up against him, her hat smashing against his temple.

"I missed you," she giggled in his ear. "What, you couldn't call me back?"

"Sorry. I've been busy," he replied. "It's good to see you."

He disentangled himself and stepped away, joining his father and Mr. Thornton at the trunk of the car to deal with the luggage. For the next twenty minutes, there was a flurry of bringing things inside, showing the guests to their rooms, and pouring drinks, and finally, they were seated in the living room.

Katherine sat beside him, her knees pointed towards his and her manicured hand on his left forearm. He didn't pull away from her cool fingers. Instead, he rested a palm on her knee, and she smiled at him, her brown eyes going soft and hopeful.

It's called acting, he told himself. The thought reminded him of Jack, and the scripts they'd read together. He could do this and make it work, and tell Jack all about his new skills in two weeks.

After some polite catching up — *Katherine has been looking forward to this trip, I think she's bored with the beaches in the Hamptons already; Emily planned a very successful benefit with her Daughters of the American Revolution chapter in June; Joe shot two under par the other day* — the focus turned to Cal.

"Calloway," Mr. Thornton said, "your father tells me you've been working at the office this summer. How are you liking it?"

"It's interesting, sir," Cal said.

"Glad to hear it. That's the kind of thing a father wants to see: his son taking to his business. I'm sure you'll be ready to run the place in a few years, let your father retire in style."

"If his business strategies work, you may be right," Theodore said. "Calloway has been broadening our investment contacts this summer."

"Oh?" Mr. Thornton looked interested. "Anything I should tap into?"

"You know these youngsters. They're worldly now," Theodore said. "Calloway has been ignoring the old club and forging relationships with a set of up-and-coming movie stars."

"Hollywood money," Mr. Thornton said, nodding. "My firm is dipping into that as well. The cash certainly seems to be flowing out west, and people with money to spend may as well invest it."

"Movie stars in Westerly?" Katherine asked, her eyes sparkling. "Who?"

Mrs. Thornton clucked her tongue. "Hollywood seems so fickle. Too willing to chase the trends, not steady enough for long term investment. And...the stories you hear about Hollywood types. Disgraceful."

Judith rolled her eyes. "I happen to agree with you," she said. "But Theodore—"

"You're worrying too much," Theodore said. "That one boy had fine manners."

"Who?" Katherine asked again.

"What was his name, Calloway?" Theodore asked. "Jack Something."

"Jack Francis," Cal said.

Katherine squealed. "Jack Francis? Here? That's so far out, can you introduce me?"

Cal froze like a deer in headlights. Jack meeting Katherine? He'd rather—

"Please, Calloway," Katherine said. "I know — you can invite him out on the yacht with us tomorrow. Would that be okay?" She turned to the adults. "If he joined us?"

"Yes, invite the boy," Mr. Thornton said. "Let's see about this new investment strategy."

"Fine by me," Theodore said. "Calloway can call over next door after dinner."

"He's right next door? Oh, Calloway, how can you stand it?" Katherine bounced in her seat. "He's so dreamy."

Cal swallowed. "I'll call him after dinner. He may already have plans."

"Worth a try," Theodore said.

"You can convince him, Calloway. If you're friends. Tell him how nice the yacht is." Katherine was gripping Cal's arm tightly, and now he did pull away. He disguised the move by draping his arm on the back of the sofa behind her, and she shifted closer.

He did his best not to grimace.

THE PHONE RANG six times before Penny picked it up.

"'Lo," she said. It sounded like she was chewing gum.

"Hi, Penny? This is Cal—"

"Hey, Cal, where are you? We've got a whole darts tournament going on tonight, you'd kill it. Winner gets bragging rights and the last bottle of scotch in the house."

"I'm home," Cal said, wishing more than anything he could just roll on over. "Is Jack busy?"

"I'll get him."

There was a clatter as she dropped the handset on the desk, and then a couple of minutes of background music and voices. Finally, Jack's voice floated through the line.

"Cal?"

Cal smiled. He couldn't help it.

"Hi."

"It hasn't even been a day. You miss me already?" Jack asked, his voice dropping into a coarse, suggestive tone.

"Yeah." It was true. Hearing Jack's voice simply increased the longing he'd been feeling all day and all evening. "Do you miss me?"

"You know I do. What's going on? I figured I wouldn't hear from you for a few days, at least." There was a touch of concern in Jack's voice now, and Cal's chest warmed.

"Well, I have a proposition for you," Cal said. He glanced at the door to his father's office, glad he'd had the foresight to close it. "You can say no."

"What is it?" Jack sounded curious now.

"My father mentioned to the Thorntons that you were living next door," Cal said. "Sorry about that, but he's got this idea that I'm wooing you for business investments."

"Is that what you're doing?" Jack asked. "'Wooing' me?"

Cal snorted. "For business only."

"Of course. Business. I must have been confused because you had my cock in your mouth for a half hour this morning."

Cal closed his eyes, trying to staunch the immediate desire that the memory brought.

"Anyway," he said, once he had things under control. "Katherine wants to meet you. So everyone decided I should invite you to come out with us for the day on the yacht tomorrow."

There was a stretch of silence. Then Jack laughed.

"You think that's a good idea?" he asked. "To trap me on a fucking boat with your girlfriend for eight hours? I'm jealous, after all."

"It's probably a terrible idea," Cal said. "But I want you to say yes."

"Really?"

"Yeah," Cal said, suddenly knowing without a doubt it was true. "I mean, obviously we'll have to be very careful, but I want to see you. And this way, even though we can't...you know...at least we get to spend a day together. And if it goes well, then I could bring Katherine over to the house sometimes and maybe—"

"Hang on, one step at a time," Jack said, laughing. "I'll go."

"You will?" Cal grinned.

"Yes. I'm curious about this girlfriend. I'll get to hang with you. And hey, a day on a yacht. Can't be too terrible."

"The Wallaces will be there too," Cal said. "So you'll know a couple of people."

"I'll bring J.C., then," Jack said. "Richie will be happy and I guess I could make Sally's day by paying a little attention to her."

"Okay. So I'll pick you up in the morning. At nine-thirty," Cal said. "Bring your swimsuit, we'll drop anchor and swim at some point."

"I'll be waiting," Jack said. "Whether I'm ready or not."

They chatted another couple of minutes before Cal reluctantly said goodbye so he could join the rest of the house for after-dinner drinks and share the good news.

He had no idea what he was getting into, but one way or the other, the holiday was going to be interesting.

CHAPTER 11

*I*ndependence Day dawned bright and sunny. It was the sort of July day that promised to be a true scorcher. The sea glittered and the land was blanketed in a shimmery haze, the air already hot and muggy before the first cups of coffee were drained.

In other words, a perfect day to be out on the water, where it was bound to be a few degrees cooler and the breeze would keep the sweat from lingering on the skin.

Cal left home a few minutes before nine-thirty to pick up Jack and J.C. next door. Katherine sat shotgun in his Azure Blue Ford Thunderbird, a red scarf tied around her hair and wide sunglasses perched on her narrow face.

He'd tried to slip out on his own, hoping for some freedom with Jack, but she'd jumped at the chance to ride to the yacht club with him and meet the man as soon as humanly possible.

"Tell me about him," she demanded, after he'd settled into the driver's seat. "Is he as adorable in person as he is on film and in magazines?"

Better, Cal thought.

But he just shrugged. "I don't know. He looks the same. I recognized him right away."

"How did you meet him? I can't believe he's right next door, that's so unreal."

Cal put the gear shift into first position and eased onto the drive. He thought back to that late night walk on the beach, where Jack had been delightfully drunk and flirting, and smiled.

He'd been so embarrassed that night. How far they'd come.

"I met him on the beach," was all he said.

"Did you approach him? Or—"

"He talked to me," Cal said, pulling onto the street. "He's just a person. Friendly. Was meeting a neighbor. It's really not a big deal."

"But your father said you spend a lot of time together?" Katherine asked.

Cal hesitated. That was true, and his father had indicated that; he just had to be careful what he said.

"I spend time with the whole crew," he said. "It's not just him. There are fifteen of them staying for the summer. He's just the most well-known."

He turned up the drive to Jack's house.

"Hey, can you do me a favor?" he asked suddenly.

"Of course," Katherine said.

"Can you be normal? Just act like you're meeting anyone. Don't freak out. It'll make him uncomfortable," Cal lied. He knew Jack liked a little gushing now and then, but he really didn't want to watch it happen, not with Katherine.

"I can be in the groove," she said, flashing him a smile.

"Thanks."

Cal put the car in park outside Jack's house.

"Wait here," he instructed, when she moved to open her door.

He got out of the car, jogged up to the front door, and rang the bell. It was only a few moments before the door swung open. J.C. grinned at him.

"Heya, Cal. Thanks for the invite. A day on a yacht, that's fab."

"Well, we'll be stuck with my parents, so don't get your hopes too high," Cal warned her.

"Not to worry. Parents love me."

"Everyone loves you," Cal said.

"That is a true statement," she replied, poking him in the chest. She craned her neck to peer over his shoulder. "That her?"

"That's Katherine," Cal said. "Be nice to her, or my life becomes more difficult."

She whacked him on the shoulder. "I'm nice to everyone." She turned back inside the house, and yelled for Jack.

He appeared a moment later, a stuffed tote in hand.

"I'm here, you don't have to yell," he said. His eyes landed on Cal and his face lit up in a way that made Cal's heart soar. "Hi."

"Hi," Cal said, grinning back.

Jack walked backwards into the house, beckoning Cal inside. Cal followed him into the front hall and around the corner, then found himself pushed up against a wall and Jack attacking his mouth.

"Sorry," Jack said, when he came up for air. "You look good this morning, and if I didn't get that out of my system —"

Cal shut him up with another kiss, and Jack received him with a groan.

After a few minutes of this, J.C. cleared her throat loudly.

Cal pulled away from Jack, and J.C. rolled her eyes and heaved a sigh. "Get it together, boys," she said. "Someone is waiting in the car, and she looks like she's the kind to be impatient." She spun around and bounded out the open door.

"Right," Jack said, straightening up and wiping at his mouth. "We're just buddies. Pals. Chums. I barely know you and don't even like you." He reached out and smoothed a palm over the curve of Cal's ass. "Don't like you at all."

Cal snorted. "Come on, she's going to do her best not to jump you, let's not keep her waiting any longer."

Jack closed the door behind him and they made their way to the car, where J.C. was already chatting up Katherine, one hand on her hip and her hair bouncing as she talked.

For her part, Katherine looked overwhelmed by J.C. She looked up as the boys approached, and her cheeks flushed pink. She pushed open her door and slid out of the car, slipping her sunglasses off and extending a hand.

"Jack, it's nice to meet you. I've seen all of your films, and am a big fan," she said. Cal smirked. He should have known that Katherine's breeding would allow her to keep herself under control.

Jack paused for a moment, looking her over, before he responded.

"Hi. Katherine, right? Call me Jack." He took her hand, and then leaned in to kiss her cheeks. She let out a breathy giggle. "Cal has told me so much about you."

"Oh, he's talked about you, too," Katherine said.

Jack shot Cal a glance, and then, with a sly smile, said, "Then I'm sure he's mentioned that I get car sick?"

"Car sick?" Katherine asked, her brows bunching together in confusion.

"I need to sit shotgun," he said. "Or else…"

"Oh. Oh! Of course," Katherine said.

Cal bit back a laugh at the blatant fib.

The drive to the yacht club was mostly uneventful, aside from a patch of traffic that slowed them down. Holiday beachgoers clogged up the main roadway that led to the club, and there was nothing to do but take their place in the line of automobiles, enjoy the sunshine, and wait it out.

J.C. chattered away, focusing Katherine's attention by asking her a string of questions — *what are you studying in school, where is your family from, what designer made that stunning dress* — and, as predicted, Katherine appeared charmed.

Jack sat quietly beside Cal, his elbow on the edge of the door, watching the passing scenery as his curls were tossed by the breeze. Cal glanced over at him, and he couldn't help but imagine how free it would feel to take a long drive, top down like this, with Jack by his side.

When they finally arrived, Cal and Jack grabbed the bags from the trunk and they made their way to the yacht. The hot day was getting hotter, the sun beating down at an angle, and Katherine commented that it was a perfect day to be out on the water.

"It'll be cooler," she explained. "Have you been yachting before?"

"I've been on a yacht," Jack said. "But not yachting. As such." He caught Cal's eye, his lip quirking up. "You'll have to show me the ropes. Wouldn't want to embarrass myself."

"You can't," Katherine said. "Nothing for you to do but hang loose and enjoy yourself."

Cal watched them interact, his eye twitching.

They were the last to board. After a round of greetings and introductions, Theodore shook his head, aiming a look at Cal.

"You're late, son. We're behind schedule, and we haven't even begun." He raised an eyebrow, a signal that he expected a response.

"Sorry, sir," Cal said. "There was some holiday traffic—"

"Sounds like something you could have anticipated, left a bit earlier."

Cal nodded. "Yes, Sir. I apologize."

"It's my fault," Jack said, jumping in. "I wasn't ready when Cal arrived." He shrugged. "But it's a holiday."

Theodore eyed him a moment, then turned to give the captain the signal to depart, and they were off.

The parents took cocktails out to the aft deck, and the girls decided they wanted to spend the time before lunch in the sun before it got too hot to stand. Katherine and Sally dragged J.C. down to the lower cabin to change, leaving the guys on the fore deck.

Once they had stripped down to their swim trunks, Cal passed around beers and they settled onto the bench seating around the edge.

"Are you glad to see Katherine?" Richie asked.

"Sure," Cal said, glancing at Jack, who was studying his beer intently.

"You must be, she's looking like a fox these days. The Hamptons beaches have been good for her." Richie nudged at Cal with his elbow.

"Are the Hamptons beaches anything like ours?" Jack asked. "I've never been."

"Ours are better," Cal said, and Richie agreed.

The girls returned, clad in brightly colored bikinis. Richie let out a wolf whistle, and J.C. struck a modeling pose, then launched into a catwalk strut, landing in front of him with a hand extended.

"Sit with me, you big hunk," she said.

"You don't have to ask me twice," said Richie, following her to the lounge chairs.

Cal rolled his eyes, but when Katherine took his hand, he let her lead him to the chairs on the opposite side. After a moment, Sally and Jack joined the group in the chairs between the two couples, Jack closest to Cal.

The conversation began light and easy. Richie and Sally had been to a movie Katherine had also seen, and it turned out Jack and J.C. knew one of the actresses in it. There was a light-hearted comparison between beaches in Westerly, the Cape, the Hamptons, and California. Jack had taken surfing lessons but J.C. had been surfing since she was a kid. Cal thought he'd be terrible at surfing since he was so tall, Jack pointed out that if he was a good downhill skier (he was) there was no real reason he couldn't find a way to stay up on a board.

As they talked, Katherine reached an arm across and took Cal's hand, dangling their linked hands between them. It was casual, and comfortable, and he didn't think much of it.

...until he glanced over and saw Jack watching him, his eyes stormy. Feeling suddenly on edge, Cal gently dropped Katherine's hand and stood up. Jack's gaze flickered up to his.

"It's pretty warm," Cal said. "I think I need to get out of the sun for a minute." He raised a brow at Jack, who looked away. "Jack, you want to go with me to grab some sodas?"

"Sure," Jack said, sounding surprised. He followed Cal off of the deck and into the main cabin, where the hired chef was preparing trays of sandwiches for lunch. "You didn't have to do that," he said quietly, once the glass door swung shut behind them.

"I was afraid not to," Cal replied in a whisper. "But you know it's not real. Don't let it bother you."

Jack chewed on his lower lip. "I can't seem to help it," he said.

Cal stared at Jack in wonder. "You really are jealous," he murmured, glancing at the chef, who seemed entirely focused on making up a batch of chicken salad. "Come on."

He led the way down the stairs to the lower cabin, and checked that the bedrooms were empty before turning back to Jack.

"I'm not into her. It's just a show. Meaningless. Like...like when we go out with J.C. and Ginny and pretend," Cal said. "You don't get jealous then."

"That's different," Jack said. "J.C. knows about us and isn't trying to seduce you."

Cal burst out laughing, and then sobered up at the pained look on Jack's face. "Katherine isn't trying to seduce me either. She's not like that, she's just...it's affection. She was only holding my hand."

Jack scowled. "I know it's not real for you, but I keep thinking that it's real for her, and I hate that it's her and not me who—" He snapped his mouth shut. "I just don't like it."

Cal sighed. On the one hand, Jack's sudden fierce jealousy was flattering and made his stomach tingle. On the other hand, if Jack kept shooting daggers at Katherine, someone was going to wonder why.

"Look," he said, "it's going to keep happening. She's going to keep being my girlfriend. Are you going to be able to keep it together?"

"Maybe," Jack said, pouting.

"You're an actor. Try. Or people are going to start asking questions."

Jack closed his eyes and took a deep breath before opening them. "I shouldn't have come."

Cal reached out and tangled his fingers in Jack's curls. "I'm glad you're here. Like we said, it's great to be able to spend the day together."

Jack's face cleared a bit, and he smiled slightly. "Yeah. You're right. What's fucking wrong with me? Sorry. I'll be fine."

Cal glanced at the stairs, and then pushed Jack into one of

the bedrooms. He swooped down and claimed Jack's mouth in a hard, thorough kiss.

When he pulled away, he said, "We better get back. Just...when she puts her hands on me, imagine what you'll do next time we're alone to erase it all."

"I'm going to lick every inch of your skin. Watch me spend the rest of the day imagining that." Jack smirked, and Cal laughed.

Lunch was an elaborate spread of sandwiches, chips, and fruit salad. Everyone gathered on the aft deck, where the breeze was cool in the shade of the canopy and the views of the water were spectacular.

With the elder Buchanans, Thorntons, and Wallaces present, there was standard chatter about plans for the future. Joe Thornton asked Cal how he was liking working for his father, and Cal did his best to feign enthusiasm. Theodore pointed out that Cal only worked in the office a couple of mornings a week, and how different things had been for him, where his father had expected him every day during every break from school all the way through college.

"I've been too easy on the boy, I fear," he said. "You know how kids are today, Joe. No appreciation for the value of hard work."

Cal focused on the thick bacon in his club sandwich, tuning out the griping. He knew there was no point in arguing, and if he left it alone, they'd move on. Besides, Richard was turning his attention to Richie with a similar commentary, and Cal didn't want to make things more difficult for him.

"Isn't Calloway top of his class at Harvard?" Jack asked suddenly, sitting back on the bench seating, his half-eaten chicken sandwich in one hand and a beer in the other. "And Richie is in a similar position at Princeton, I think."

Cal shot Jack a warning look, but Jack just shrugged.

"Doesn't seem to me like something that could happen without hard work." He took a large bite of his sandwich, and then spoke around it. "Just an observation."

Theodore huffed. "Were you at university, Jack?"

"No, sir," Jack said. "Went straight to L.A. after high school, where I got a job washing dishes at a studio commissary, and started auditioning for anything I could."

"You've had good success, I hear," Richard Senior commented.

"Yes. I was lucky to get the job I did, because I got promoted to waiting tables and was able to talk to a lot of people. Some of them were the right people."

"I don't think I ever considered how much of Hollywood involves networking," Richard commented.

The conversation shifted then with the Wallaces curious about the movie business. Cal relaxed and enjoyed the sun on his shoulders and the sound of Jack's voice mixed with that of the waves below and the gulls overhead.

After lunch, they dropped anchor for some swimming. Katherine used the opportunity to cling to Cal, squealing as Richie splashed her. Jack joined in, pushing the water so that a wave drenched her, leaving her dripping and coughing.

"Sorry," he said. "I didn't know it would make such a big wave."

Cal snorted, and covered it up with a cough of his own.

When they tired of swimming and lounging, they took turns showering and changing into dry clothes for dinner. Cal was fastening his belt in one of the bedrooms when there was a knock on the door.

"Come in," he called.

He was expecting Jack, or maybe Katherine. He was not expecting his mother. She closed the door behind her and smiled.

"You're having a nice day?" she asked.

"Yes," he said, mildly surprised at the question. It was one she hadn't asked him in a long time. He'd assumed she'd stopped caring how much he enjoyed anything, focused only on how he looked and acted, how he reflected on her.

"It's so good to spend time with the Thorntons again," she said. "And it makes me — and Emily — so happy that you and Katherine have come together. We used to talk about it, you know, when you were little."

"You talked about Katherine and me? Together?" Cal asked.

"Yes." Her eyes went far away, sinking into the memory. "We'd watch you play and dream that maybe one day you'd choose each other. You really are a perfect match. She's a lovely girl, with such poise, and so tall and pretty and bright. Your children will be stunning."

Cal swallowed. "Our children? Mother—"

But Judith was still talking. "It's such a perfect day. I thought you might...I brought this, in case."

She crossed the small space, drawing a hand out of her pocket and unfolding it, revealing a glittering jewel on her palm. Cal stopped himself from taking a step backward, barely.

"What..." His stomach turned. "Is that a ring?"

"My mother's," Judith said. "I asked her for it last time I visited. I knew it was almost time, and I wanted you to have it."

"Almost time? For me to..." A band began to tighten around Cal's chest, and he struggled to pull in a breath. "You think I should propose to Katherine."

"Of course. Tonight could be perfect," Judith said. "You're clearly enjoying each other so much, and with all of us here...I thought maybe over dinner, or while we were watching the fireworks show. Think of it, how romantic. She'll be thrilled."

Cal cleared his throat. It felt thick, like something was stuck in it. "Mother, I hadn't...we haven't talked about getting married. I'm not sure she—"

"Nonsense," Judith said, brushing off his protest. "Obviously she wants to marry you. Why wouldn't she?"

"I'm just saying that I don't think tonight is the night," Cal said. "They're here for a couple of weeks, can I just...I wasn't thinking about that today, and I'm not prepared."

Judith's smile softened. "You want to plan it out, what to say," she said. "I promise she'll be thrilled no matter what, but that's thoughtful of you to want it to be perfect."

"Yes," Cal said. "I don't want it to be rushed."

"Well, why don't you hang onto this, just in case," Judith said, pressing the diamond ring into his palm and closing his fingers around it. "If you change your mind...and otherwise, you can keep it with you for when the right moment arises."

"Thank you," Cal said. The ring bit into his flesh as he clenched a fist around it. "Could you give me a minute? I'll be up shortly."

"Certainly," Judith said. She reached up and patted his cheek. "I'm proud of you, darling. You've chosen well."

She retreated then, leaving the door ajar. Cal carefully opened his fist and stared at the jewel.

It was a large, high quality gem, brilliant cut, set in an elaborate platinum Art Deco setting. There were smaller baguette diamonds flanking it, and additional single cut diamonds glittering from the setting.

It was a beautiful ring, that was certain. Katherine would love it, and she'd love that it was from the early part of the century. She'd be thrilled to wear it, showing it off however she could.

And the idea made him sick to his stomach.

He had known, on some level, that Katherine expected them to marry someday. He'd worried about it occasionally, but it seemed so far off that he'd shoved it deep down and pretended it didn't really exist. Maybe he shouldn't have stayed with Katherine for so long. But it was simple. They were friends, and he knew what to expect from her. Dating someone new would be...difficult.

With a sigh, he plucked the ring from his palm and held it up to the light coming in from the small windows. He tried to imagine proposing, getting married, what would happen after that. Tried to get used to the idea, since it was unlikely he'd be able to avoid it forever. And in that case, perhaps Katherine was—

The door opened. He turned to ask whoever it was to leave him alone, and froze.

"There you are. People were asking where you'd gone off to..." Jack trailed off, hand still on the doorknob, eyes fastened on the ring in Cal's hand. "What is *that?*"

"It's nothing. It's—" Cal sighed, his shoulders slumping slightly. He didn't want to lie to Jack, not after he'd accidentally concealed Katherine's existence in the first place. "It's my grandmother's engagement ring."

"Why do you have it?" Jack asked. His eyes widened, and he stepped into the room and closed the door. "Wait. Are you...were you going to propose to Katherine? Today?"

"No," Cal said. "No. I would have told you if — my mother gave it to me. Just now."

Understanding dawned, and Jack grimaced. "She wants you to propose."

"Yeah," Cal said. "I swear I had no idea."

"I believe you," Jack said. "So are you going to? Propose?"

"Not today." Cal shook his head. "I told my mother I needed more time."

"But you might? In the future?"

"I don't know," Cal said. He closed his eyes for a moment, took a breath. "I guess I have to marry someone at

161

some point. I just didn't think I'd have to think about it so soon."

Jack frowned. "Do you? Have to marry someone?"

Did he? Cal tried to imagine not getting married, the opposite of what he'd tried to picture a few minutes earlier. It was just as hard to envision, but not nearly as distressing.

"I always thought I would," Cal said at last. "It's what everyone expects."

"Yeah." Jack chewed on his lip. "I guess."

"What about you?" Cal asked. "Think you'll get married?"

Jack let out a laugh. "No idea. Commitment isn't really my thing. I've never thought much about it."

Cal wondered, for the millionth time since meeting Jack, how it must feel to be completely your own person, to have your future be yours, and not some obligatory path laid out for you before you were born.

A stab of envy hit him in the gut. He shook it off, because it wasn't going to do him any good.

"Does Katherine expect you to marry her?" Jack asked.

"Probably," Cal said.

Jack reached out and took the ring from Cal. He flipped it between his fingers, squinting at it.

"This is nice," he said.

"Yeah."

With a smirk, Jack slipped the ring onto his finger. It wouldn't go past his second knuckle, and he held his hand up, turning it this way and that to catch the light. Cal's breath caught in his throat.

But then Jack pulled the ring off and handed it back to Cal.

"I feel sort of bad for Katherine," he said. "She thinks she's getting her fairy tale prince, and you'll never be...you know."

"Yeah," Cal said. And here was the guilt. *Fantastic.* "We should head up."

"One second," Jack said.

He stepped close, took Cal's face in his hands, and kissed him gently. Cal gratefully let him, allowing the feel of this man to smooth out his nerves and make him forget, for a moment, about everything else.

There simply wasn't room for anything else when he was kissing Jack.

When Jack broke the kiss and stepped back, he examined Cal's features and smiled. "There," he said. "Much better. I'll go up first, you follow in a minute."

He slipped back out the door with one last wink over his shoulder. Cal watched him go, feeling an ache rising in his chest, a familiar emptiness that he'd almost forgotten about this summer, with Jack to fill its space.

He shoved the ring in his pocket and went up to join the others.

BY THE TIME dinner rolled around, they'd returned to the dock, the sun had begun to sink towards the horizon, and the oranges and pinks streaked across the sky and sea like a painting.

The table was set on the fore deck with linen and champagne, and the party settled in for Independence Day supper and to watch the fireworks that would follow. The chef served up a lobster bisque as a first course, and everyone dug in, eating in silence for a few minutes, tired from the long day in the sun.

During the salad course, quiet chatter began in pockets around the table. Emily, Judith, and Felicia began to plan the social activities for the next couple of weeks. Theodore and Joe entertained Richard Senior with tales from their youth. J.C. and Richie seemed to be having an intense, whispered discussion, and Sally was talking to Jack about something that had him plastering a neutral expression in his face and nodding every now and then.

From her seat beside Cal, Katherine sighed happily.

"What a great day," she said. "Don't you think?"

"Sure," said Cal. "The weather was good."

She hummed. "And the company."

He paused while slicing up his wedge salad and looked at her. She was smiling, an affectionate smile, her eyes shining in the setting sunlight. She leaned towards him and kissed his cheek.

The glance he shot at Jack was instinct. The look on Jack's face was devastating, and was gone in an instant.

"Calloway will take over one day." Theodore raised his voice slightly, commanding the attention of the table.

Cal was suddenly on high alert. He could hear the alcohol crackling around the edges of his father's tone, and that usually meant —

"If he proves himself, of course," Theodore said. He set his water glass on the table with a bang. "He's been taking his time in doing so, but I think he's a late bloomer. Isn't that right, son?"

"I hope so, sir," Cal mumbled.

Theodore peered at him a moment, and then Judith asked if anyone needed more champagne, and the conversation moved on to something else.

Cal relaxed — at least as much as he could with Katherine touching him constantly, and Jack watching from his place across the table beside Theodore — and tried to concentrate on Katherine's quiet chatter.

It wasn't until the dishes with the remnants of Steak Diane and roasted potatoes were cleared, and the chef had brought out plates of individual strawberry shortcakes, that Theodore fastened on Cal again.

"Every so often I catch a glimpse of something that tells me he's got the Buchanan business intuition. But other times, I wonder how much is a façade." Theodore narrowed his eyes at Cal, who went still.

"A façade?" Joe asked.

"Feigned interest," Theodore said. "You'd think he'd be grateful for the opportunities he was born into, but there are times I get the sense he looks at the legacy I'm providing as a burden instead of a gift."

"No, sir. That's not true," Cal said, even though it was. "I apologize if it seems that way."

"I've built all of this for you," Theodore said. "You can walk in and pick up the mantle and make me proud, or you can sulk around like a—"

"Would you just shut up?"

Heads whipped to Jack, who set down his fork with a clatter.

"Excuse me?" Theodore said.

"You've been picking on him all day. All day. It's tired. Move on." Jack's jaw set, his eyes glittering.

Cal's heart sped up. Out of fear or desire, he wasn't sure.

"He's my son, and it's none of your business," Theodore snapped, getting to his feet.

"You're making it all of our business by talking about it," Jack said, rising beside him.

"If he acted more like a Buchanan, I wouldn't have to. Instead, he larks about like a —"

Jack's fist flew through the air and landed squarely on Theodore's right cheek. His head snapped back, and he stumbled. Judith let out a shrill yell.

J.C. jumped up and wrapped her arms around Jack's waist, pulling him backwards. Cal dashed around the table to check on his father, who'd crashed against the railing and was holding his hand to his face. His eyes were unfocused, and he was cursing under his breath.

Cal caught J.C.'s eye and gestured with his head towards the main cabin. She nodded and steered Jack to the doors. He didn't put up a fight, instead seeming to slump inward as she pulled him out of sight.

"Are you all right?" Cal asked his father.

"He punched me," Theodore said. There was less anger and more awe in his tone. "The little punk punched me."

"Well, Theodore, you were being a bit of an ass." Richard Senior approached and peered at Theodore's face. "He got you good, but he just caught your cheek. I don't think you'll get a black eye."

"I can't believe that just happened," Judith said, crowding in to get her own look at the damage. "Of all the things, and we were having such a nice time. I should call the police."

Cal's stomach seized. *No.*

But Joe Thornton spoke up. "That's probably not necessary. It's not a party until there's one good fistfight, right Theodore? Just like the good old days."

"Here, sit back down," Katherine helped Theodore back to the table and into his seat. She pushed his water glass towards him. "Drink some water."

Deciding things were momentarily under control, Cal slipped away, descending to the main cabin. He found Jack and J.C. there, sitting in the corner. Jack's head was in his hands, and J.C. rested her palm on his back.

"Hey," he said, crossing the room and sitting on Jack's other side.

Jack looked up, his eyes a storm of uncertainty and worry. "I'm so sorry," he mumbled. "I fucked that up. I don't know what I was thinking."

"Yeah, what was that?" Cal asked quietly. He took Jack's

right hand in his, examined his knuckles, which were reddened and beginning to bruise. "You okay?"

Jack blinked rapidly, shaking his head. "I was just so angry. He wouldn't stop picking on you. And nothing he was saying was true, and I couldn't stand listening to it anymore, or the way it was making you look. I was already on edge from...you know...and I guess I just snapped. Fuck."

Cal brushed his thumb across Jack's knuckles, and Jack hissed. Then he brought Jack's hand up to his lips and kissed his knuckles gently, one by one.

Jack had punched his father. Because Theodore was picking on Cal. It wasn't anything Cal couldn't handle — that he hadn't been handling his whole life — but for someone else to care enough to get angry...Cal couldn't quite digest it.

He looked up, straight into Jack's eyes, which were large and dark and shining. "Thank you for doing that," he said. "For me."

"You're welcome," Jack said, his voice a little breathy. "But now what? They'll never let you associate with me again."

"We'll work it out," Cal said. "I promise."

They stared at each other for a long moment. Then there was a clatter on the stairs from the upper deck, and the door swung open. Jack snatched his hand back and Cal slid a few inches away as Katherine entered.

"Good, there you are," she said. "I think it's probably best if we leave, take you guys home. Everyone else is going to stay and watch the fireworks."

"You want to miss the fireworks?" Cal asked, surprised.

"We can see them from your house just as well," Katherine said. "Let's get Jack and J.C. home and let your parents cool off for a while."

"Are they furious?" Jack asked. "Should I apologize?"

"Maybe tomorrow?" Katherine said. "It's actually not as bad as you might think. My dad has Theodore convinced that you're just like they were in college, and that a little rough and tumble is an admirable trait." She smirked. "He also said that if you hadn't done it, he might have, because Theodore was running his mouth and making everyone uncomfortable."

"I might love your dad," Jack said, clearly stunned.

"What about my mother?" Cal asked. "Does she still want to call the police?"

"Oh, fuck," Jack said. "My agent is really gonna kill me."

"No police," Katherine said. "Sally and I talked her out of it. I think it'll end up okay. But we should leave now, give them some space. My dad and Sally are going to keep smoothing things over."

"Thanks," Jack said, rising from his seat. "Really, thank you."

"No sweat," Katherine said.

They disembarked and made their way back to Cal's car in silence. J.C. and Katherine climbed in back, and Cal and Jack in front, and they drove to Jack's house in more silence. Cal watched Jack out of the corner of his eye, and he seemed to draw further in on himself the closer they got to home.

When they arrived, Jack glanced at Cal, muttered "goodnight," and bolted for the house. Cal watched him go, feeling helpless. J.C. climbed out of the back, shrugged, and ran after him.

Katherine took Jack's place beside Cal and sighed. "He'll be okay," she said. "Let's go home. Fireworks will be starting soon."

She was right. It was fully dark, almost time for the celebrations. He drove them around to his place, wishing he was feeling more like celebrating, and they crossed through the house and out to the back deck.

"We'll be able to see better from the beach, I think," she

said. She grabbed a blanket off the outside sofa and held out a hand. "Walk with me."

He placed his hand in hers and let her lead him off the deck, across the lawn, and down the steps to the sand. She picked out a spot, and they spread the blanket out and settled onto it.

They sat in silence for a while, not touching. She stretched her legs out, kicked off her sandals, and stuck her toes in the sand while he drew a knee up to his chest and rested his chin on it. The waves were gentle, making a soft *whoosh-slap* against the shore. The moon was a few days past full, floating in the sky like a pale yellow bowling ball.

Cal was trying to find the face in the craters when Katherine spoke.

"Are you okay?" she asked.

He shrugged. "I'm not sure. If you want me to be honest."

"I always do," she said softly. "Even when it's hard. You know you can be honest with me, right? About whatever. We've been friends for long enough that I hope you realize that."

"I do," he said, but something in her tone made him pause. "Is there...do you think I'm not? About something specific?"

It was her turn to shrug. "Maybe."

He tried to think what she could be talking about. Unless she knew that Judith was giving him his grandmother's ring, and that she had wanted him to propose. He didn't want to bring it up, because he didn't want to get her hopes up by talking about marriage when he wasn't sure what he wanted and wasn't in a state of mind to figure it out.

"Cal..."

Cal looked up, momentarily distracted by her use of his nickname, something she hadn't done since they were kids. She was wearing a wry, sad smile, and sighed.

"I know."

"You…" Cal's breath caught. So she did know about the ring? Or…he decided to be cautious. "You know what?"

"I know," she said. "About you. What you like. Who you like."

Oh, fuck.

Cal's heart thudded hard, and then stopped altogether, his chest and stomach turning to ice. He must have looked stunned, horrified, sick…because she let out a gentle laugh and placed a hand on his arm.

"It's okay," she said. "I'm not planning to tell anyone. You're safe."

Cal tried to swallow, and it got stuck halfway down his throat. He coughed, tried to work up some moisture before swallowing again. He thought about pretending he didn't know what she meant, denying it, anything.

But he could see from the expression on her face that she was telling the truth. She knew.

"When? How did you find out?" His voice was a raspy whisper, sandpaper on sand.

She shrugged. "I've known a long time," she said. "It wasn't that hard to guess that you weren't that interested in me. Even when I…well, let's say I could tell your interest in me was purely platonic from pretty much as soon as we started seeing each other. But I wasn't sure until Cam."

"Cam…" Cal frowned, searching his memory. "Cam Hornsby?"

Cameron Hornsby had been a senior at Harvard who Cal had briefly fooled around with at the beginning of sophomore year. It hadn't lasted long, a month or so, before Cam had decided he needed to focus on school and graduating and Cal was too distracting.

"You knew about me and Cam?" Cal asked. They'd been so careful…or so he thought.

"I already suspected that you were...and then I saw the way you and he interacted. It just confirmed it."

"You never said anything."

"No. I hoped that maybe you'd — eventually — come around on me."

She looked sad, and he suddenly felt guilty. Guilty for having led her on, guilty for lying, guilty for not being what she wanted him to be. It ate at his gut like acid, that he couldn't help it, and would continue to do it, to other women for the rest of his life.

"I'm sorry," he mumbled, his gaze dropping to his hands. "I didn't mean to deceive you. Or lead you on."

She sighed. "I know. And you aren't leading me on, now that I know that it will never happen. You'll never look at me the way you look at him."

"At Cam?"

"At Jack."

Cal stilled. "Oh." He didn't deny it. It wouldn't do any good. She'd seen through them. "It was obvious?"

"Cal, you — both of you — look at each other like there's no one else around."

He peered at her. "Do you think the others can tell?"

She thought for a moment, and then shook her head. "I don't think so. I was looking for it, and knew what to look for. I don't think anyone else has caught on."

He shook his head. "You're being very calm about this," he said.

She frowned. "Am I? I guess I've had a long time to get used to the idea. But I don't understand it, why you'd want that instead of girls."

He smirked. "Probably for the same reason you want that instead of girls."

She let out a surprised laugh. "That's a fair point. I guess we have even more in common than we thought."

He sighed. "So. What now? We tell our parents that we decided to break up? Should we wait until after you all leave?"

"Who said anything about breaking up?" she asked. "I'm sure I didn't."

The first *boom-crackle* of fireworks burst overhead, and they both looked up at the green lights streaking across the night sky.

Cal turned back to Katherine. "You don't want to break up? Why?"

"Shhh. Let's watch for a minute."

He sat beside her, too distracted by the explosions going on in his chest to focus on the explosions above his head. He shifted on the blanket, antsy to continue the conversation. Finally, she spoke without looking at him.

"We could help each other," she said. "Think about it. If I know about you, and am willing to accept it? I can help you."

"You can?"

Now she did turn back to him. "I can. I can be your cover. No one will suspect, because you'll have a wife."

"A wife?" His heart pounded again.

"A wife. Come on, Cal. We both know that's where we were headed. My mom told me that Judith was getting your grandmother's ring for you. I half expected you to propose today."

"My mother wanted me to," Cal admitted.

"I thought so. I know why you hesitated. But it wouldn't have to be so bad, would it? We're friends. We've known each other forever, we get along well." She swiveled so that her legs were tucked under her and her torso was fully facing him. "All that stuff you hate? The social obligations and all? I can take care of all of that. Make you look good. I'd be such a good wife, Cal. I could make you proud."

"But we wouldn't really be...it would be fake," he said.

"And no one has to know that but us. I can give you the freedom you need. And children. I know you want children, and I can give that to you. Someone to carry on your name. So you can leave your own legacy."

"What about you?" Cal said. "Wouldn't you hate not having a chance at something real?"

She shrugged one shoulder. "I don't think so. I get something here, too. Your name. The social position I want to be in. And if I look the other way for you, you could look the other way for me."

Cal tried to figure out what she was suggesting. "You mean you'd have affairs?"

"Sure," she said. She smiled. "You want to know what I've been doing in the Hamptons while you've been falling for a movie star?"

"I haven't been falling—"

"I've been sneaking around with the guy who cuts our lawn. It's a total cliché but I don't even care. So yes, I would have affairs."

Cal looked up at the colorful, glittering lights and tried to envision the picture she was painting. Could he do that? Marry Katherine, continue to have her as his public partner, and then secretly be able to pursue his true interests without having to lie to her? Would she be happy or would she end up resenting him? Would he resent her?

She'd said being married would give him freedom. In his gut, he knew that was a lie.

"So..." she said, sounding timid once more. "What do you think?"

"I think—" A cluster of explosions burst overhead. "I think I need to think about it."

After a beat, she nodded. "That's fine. Take your time, it's not a rush. You don't even have to decide during this visit.

We can always tell everyone at Christmas that you proposed right before the break."

"Yeah. Maybe," he agreed.

"Do you have the ring? With you right now? I'm kind of curious."

He dug into his pocket and pulled out the jewelry, handing it over to her wordlessly. She turned it over in her fingers, the diamond lighting up with the colors of the fireworks as the show hit its crescendo.

"It's beautiful," she murmured. Then she slipped it on her finger.

Cal's gut clenched at the sight, and he held his breath until she slid it off and handed it back to him.

The finale ended, the last crackling of sparks subsiding into nothing. Cheers could be heard from up and down the beach, a particularly loud burst from the deck of the house next door. Cal tucked the ring back in his pocket and got to his feet. He held a hand out to Katherine to help her up, and they shook out and folded the blanket.

"Why don't I show you what an asset I can be," she said suddenly. She glanced to the right, towards Jack's house. "I know you're worried about him and want to check on him. Go."

"I can't," Cal said. "My parents — and yours — will be home soon."

"I'll tell them you weren't feeling well and went to bed." She smiled smugly. "And I'll tell them they should leave you alone because I already checked in on you and you needed to rest."

"And they'll believe you?"

"Why wouldn't they? For all they know, I'm a devoted girlfriend, almost-fiancé. I've no reason to lie to them."

Cal hesitated, but only for a moment. He wanted to see Jack. Needed it.

"Okay," he said. "Katherine...thank you."

"Go," she said.

He turned and ran for the steps. Once he'd decided to follow her advice, he couldn't wait another second. He took the stairs up to Jack's house two at a time, then sprinted across the back lawn.

When he reached the back deck, he scanned the people littered across it, but didn't detect that familiar mop of black curls.

"Cal!" called Graham. "Happy freedom day, buddy."

"Yeah, you too," Cal said. "Do you know where—"

"Haven't seen him," Graham said. "I thought he was with you."

Cal nodded and headed into the noisy house, where music was once again blasting. After a moment's consideration, he ignored the crowded rooms and went straight for the stairs, following a hunch.

Jack's bedroom door was closed. Instead of knocking, Cal turned the knob slowly and then pushed open the door, peeking inside.

There, curled up on his side, still wearing his clothes from dinner, was Jack. The moonlight streaming in the windows illuminated his pale skin, his sleeping features marred by a small frown.

Cal slipped inside and closed the door behind him with a soft *click*. He approached the bed, trying to determine his best move. Should he wake Jack up?

He kicked off his shoes and crawled onto the bed behind Jack, curling his body around the man's sleeping form. He placed a small kiss on Jack's neck and then breathed deeply, the scent of this man enough to relax him immediately.

Jack sighed and snuggled back into Cal's embrace, and Cal smiled into his curls. A few minutes passed like this, until

Jack's breathing changed ever so slightly and he stiffened for a moment.

"Cal?" he whispered.

"Yeah. It's me." Cal replied, pitching his voice into that low rumble that he knew made Jack shiver.

He wasn't disappointed, as the man in his arms gave a tremble.

"What are you doing here?" Jack asked.

"I wanted to be here."

"But what about—"

"Shhhh." Cal moved, rolling Jack onto his back and silencing him with a deep kiss.

When he withdrew, Jack blinked up at him, his eyes troubled. There were telltale shiny tracks leading away from his eyes, and Cal's heart broke. Jack had been crying.

"I'm so sorry about today," Jack said. "I'm so sorry I—"

"Stop." Cal kissed Jack again. "Let's not. I don't care. Can I just…" He began to trail tiny kisses and licks down Jack's neck. "Let me show you what I care about."

He sat up and waited for Jack's nod, and then — slowly — began to undress him. He unbuttoned Jack's shirt and pulled it off. The tee-shirt underneath followed. Next came the belt, followed by his linen pants and boxers.

Once Jack was laid bare before him, he wasted no time. He wasn't sure how to explain what he was feeling, and so he was going to do the second best thing…show Jack.

He skimmed his lips over Jack's skin, reveling in the breathy moans that evoked. His fingers brushed over gooseflesh, his tongue tasted all the pockets and crevices it could find. He plucked and stroked and teased until Jack was shivering and gasping beneath him.

Jack moaned. "Don't stop," he said. "Please."

"Do you get it yet?" Cal asked, lowering himself on top of Jack and nuzzling at his neck.

"Get — ah —what?" Jack asked.

"Get what I'm trying to show you."

"What? I'm not—"

Cal bit into Jack's earlobe and tugged. "Guess I'll have to keep going, then."

For the next half hour, he granted Jack's request and didn't stop. Once he'd put his hands and mouth on every inch of the man's body, he simply started all over again. He couldn't get enough — enough of Jack writhing beneath him, enough of the sounds he made, enough of the way he said *Cal* such that it sounded like a half-prayer, half-plea.

Eventually, he shed his own clothes and draped himself over Jack, aligning their bodies from head to toe.

"*Now* do you get it?" Cal asked.

Jack shivered and turned his head into Cal's neck. "I don't know what I'm supposed to be getting."

"That I don't care what happened today. It'll work out. The only thing I care about here…" He swooped in and kissed Jack, kissed him so long he nearly lost track of the sentence. "…the only thing I care about here is you."

Jack groaned, and then grabbed at Cal's ass and pulled, so that Cal's hips shifted and they slid together. Now it was Cal's turn to moan. He moved his hips in a steady rhythm, and within minutes his orgasm rushed in, exploding out of him on a shout. He heard Jack come apart beneath him, and grinned, gasping.

He leaned down and snagged Jack's discarded tee-shirt from the floor, using it to wipe them clean before pulling the blankets on the bed back and gathering Jack close beneath them.

They were quiet for a while, and then Jack spoke.

"Shit, that was…unreal."

Cal laughed. "Yeah."

"I mean, for not fucking, that was like…"

"Yeah."

Jack sighed. "So I'm glad you're here. Obviously. But...how? You didn't let me ask before."

Cal thought for a moment. How much should he tell Jack? He sighed.

"Katherine covered for me," he said quietly.

"She what?" Jack pushed himself up on one elbow and peered down at Cal, his brow furrowed in confusion. "What does she think she's covering you for?"

"This," Cal said. "She knows."

Jack's eyes widened. "She knows about—"

"Well, about me. But also about us."

"How did she figure it out?" Jack asked.

"Apparently she's known about me for years." He let out a short laugh. "And with us? I guess it's pretty obvious if you know what to look for."

"Fuck," Jack muttered. He slid back down onto the pillow. "Do I have to be worried about this? Call my agent, tell him to get ready for another scandal?"

"I don't think so," said Cal. "She said she isn't planning to tell anyone about me, and I guess that covers you, too." He paused. "She was surprisingly understanding."

"So why is she still hanging around?" Jack asked. "Why is she still pretending you're into her?"

"She wants to get married," Cal said. "She thinks it would benefit us both. She'd get the name and status she craves, while I get a perfect wife to show off so no one is the wiser about who I really am."

"Wow," Jack said. "Ambitious. That tracks."

"She made some good points," Cal acknowledged. "It would take the pressure off, remove any scrutiny that might come my way. She'd look the other way so I could still date. It could work. And it would be nice not to have to lie."

"Is that what you really want?" Jack asked. "To have a fake marriage and a secret life?"

"Do I have a choice?" Cal rolled onto his back, staring up at the ceiling. "It's not like I could do what I really want to do."

"What do you really want to do?"

"I don't know. Not that."

"But if you could have whatever life you wanted?" Jack asked. He placed a palm on Cal's chest, and Cal wondered if Jack could feel the way his heart sped up at the simple touch.

Follow you back to L.A. in the fall, Cal thought desperately. He didn't say it. Couldn't say it, because saying it would make him want it even more, and make the fact that he couldn't have it completely unbearable.

Besides, it would scare Jack off. The guy had said just that day that commitment wasn't his thing. He's probably run screaming at the very suggestion.

So Cal just said, "No idea. Really, I don't think about it much, because when I do...it just makes me..."

Jack shifted so that his head was on Cal's chest and his arm was wrapped around Cal's waist. He sighed.

"I get it," he said. "I do. You probably think I don't give a fuck what anyone thinks, and that's mostly true. But there are some things I have to care about, if I want the things I want, like my career."

Another stretch of quiet. Cal thought about what Jack had said. As carefree as he seemed, he obviously had things he worried about, and things he needed to be cautious of, if he wanted to be successful in Hollywood.

So they both had to live in a world that told them they weren't quite right, were never going to be accepted as they were.

"I'm probably going to marry her," he said, after a while.

Jack didn't respond right away. Cal listened to the music

pulsing through the walls from downstairs, watched the moonlight flicker in the window, felt Jack's curls under his chin.

Suddenly Jack surged up and kissed him fiercely.

"Then it's like we said," said Jack, his lips brushing against Cal. "We have the summer. Let's make the most of it."

Jack took control, attacking Cal with his mouth and hands, and all Cal could do was take it. The night expanded around them, and he told himself to just enjoy each moment as it came, and not think too hard about what lay beyond.

And yet, with each passing second, he knew that his freedom was merely temporary, and that future he'd been dumb enough to let himself want was going to crumble away into nothing.

CHAPTER 12

fter Independence Day, Cal's carefully constructed and manicured life began to take on a funhouse quality. Everything was just slightly off, like a representation of reality distorted to expose flaws that were at times comical and at other times hideous.

His house, the beautiful seaside mansion that was the envy of Westerly, became a prison fraught with hazards, as he navigated the aftermath of the yacht trip disaster. Theodore, who had escaped the encounter with a slight bruise on his cheek, rarely let a meal go by without making a snide remark about the house next door. Judith spent all her time hinting at weddings; her lack of subtlety would have been embarrassing if he cared enough for it to be.

Katherine, for her part, demonstrated extreme poise and cleverness at every turn like he had never seen before. She handled Judith with ease, placated Theodore, and managed to praise Cal enough that he even began to think his parents were seeing him in a different light.

"Well, I wouldn't know," she said one evening over oxtail soup while the parents were discussing Kennedy's deployment of National Guard troops to desegregate the University of Alabama. "I never bother myself with such things. Calloway may have some insight, however."

Joe Thornton turned to Cal. "What do you think?" he asked. "Should universities be forced to desegregate?"

"Harvard has black students," Cal said. "And from my experience, they have not only earned their places, but contribute to the marketplace of ideas with valuable perspectives that deepen every student's experience. Isn't that the point of a university?"

"Perhaps," Theodore said. "But Harvard has willingly admitted black students for a hundred years—"

"Not many," Cal countered. "My class has nearly twenty, I believe, many more than usual."

"Emphasis on the word *willingly*," Theodore said with a withering stare. "The question is whether universities should be forced to desegregate, not whether desegregation has educational benefits. Surely, if having black students improves the educational quality of a university, the best students will choose desegregated schools and the problem will resolve itself."

Recognizing his father's tone of dismissal, Cal was ready to let it go, but Katherine jumped in again.

"Calloway, what were you saying to me the other day?" she asked. He racked his brain, but couldn't come up with a single conversation they'd ever had about desegregation, let alone in the last week. "Something about equal protection?" she prompted.

"Well," he fumbled, "that equal protection is the basis for desegregation in general?" She nodded encouragingly, and he continued. "And if the point is to provide black students with equal opportunities in education, they benefit from the marketplace of ideas as well. Keeping them from a government-provided marketplace cannot be equal. Which is what the Supreme Court said. Surely, the Supreme Court's ruling should be respected, and if a university refuses, the ruling can be enforced? If not, what good is the ruling?"

Joe Thornton nodded. "I suppose that makes sense."

"Seems an overreach by Kennedy," Theodore said. "Using the National Guard like that. But perhaps you're right."

Cal stared down at his soup in disbelief. The conversation shifted, but he shot Katherine a grateful smile, and she winked in return. He suddenly felt like they had this partnership, and it was comforting, but also unsettling.

Interactions with his longtime friends were also somewhat strained. It was like they could sense, for the first time, that Cal was feigning interest in most of what they talked about or did. Katherine helped there, too, and he let her take the reins in the socializing that no longer held the escape from his parents or his impending future that it once had.

He couldn't help it. He saw all of them morphing into versions of their parents. Every discussion, every outing suggested, every reminiscence felt like he was stepping into Theodore's shoes and putting on a costume he didn't want but couldn't seem to avoid. It left a bad taste in his mouth and a churning in his stomach, so he yielded to Katherine's social graces and let her make apologies (*he's had a rough morning; a small row with his father; he had a touch too much to drink last night; the heat makes everyone a little restless*).

Even time spent next door was altered. With his help, Katherine had tentatively found her place among Jack's crowd. He confided in J.C. that Katherine knew his secret, and J.C. took Katherine under her wing as a co-conspirator.

"I'll teach her everything she needs to know, Cals," J.C. said the first night, over cold beer on the back patio. "Don't worry about a thing. By the time she goes back to her fancy beaches in New York, she'll be well on her way to being a pro."

"Thanks," Cal said. "But don't call me 'Cals.'"

"Sure thing, Cal-o." J.C. kissed him on the cheek and bounced away, leaving Cal rolling his eyes in her wake.

Since Katherine was now around all the time, however, he felt less free at Jack's than he had before. Jack noticed.

"You're so...tense," he said one afternoon, peering down at Cal. Jack was straddling his waist, and they'd been in the middle of a good makeout session when Jack had abruptly stopped and sat up with a frown. "What's going on?"

"Nothing," Cal said quickly. He was desperate not to ruin the time they had left, and it suddenly felt like there wasn't enough of it, as if it was whizzing by like cars on the new interstate.

"It's not nothing," Jack said. He slid to the side and curled up against Cal, tucking his nose into the place where Cal's neck met his shoulder, a favorite spot of his. "Come on. Talk to me. What's got you wound up?"

"I don't know," Cal said. "I think I'm just...it's weird with Katherine around. Isn't it?"

"Not really," Jack said. "Not for me, not now. But then, I haven't known her my whole life. Maybe it's just hard for you to adjust to the way she is now? The role she's playing?"

"She's part of the other me." Cal searched for words to explain his hesitation. "She represents the Cal that is for public consumption. Calloway, the Buchanan heir. She doesn't belong here. In this space, with us. With who I am here. And so it feels weird to let her see this me and not be hiding it. It's like I'm too exposed and it's...weird."

"You'll get used to it," Jack said reassuringly. "It's a change, that's all."

"I just keep feeling like I'm doing something wrong."

"Wrong...with me?" Jack asked.

"No. Yes. I don't know. I know most people think it's wrong — what we do — that's been clear to me my whole life. But before, I just accepted it, that I was going to do this wrong thing, that *I* was wrong, but as long as no one knew and it wasn't hurting anyone, I was okay with that and it didn't feel wrong, inside. But now, with Katherine knowing? It's a link. To the rest of my life."

"That worries you," Jack said.

"If she gets mad at me, it's all over. She could ruin me."

Jack was quiet for a minute, and then asked, "Do you trust her?"

"Maybe?" Cal sighed. "Yes, mostly. I guess I don't have much choice. She already knows so there isn't a thing I can do about that. I just don't like someone else..."

"Having power over you?" Jack asked.

"Yeah. Like it's out of my control. Before, the only people who knew were also like me. So it was mutually assured destruction. But it's different with Katherine, because there isn't that balance."

"Sometimes, you have to accept that people have power over you, in certain ways," Jack said. "I have."

"Yeah?" Cal asked. "Like how?"

"Getting involved with you was a risk for me. More than you know." Jack kissed Cal's neck. "A good risk. Worth it. But a risk nonetheless."

Cal turned that over in his mind. He'd been thinking he was the one taking all the risks, involving himself with a man in his home environment where he could be so easily discovered. He hadn't considered Jack's risks.

"Tell me more," he said. "If you want."

"I told you I had to get out of L.A. for a while," Jack began. Cal made a noise of assent. Jack had said that, and alluded to some problem back home. He'd wondered about it. "There was a scandal. Or an almost scandal. I'd been seeing this producer — on the down low, of course, and nothing serious

— for a couple of months. It was fun, he was fun. Until his wife found out."

"Fuck," Cal said, feeling an empathetic surge of anxiety even as he squashed the jealousy at the idea of Jack with another man. "How did she find out?"

Jack laughed. "She walked in on me blowing him in his pool house. Not my best moment. Or his."

"What did you do?"

"Well, it turned out to be a set-up. She'd suspected he was cheating and told him she was going out of town, then circled back with a Polaroid camera, intending to use it to ask for a divorce. When she found me, and not some busty blonde, I think it threw her for a loop. But she shifted gears and immediately moved to blackmail."

"Fuck," Cal said again.

"Yeah. She said I could keep fucking her husband if we paid her monthly. I decided it wasn't worth it — it was running its course anyhow — and said no way. But she threatened to leak the photographs to the press, and..." Jack ran a hand through his hair. "My agent was furious. *Fuck who you want but be discrete, Jack.* He yelled at me for an hour, and then told me to leave town and he'd handle it."

"Did he?" Cal asked.

"I assume so. I haven't seen any photos of me on my knees with that prick's dick in my mouth in the papers."

Cal flinched at the visual. "Well, that's good."

"Yeah. But I was supposed to lay low this summer. My agent encouraged me to party it up...with women. *Have ten women. Hell, have twenty*, he said. I was definitely not supposed to find a boy to enjoy."

"Why did you?" Cal asked. "I mean, if you're taking a pretty big risk, why would you bother?"

Jack propped himself up on an elbow and smiled. He trailed his finger along Cal's lips one by one.

"What kind of a question is that?" Jack asked softly. "I met you. There was really no other choice to be made. I told you, sometimes you have to accept that someone else has power over you."

He leaned down and touched his lips to Cal's, and then bounced up and off the bed.

"Let's do something," he said. "I need to move."

"Do what?" asked Cal.

"I don't know. You live here. What haven't we done? Take me somewhere." Jack grinned and tugged at his curls. "Take me on a date."

Cal's heart leapt at the phrasing, but he hesitated. "It's risky," he said. "Speaking of risks."

"So it'll be good practice for Katherine. Come on, I want to go somewhere. With you."

Jack's enthusiasm was infectious, and Cal couldn't help but smile. "We could go up to Providence, have dinner on Federal Hill," he suggested. "You like Italian."

"Not just dinner," Jack said. Isn't there somewhere we could move around? I need to burn off some energy."

Cal thought for a moment, and then had an idea. "How do you feel about chowder and clamcakes? And ferris wheels?"

Jack's face lit up. "A carnival?"

"Better," Cal said. "Let's go to Rocky Point."

AN HOUR LATER, they were speeding up the Interstate towards Rocky Point Beach. Katherine was chattering excitedly to J.C. in the back seat.

"You're going to love this," she said. "Seriously, what a great idea. The food is incredible and the park is so much fun."

"What is it, exactly?" J.C. said. "Jack said carnival."

"It's not temporary like a carnival," Katherine explained. "This place is always there, and they have amusement rides and midway games. I heard there's a new one this year, a haunted house."

"Are you going to be okay going into the haunted house with tiny little me and not the Jolly Green Giant?" J.C. asked. "I'm not going to hold you close."

Katherine laughed. "I'm made of stronger stuff than you think," she said. "Maybe I'll protect you."

Cal listened to the conversation and glanced at Jack beside him. "What do you think?" he asked. "Will you protect me in the haunted house?"

Jack snorted. "Sure, just tuck yourself behind me, and I'll shield you, baby."

They were seated at long tables in the Shore Dinner Hall just as the sun began to dip towards the horizon. There was still an hour or so until sunset, but the light began to take on that late evening look, with faint pinks and oranges beginning to show in the sky above the waves of the Narragansett Bay.

The servers came by with giant platters of clamcakes, steamed clams, bread, corn on the cob, lobster, watermelon and bowls of clam chowder. Jack's eyes went wide at the sheer quantity of food being deposited in front of them.

"Holy fuck," he said.

"First time here?" asked a girl to his right.

"Yeah," he said. "I'm from out of town."

"Well, it's all you can eat, so dig in. Hey, anyone ever tell you that you look like...what's his name...that actor guy? Jack something?" She squinted at him.

"All the time," he said, wiggling his eyebrows. "I should thank the guy someday. He helps me get dates."

Across the table, Katherine giggled. Cal snorted into his clam chowder.

They struck up a conversation with their table mates as they took advantage of the "all you can eat" policy. The group had been to the park a few times that season already and were full of recommendations.

"The Flume is always our first stop," said one guy. "But the new Castle of Terror is boss."

"I've been to haunted houses," Jack said. "What makes this one special?"

"It's not just a haunted house," one of the girls said. "It's a ride. And it's in the dark and super spooky."

"Your ladies will want to stay close," said the guy with a wink.

"Maybe the guys will want to stay close," Cal said. "Equal rights and all."

Jack kicked Cal's foot under the table and Cal hid his smirk behind his corn on the cob.

After dinner, Jack complained about the amount of food he'd eaten. "I'm bursting at the seams," he groaned. "Why didn't you stop me?"

"That's half the fun," Cal said. "You'll be fine in an hour. We can hit the midway games until we've digested."

After miserably failing to knock cans off of pedestals or pitch tiny rings onto soda bottle necks for a while, Jack huffed.

"You're going to go broke paying for all these games," Jack said.

"He can't go broke," said Katherine. "Don't worry about it."

"What do you mean?" Jack asked.

"He's got the trust fund," she said.

Cal rolled his eyes as Jack raised an eyebrow.

"I get it in August," Cal explained. "When I turn twenty-one."

"No wonder you toe the line with your parents," Jack said.

"Oh, my parents can't touch the trust," Cal said. "My grandfather set it up. It has nothing to do with my father or my mother."

"That's lucky," Jack said. "Well, even so, these are rigged, I think," he said indignantly, turning back to glare at the midway operator.

J.C. laughed. "There's a duck pond over there. We can fish out a plastic duck for you. Everyone wins a prize, it says. You might get a keychain."

Jack rolled his eyes. "I'm not that desperate. Yet. Let's try again later, I want that big stuffed lobster."

They bought books of tickets and hit the Castle of Terror first. As they stood in line, Katherine shuffled next to Cal, and he took the cue and put his arm around her shoulders.

"This looks so good," she said. "Jack, do you like haunted houses?"

"Sure," Jack said. "Who doesn't like to be scared?"

"I don't," J.C. said. She stood on her toes to peer over the line, and eyed the two-person carts that rumbled along the track and disappeared into the castle behind swinging doors. "In fact, I'm having second thoughts."

"Don't make me go alone," Katherine said. "It'll be fine, I promise. It's probably cute and not actually scary. And why don't you like to be scared?"

"I just don't see the need in being fake scared when there are plenty of real life things to be scared about, like nuclear war and pesticides in our food." J.C. grimaced. "Sorry, I don't mean to be a drag."

"You've read *Silent Spring*," Katherine said.

"Yeah. Did you?" J.C. asked.

Katherine pushed away from Cal and moved up to talk to J.C., pushing Jack behind her. "It scared me, and not in a good way."

Jack fell in place beside Cal and let his knuckles brush

against Cal's hip. "Well look at that," he said. "The girls seem to be getting along."

"That's lucky," Cal said. "Think we should let them take the ride together?"

"Might as well," Jack said.

Cal grinned. It seemed like a natural conversation. Had the girls planned it? Katherine shot him a wink, and he grinned harder.

Cal had to fold himself into the tiny cart, and Jack giggled away at the sight.

"Hurry up, it's going to get to the doors before you're in," he said.

Cal finally managed to squeeze his knees into place — at an angle — and reached out for Jack's hand to help him in. Because of the angle of his knees, they ended up smooshed together on one side of the cart.

"Good thing you're skinny," Cal observed.

"Too bad you're huge," Jack fired back.

Cal glanced behind them, where the girls were already settled. J.C. gave a wave, and the carts lurched forward into the castle.

Katherine had been right. The Castle of Terror wasn't that scary, a lot of small jump scares and cartoony horror murals on the walls. But it was dark, and Jack grabbed Cal's hands and didn't have to let go.

They went up a ramp, gears clanking ominously beneath them, and hurtled out of the Castle onto an overlook. Jack still didn't let go, and Cal didn't worry about it.

When they re-entered the Castle, they were in complete darkness. Chains rattled around them, along with the wailing of ghosts.

"Cal," Jack said. "Look at me."

"I can't," Cal said, turning his head into the black. "There's no light, so mmph—"

Jack's mouth closed over his urgently. Cal's stomach somersaulted. *Public*, his mind whirred. *Dark*, was the thought that followed. He kissed Jack back until they thumped through another set of doors and back into the light at a second overlook, breathing rapidly.

He glanced at Jack, who was enjoying the view of the park and smiling a smug smile. Cal laughed.

As he climbed out of the cart at the end of the ride, Cal's cheeks were flushed. Jack had taken advantage of every dark spot in the ride.

"Want to go again?" he asked, and Jack laughed.

"Later. Definitely."

They rode the Flume next, floating along the elevated half-tubes and laughing down all the dips. The watery track wound its way through the trees, and there was no one around, so Cal scooted forward and wrapped his arms around Jack's waist until they got to the final plunge.

They all rode the Tilt-a-Whirl together, then the Music Express and the Spider, and afterwards took a break for cotton candy and doughboys.

"How am I even eating?" Jack asked, breaking off a piece of doughboy and shoving it in his mouth. Cal did the same, enjoying the crunch of the sugar and the gooeyness of the hot fried dough.

"Rocky Point magic," Cal said. "Ferris wheel next, now that it's dark."

They rode the ferris wheel twice. The first time, they each rode with their girls.

"Thanks for including me in this," Katherine said, as they rotated up into the air and back down. "Thanks for giving me a chance."

"I should be thanking you," Cal said. "You're the one doing me a favor."

"I'm having fun," Katherine said. "It's nice. There's no

pressure on me, and I can just hang out with J.C., who I actually like."

The cart stopped near the top, and Cal looked out over the lights of the park. The anxiety he'd been feeling earlier, the unsettled, slightly off feeling, began to dissolve. "You've been so great about everything," he said. "I can't...you don't have any idea how much this means to me, what you're doing for me, right now."

"I think I do," Katherine said. "I can see how much you care about each other." She nudged him with her shoulder. "Do you love him?"

Cal's breath caught in his throat. "It would be stupid of me if I did," he said. "Wouldn't it? It's only for the summer, and then we'll both return to our lives."

"Love is never stupid, I don't think," Katherine said. "I loved you, or...no, I did. I do, still, even if it's not romantic. And I don't regret that. It's not a bad thing, to love and be loved."

"I'm sorry I couldn't—"

"I said I don't regret it, silly," Katherine chided. "No need to be sorry. So do you? Love him?"

The wheel started up again, and Cal chose to remain silent. He was silent as they unloaded, returned to the line, reshuffled, and loaded a second time. As he settled into the cart with Jack, Jack eyed him.

"You okay?" he asked as they moved up to the next level and stopped. "Did something happen? Did Katherine—"

"She's fine," Cal said. "Great, in fact. I think this might...I think it might work, what she's proposed."

He tried to imagine his life with her at his side, doing the things she'd been doing all week. Supporting him and his choices, easing the way, sharing the burden. There was something comforting about it...but at the same time, the comfort was distorted.

Because he couldn't quite imagine anyone besides Jack as the third person in their triangle, and that was going to be a problem.

The cart moved up again, stopped again.

"No," Jack said. "Something is off. What did she say to you?"

He reached over and took Cal's hand, and Cal stared at their laced fingers. He tried to imagine riding this ferris wheel and holding someone else's hand, and it made him sick to his stomach.

"Nothing," Cal said. "I just…you…" He turned to Jack. What was he supposed to say? What do you say when you realize you're in love with someone you can't have?

The cart continued up towards the top.

"Cal." Jack took Cal's face in his hands. "Come on. Something is going on, can you just let me in on it? Let me help."

Cal locked his gaze onto golden-green eyes full of concern. One more shift, and the cart came to a halt, swinging back and forth at the top of the wheel.

Commitment isn't really my thing, Jack had said. He'd also been clear about the time constraints on their relationship: *we have the summer,* he'd said. *He'll get distracted by someone eventually, he always does,* Ginny had said.

At the end of the summer, Jack would go back to L.A. and his producers and actors and Hollywood life. At the end of the summer, Cal would return to Harvard and take the final steps into the mold that had been waiting for him since the day he was born.

At the end of the summer, he'd have to let go. But maybe in the meantime…

Love is never stupid, Katherine had said.

Cal looked into Jack's eyes, the eyes filled with concern, and thought about the other side. How Jack had been jealous, how he'd stuck up for Cal in front of Theodore, how he seemed to always know how Cal was feeling.

Getting involved with you was a risk for me. Worth it, Jack had said. *Sometimes you have to accept that someone else has power over you.*

Suddenly, nothing was off. It all clicked back into place, and Cal's vision was clear.

"I think I'm in love with you," he said quietly.

Jack's lips parted.

"I'm sorry," Cal said.

"What are you sorry for?" Jack's lips curved into a smile.

"I don't mean to put pressure on you. I know we—"

"I don't feel pressure," Jack said. "The only thing I feel is — Cal, I'm in love with you, too. I think I have been since that day we walked the beach in the rain."

Cal's heart pounded hard twice, and he surged forward, capturing Jack's lips. They kissed until the wheel began to rotate again, reluctantly pulling apart as they sank into view of the rest of the park.

"Now what?" Cal asked, breathless, as they swooped towards the top again.

"Now you're going to win me that stuffed lobster, and then take me home and show me a good time." Jack grinned at him. "That's what boyfriends do, after all, or so I hear."

Boyfriend. Cal grinned back.

"It's a deal."

The lights of the park twinkled around them, brilliant and undistorted. Cal didn't have a clear view of what his life was going to look like after August, but for now, for the summer...

...he was in love, and that was clear enough.

CHAPTER 13

*J*uly turned into August.

The air grew heavy and oppressive as the temperature climbed into the high nineties and the humidity climbed along with it. Days were spent horizontal, fans whirring constantly and cold beverages dripping with condensation.

Jack complained about it.

"Why is it so hot here?" he asked one morning. They'd tried the beach, but even the breeze off the ocean seemed to have taken a break, and the summer sun was relentless. After an hour they'd retreated into the house, flopped onto the sofas and chairs in their swimsuits, limbs spread wide, trying to expose as much bare skin to the air as possible.

Cal accepted the joint Grant passed him and took a hit. "It's August," he said, his voice choked as he tried to hold in the smoke.

"It's not this hot in California," Jack whined. "This is like it is in New York in August. But the ocean here is supposed to make it better."

"It'll cool off in a few days, once a storm rolls through," Cal said. He took a second hit, then offered the joint to Jack, who waved it away.

"I'm too high to be hot," he said. Then he shook his head. "I mean, I'm too hot to be high. Fuck."

"Your problem is that you're usually cold," Cal said. "So you can't handle it when you're not."

"I wish I was cold right now. Bring on the snow."

Cal hesitated as an idea popped into his mind. Maybe it was the weed, or the heat, or the way Jack's nose scrunched when he pouted, but he knew exactly what he wanted at that moment.

He handed the joint back to Grant, got to his feet, and stood over Jack.

"What?" Jack asked, peering up at him with a scowl.

Cal hauled Jack up and then, in a quick move, tossed him over his shoulder.

"Hey," Jack said, smacking Cal's back and kicking his legs into the air. "What the fuck."

Cal wrapped an arm around Jack's thighs and ignored the beating his back was taking.

"You want to be cold, let's make you cold."

He climbed the stairs two at a time as Jack sagged against him, running out of energy.

"You're hotter than I am," he grumbled. "I'm sweating into my eyes now, and can't even admire your ass."

Cal snorted and continued down the hall to the bathroom. He turned the shower on cold, then dumped Jack onto his feet in the bathtub.

"Hey," Jack sputtered.

"Cool off," Cal said. Jack shook his hair out of his eyes and pouted up at Cal through the streaming water, and Cal laughed. "It feels good, though, right?"

"Yeah." Jack's pout turned into a grin. "Join me."

He reached out and grabbed the waistband of Cal's swim-suit, pulling him forward until he stepped into the bathtub, the cool water hitting his chest and stomach. He sighed with relief as the water cascaded over him. He ducked his head under the stream and then smoothed his hair back.

Jack hummed. "You're always so delicious when you're wet," he said.

He leaned in and sucked on Cal's collarbone, licked his way up his neck, and landed on his lips with a soft kiss.

"It's too hot to fuck," Cal whispered against Jack's mouth, even as Jack yanked his swimsuit down and shimmied out of his own.

"You're too hot not to fuck," Jack said. But he contented himself with just running his hands over Cal's skin and sipping water from his shoulder.

After a few minutes, Jack shivered, and Cal turned off the water and stepped out of the bathtub, pulling Jack with him.

He draped their dripping suits over the faucet and then grabbed a towel.

"Don't dry off," Jack said. "We'll stay cool longer."

"We'll drip all over the house," Cal said.

"So what? It'll dry."

"We're naked." Cal gestured at himself and Jack, as if to remind him of the obvious.

Jack opened the bathroom door a crack and peered out. "Come on, the coast is clear."

He grabbed Cal's hand and darted into the hallway. Cal stumbled after him, cheeks flaming. He looked around wildly as they ran down the hall, the air brushing against his skin and making him shiver.

By the time they reached Jack's bedroom and closed the door behind them, they were both laughing. They tumbled onto the bed to catch their breath, but every time Cal looked at Jack snickering beside him, another wave of laughter would bubble up.

Finally, it subsided, and they lay side by side, breath evening out and the heat of the day settling over them once more.

"Let's go to Boston." Jack said suddenly. He rolled his head to the side and squinted at Cal.

"Now? Why?"

"It might be fun," Jack said. "And it's so hot."

"You'll be hot there, too." Cal shifted up onto an elbow. "It's north, but not north enough to matter."

"But I'll at least be hot in a different place. It'll be a distraction. Come on, I've never been."

"Really?" Cal laughed. "Never? Your whole life? It's not that far from New York."

Jack shrugged. "I'm a New Yorker. Why would I need to leave to go to Boston?"

Cal rolled his eyes. "If you really want to, I guess we can go up tomorrow."

"No, let's go now. Today. We can stay the night." Jack sat up. "Let's get out of here."

Cal regarded him. Jack looked suddenly determined, fierce. Like this was vitally important. And there was no way Cal could say no to that look.

"Okay," Cal said.

"Okay? Really?" Jack bounced once on the mattress.

"Yes," Cal said, laughing. "We can stay at my House. For a night. Two, if it'll make you happy."

"Your house?" Jack asked.

Cal reached out and smoothed the confused wrinkle between his eyebrows.

"Not actually mine. Eliot. My House where I live at Harvard."

Jack grinned. "I'll get to see where you live?"

"Sure. It's not very exciting. It's just a dormitory. And it'll be mostly empty."

"Good." Jack jumped to his feet. "Ugh. This means we have to put clothes on."

"Yes, Harvard generally prefers that its residents be clothed." Cal rolled off the bed. "Pack a bag. I'll run home, set it up, and come back with the car in an hour."

"It'll be okay?" Jack asked suddenly. "With your parents?"

"My parents will be thrilled if I tell them I want to go up and meet with my professors early this year." Cal leaned down and kissed Jack. "Don't worry. This kind of trip is sanctioned, so long as they don't know you're going along."

Cal didn't miss the cloud that passed over Jack's face, even though it was gone in an instant and replaced with a brilliant grin.

"Far out."

THEY DROVE up in Cal's car rather than worrying about train schedules. With the top down, the wind whipped by them, and the journey on the freeways was both cooler and exhilarating. It was also loud, with the cars roaring around them. Instead of talking, they sat contentedly side by side, exchanging sunglasses-covered glances and the occasional brush of a hand on a thigh or an arm.

There was a peace to it, a casual intimacy that made Cal's chest ache with simultaneous yearning and satisfaction.

The familiar streets of Cambridge also introduced a dichotomy of emotion. Their familiarity was both comforting and irritating. He liked Harvard, most of the time. For one thing, it wasn't home. Studying didn't bother him, and he was enriched by the conversations he had in classes and over drinks. He enjoyed the casual company of the friends he'd made.

What it represented was another matter entirely. He hadn't chosen Harvard; it had been chosen for him. He hadn't chosen his coursework; it was expected that he'd study what he needed to understand the business. He hadn't even chosen his house; Eliot was where he was expected to live.

You'll make as many contacts in the residence as in the class-rooms, Calloway. These men will be able to move you forward in your life, so treat them accordingly.

It was solid advice, for its intent. If Cal had been passionate about the family business and ambitious enough to feel driven by a desire to climb to the top of…whatever, it would serve him well.

In the end, what he felt about Harvard was a complicated mix of fondness and resentment, which was confusing at best. As he drove across the Anderson Bridge and onto campus, he realized that he wasn't feeling the anticipation of moving back that usually hit him at this point in the summer.

A glance to his right told him all he needed to know about why that was. Jack was sitting up in his seat, looking around with interest, taking in the atmosphere with a tiny frown.

"Is this Harvard?" he asked.

"This is Harvard," Cal said. "I'll take you by the Square later. We can go for a walk."

He pulled into a student lot and sighed as the engine rattled into silence.

"Everything okay?" Jack asked, tipping his sunglasses down, his curls tumbling across his forehead.

"It feels odd to be here, I think," Cal said. "That's all. I'm fine."

They collected their bags and Cal led the way down the tree-lined street to the courtyard of Eliot House. He'd have to sign in at some point, let the Master know he was in town for the night and had a visitor. It didn't concern him much; it wasn't wholly uncommon, so no one should think anything odd.

Jack was quiet beside him as they crossed the courtyard to his entrance, as he fitted the key in the lock. He held open the door.

"In you go," he said, gesturing for Jack to precede him.

Jack fixed his sunglasses on top of his head and grinned. "Taking me home with you so soon?" he murmured under his breath.

Cal rolled his eyes. "Well, since you were so pushy about it—"

Jack smacked his chest on the way inside.

Cal's suite, which he shared with three others, was on the fourth floor. He unlocked the main door. Silence greeted him, and he shrugged, noting the open windows.

"We might be on our own for the night," he said. "But Harrison was staying for the summer, so don't...you know."

"Bend you over the sofa in the common room? Noted," Jack snickered.

The suite was warm, but with the windows open, there was a cross breeze that was pleasant. Cal took Jack's bag and tossed their things to the side while Jack collapsed onto the sofa.

"You're right," he said. "It's just as hot here."

"And here there isn't an ocean to jump in." Cal pointed out. "Changing your mind?"

"Nah." Jack rocked his head back and forth. "I'm glad we're here."

Cal sat beside him with a groan, letting his eyes close, and they listened to the muted sounds from outside: cars rumbling past, someone shouting, a siren in the distance. It wasn't as frenetic as it would be once school was fully back in session, but the noise of the city was a nice contrast to the silence of his house back in Westerly.

After a minute, Jack's hand landed softly on his. He flipped his hand palm up and curled his fingers around Jack's with a smile.

"So this is where you live. Most of the time," Jack said. "When you aren't on the beach."

Cal opened his eyes and found Jack looking the room over curiously. He tried to see it through fresh eyes: the walls with scarred white paint and scuffed molding, the wooden window casings with wavy glass panes, the red and brown rug beneath their feet, the rambling bookcases along the walls and scattered end tables piled with an assortment of the stuff of living.

The air smelled of must with a mingling of faint sweetness. He spotted a quartet of extinguished cigars in an ashtray on the coffee table and beside it, a deck of cards, an empty whiskey decanter and a tray with cracker crumbs. Harrison had had a card night recently.

It wasn't anything special, but yes, it was home, for now.

"I'm sure it doesn't seem like much," Cal said. "After Hollywood Hills mansions."

Jack didn't respond. He let go of Cal's hand and pushed to his feet, then began to circle the room. Cal watched as he ran his hands over the furniture, the books, the scratches in the paint from where they'd accidentally shoved a table too hard sophomore year. He paused at a stack of Polaroids on one of the bookshelves, shuffling through them quickly, and then more slowly.

Finally, he looked up. "Which one is your room?" He asked.

Jack crossed the common room in long strides when Cal

pointed the way, pulling open the door and sticking his head inside. Then he disappeared into the room.

Cal gave him several minutes before he grabbed the bags and followed. He found Jack sprawled face down on his bed, arms and legs flung wide.

"How did you know which bed was mine?" Cal asked, coming to sit on the edge.

Jack's reply was muffled, since his face was buried in Cal's pillow.

"What?" Cal asked.

Jack turned his head to the side and smiled. "This one smells like you." He flipped onto his back and reached for Cal. "Kiss me," he commanded.

Cal leaned in and met Jack's lips with his own, sinking into the comfortable sensation easily and without hesitation. It was a kiss with a value of its own, not leading to or from anything. Cal sighed into Jack's mouth and felt the man smile against him.

They were already breaking apart when the suite's door opened. Cal stood, and Jack rolled off the bed onto his feet as well.

"Want to meet my suite mate?" Cal asked softly. Jack nodded.

Harrison was emerging from the bathroom, wiping his face with a towel, when they entered the common room. He grinned and slung the towel around his neck. He'd clearly just come in from a jog, since his gray Harvard t-shirt and maroon shorts were drenched with sweat.

"Calloway! I didn't know you were coming back so early," Harrison said. He strode forward with his hand outstretched and grabbed up Cal's hand enthusiastically.

"It's temporary," Cal said. "Just here for a night or two; Jack wanted to see Harvard." He stepped to the side and gestured at Jack. "Harrison, this is Jack Francis. Jack, Harrison Beauchamp."

Harrison looked Jack over and shook his hand as well. "Of the Chicago Beauchamps," Harrison said. "Francis?"

"Of the Hells Kitchen Francises," Jack said, barely hiding his smirk.

Harrison looked puzzled, and Cal snorted into his hand. He kicked Jack's foot and cleared his throat.

"Jack's an actor," he explained. "Moved into the house next to my parents' for the summer. We realized he'd never been to Boston and he wanted to see it before he heads back to Los Angeles."

"An actor," Harrison said, as recognition dawned. "Of course. I saw you in *The Great Dance-Off.*"

"*The Greater Dance-Off,*" Jack corrected him. "The sequel. Richard Logan was in the first one."

"Right. Wow. So you're summering in Westerly?" Harrison asked.

"Sure," Jack said. "I mean, I call it a vacation, but—"

Cal kicked him again, and he stopped, shrugging, just as Harrison burst out laughing.

"How is Natalie?" Cal asked, attempting to distract Harrison by asking about his girlfriend.

"She's good. Taking summer classes, so she's busy a lot. What about Katherine? Have you seen her?"

Cal nodded. "She and her parents stayed with us for a couple of weeks in July. She's doing well."

"Family gathering, hmm? Have you popped the question yet?" Harrison asked.

"No, not—" Cal cleared his throat and avoided glancing at Jack. Katherine was still a sensitive subject between them, though he wasn't entirely sure why. He knew why he got a sick feeling when thinking about their future, but he didn't understand Jack's reactions. By then, Jack would have moved on. "Not just yet."

"You'll warn me when you do, though? As soon as it happens Nat will be on me for the same thing." Harrison rolled his eyes. "You know how they are."

"Yeah, sure. Maybe towards December," Cal said, voicing what he and Katherine had discussed.

"Hey, speaking of Natalie, you two have plans tonight?" Harrison asked.

"Not yet," Cal told him. "We just got here. Why, you know about some happening?"

"Nat and her housemates are having a dinner party," Harrison said. "You should come, they'll be thrilled."

Cal frowned. "You sure you want to spring two unexpected guests on her? Last time—"

"It'll be fine. I'll call over there and let them know to expect you." Harrison clapped a hand on Cal's shoulder. "Good to see you. And good to meet you," he said with a nod to Jack. "I'm going to run a shower, but if you head out, I'll see you later. Seven at Natalie's."

Before there was time for any further protest, he ducked back into the bathroom and closed the door.

As the sound of water running echoed in the space, Jack tilted his head to the side.

"I get to meet more of your friends?" he asked.

"If you want," Cal said. "Listen, if you're not interested in having a bunch of co-eds fawning over you tonight, we can do our own thing."

Jack squinted at him. "Can I decide later?"

"Sure. Want to go for a walk?"

Jack agreed, and they descended the creaky stairs down to the courtyard.

"Are these all student dorms?" Jack asked, spinning around in a circle, arms flung wide, as he walked.

"Most of it," Cal said. "But there's a dining hall over there, and that's where the Master and Tutors live. There's a library over there, some other common rooms." He hesitated. "Want to see?"

"Yes please," Jack said eagerly. Cal smiled.

He took Jack on a brief tour of the House. Jack had lots of questions. *Is this where you eat? Where do you like to sit? What's your favorite spot? Where do you have the socials? Tell me a funny story that happened in this room.* Somewhat baffled, Cal did his best to keep up, answering what he could.

Then they walked over to Harvard Square and up to the Yard. Cal pointed out his freshman housing, the Widener Library, and the Philosophy Department. They stretched out on the ground in the shade of the great elms, taking comfort in the cool blades of grass underneath them and the relative summer quiet of the space.

"Why did you show me the Philosophy Department?" Jack asked. "Have you taken a class there?"

"One," Cal said. "Freshman year. An intro course."

"Did you like it?"

"I did. It was interesting."

Jack rolled onto his side and propped his head up on his hand. "Why didn't you take more?"

Cal shrugged, his shoulder blades dragging across a half-buried root at his back. "It wasn't the plan."

"Right," Jack said. "The plan."

He rolled onto his back once more, lacing his fingers behind his head. They lay in silence for a few minutes before Jack spoke up again.

"A while ago, at the beginning of the summer, I asked you what you would choose for yourself, if given the chance. Do you remember?"

"I remember," Cal said. They'd been at the beach club, the first time Cal had brought Jack there. They'd visited the yacht, and Jack had noticed that the lifestyle didn't quite fit Cal.

"You said you didn't know, because no one had ever asked you before. Have you thought about it? If you could choose for yourself…what would you do?"

"I'd write," Cal said softly. He wasn't sure where it had come from, since he hadn't actively thought about the question in a way that got him anywhere.

But it was true.

"Really?" Jack sat up. "What would you write?"

"Not sure," Cal said. "Anything. Maybe for a newspaper, or a magazine. Or…don't laugh, okay?"

"I'm not gonna laugh at you, Cal."

"Sometimes I think about the way the world works. The way we work. And why we work that way. I feel like I have things to say about that. I audited a creative writing course last semester." He glanced at Jack and blushed. "Audited so it wouldn't show up on my transcript. But I wrote some stories, and…it was fun."

"You want to write," Jack murmured. "Then, Cal, why are you going to work for your father?"

Cal didn't answer, because he didn't have an answer. Jack didn't seem to expect one, because he sprang to his feet and held out a hand.

"Come on. I'm thirsty, let's find a drink."

They visited a dark little dive bar that wasn't picky about fake IDs, and Cal regaled Jack with various Harvard stories over lukewarm beer. Then they picked up a bottle of wine for the dinner party from a package store on the way back to the House.

"Always bring a gift when you visit someone's house," Jack said with a snort. "It really is a rule."

Harrison was already out when they got back to the dorm.

"I need another shower," Cal said.

"Me too," said Jack. "You go first, though. I want a nap."

Cal grabbed a towel, smiled at the way Jack once again face planted on his bed, and retreated to the bathroom. The shower felt good after a day of sweating, and he took his time under the cool water. When he returned to the bedroom, his towel wrapped securely around his waist, he expected to have to wake up Jack.

Instead, what he saw made him stop short in the doorway.

Jack was sitting cross-legged in the middle of the bed, leafing through a magazine. A magazine with his face all over it. He looked up when Cal entered.

"Hey," he said. "Um…what's this?"

"It's…" Cal swallowed. Where had that come from? He'd thrown his magazines in the dumpster when he left in May. "It's a magazine."

"I see that," Jack said. "It's one of mine. Why do you have it?"

"Where did you find it?" Cal asked.

"It was wedged between the bed and the wall," Jack said. "Cal, are you…did you…"

Rubbing a hand over his face, Cal entered the room and closed the door behind him. He couldn't think of a way out of this, not one that would be convincing. And he didn't really want to lie. Not to Jack.

"I used to have more," he said softly. "I thought I'd tossed them all before going home for the summer, but I guess I missed that one."

"You had more?" Jack asked. "Of…were they all kinds, or—"

"They were all you," Cal said. He wished he were wearing clothes, because Jack's body was tensed, almost like he was getting ready to run. *Fuck.* Cal couldn't let him run. "Please, it's not…I thought you were beautiful. It seems weird, but I was really just a fan. I mean, I'm still a fan, but—"

Jack sprang up, and Cal had a split second to decide whether to jump in front of him or get out of his way. Before he could make the impossible choice, he had his arms full of a laughing Jack.

Relief coursed through him, and he grabbed on tight.

"You're not mad?" he asked, as Jack kissed his cheeks. "Or freaked out?"

"You thought I was beautiful," Jack said, giggling. "That's so fucking cute, Cal. I didn't think you even knew anything about me before we met."

"I did," Cal said. "When I realized it was you, that first night, I thought I'd gone crazy and brought forth a hallucination. What I wanted but couldn't have."

"And now you have me," Jack said. "Let me ask you a question. Did you look at my pictures and—"

"I'm begging you, please stop," Cal said, flushing pink.

"That's a yes!" Jack crowed. "Man, I'm so glad we came up here."

He planted a wet kiss on Cal's mouth, then jumped to the floor. He opened the door to the room.

"I should shower. I'll leave the magazine. Just in case you want to—"

Cal snatched off his towel and snapped it at Jack's legs with a laugh. "Maybe I will, if you take too long."

"If you can hold out, I'll make it worth your while tonight." Jack wiggled his eyebrows, and then with another hoot of laughter, ran off for the bathroom.

Cal sank onto his bed with a huff. After a minute, he picked up the magazine. It was one of his favorites, with a beach shoot. Jack with a surfboard, Jack lounging on a beach chair, Jack hanging off the back of a Jeep. Jack shielding his eyes and gazing into the sunset.

He smiled. He'd seen the real life versions of these photos all summer. He didn't need this anymore, because Jack was right. He'd been lucky enough to enjoy the real thing. He could probably toss it.

And yet...he slid it into the bottom of a dresser drawer. Summer was flying by. It was already August. Once Jack went back to Los Angeles, at least he'd have this waiting for him at school.

CHAPTER 14

*T*he girls lived in a Radcliffe House on Radcliffe Quad, about a mile from Eliot House. Cal and Jack walked, taking their time winding through the streets in the waning sun of the day.

"I think it's cooler, by a few degrees, at least," Jack said, spinning in a circle. He tripped slightly on the uneven brick, and Cal reached out a hand to steady him.

"It is." Cal shielded his eyes and looked up, noting the clouds beginning to gather in the distance. "I think we're in for that storm."

"What storm?" Jack asked.

"The one that always shows up after an August heat wave." Cal laughed as Jack spun around again, tripped again. "What are you doing?"

"I suddenly have a ton of energy. Don't you? There's something in the air, like...like..."

"A storm?" Cal asked. But he knew what Jack meant, because he could feel it too. Something had shifted today, and he didn't know exactly what, but he felt like he was on the edge of something.

"Who are these people we're going to see?" Jack asked. "One of them is that Harry fellow's girlfriend?"

Cal snorted. "Harry?"

"The fact that you all insist on using your full names is ridiculous. Should I lengthen mine for the night?" He tipped his head back so he could look down his nose at Cal. "That's *Jackson* to you."

"Now that I'd pay to see," Cal said, laughing. "Yes, Natalie is Harrison's girlfriend. She's also Katherine's good friend, so you'll have that in common."

"Would you say that Katherine and I are good friends?" Jack asked. "I'd say we're more convenient acquaintances, linked by our associations with you."

Cal eyed Jack. His voice had taken on an odd note. "Anyway, Natalie lives in a House like I do, with a lot of Radcliffe girls. So I don't know who stayed for the summer or exactly who'll be there."

"Will Katherine?"

"She's back on Montauk, so I don't think so."

Jack seemed to relax at the words, and sighed. He stepped closer and let the back of his hand brush Cal's as they walked. Cal's hand twitched, and he let his pinky briefly tangle with Jack's. Jack hummed, and the sound reverberated in Cal's own chest.

"It's nice to be here on our own," Jack said.

Natalie's House, Cabot House, looked much like Eliot. Jack followed Cal inside, where they signed in.

"Tight security?" Jack asked, as they made their way through to a private dining room.

"Not especially," Cal said. "It's for appearances more than anything else, I think. There are rules about entertaining the opposite sex, but they aren't too strict about it."

"Imagine," Jack said, "what they'd say if they knew it wasn't just the opposite sex they had to worry about."

Cal shushed him as they turned the corner. The dining room was filled with noise and laughter, and it looked like they were the last to arrive.

"Calloway!" Natalie emerged from a group of girls, her dark hair pulled back and her blue sweater like a beacon amidst the muted colors of the room. She crossed to him and gave him a brief hug, pressing her lips to his cheek.

"Hi, Nat," he said with a grin.

"When Harrison told me you were coming, I was thrilled. Thrilled! I haven't seen you since the end-of-year Eliot social. How was your summer?" she asked. Cal didn't miss the way her gaze flitted to Jack and back several times. She was trying so hard not to be obvious, and it was endearing.

"It's not over yet," Cal said. "Nat, this is Jack Francis. Jack, Natalie Greene."

Jack shook her hand, and she turned pink. "I'm a huge fan," she said.

"Nice to meet a fan," Jack said, flashing her a white-toothed grin. She turned a deeper shade of pink. "Thanks for letting us crash your shindig."

She giggled. "Imagine, little old me turning down Jack Francis. Harrison said you've been summering in Westerly?"

Jack glanced at Cal, barely hiding a smirk. "Yes, that's where I've been summering," he said. "Lucky me."

Nat called over some of her friends. Cal sidled away unnoticed, letting the women fawn over his boyfriend, and joined Harrison and some of the other men over by the wet bar setup.

"Calloway, this is some trick," said Julius Barrington. "You bring a fellow who takes all the attention off of us. Now what are we supposed to do?"

"How much shall we wager that this movie star will walk out with one of our girls before the night is over?" asked Harrison.

There was good-natured grumbling. Cal did his best not to jump at the chance to take the sure bet. He smiled into his beer and just listened.

They sat down to dinner. Cal was seated between Jenny Blake on one side and Margaret Lawrence on the other, with Jack across the table. They dug into cold cucumber soup and dinner rolls with butter, and light conversation began.

After catching up on summer activities, Natalie said, "Have you boys heard what we girls have been up to? Harrison, you shush."

"What have you been up to?" Cal asked.

"We're contributing to the civil rights movement," Jenny said proudly, squaring her shoulders. "And not like our mothers, who pretend to help by organizing fancy fundraising dinners that do more for their reputations than anything else."

"Jenny has been having quite the argument with her mother over it all summer," Margaret said.

"I'm right, though," Jenny said with a sniff.

"How are you contributing?" asked Jack.

"It's so exciting," Natalie said. "Have you heard that they are marching on Washington at the end of the month to demand change?"

"They want President Kennedy to push legislation to protect the right to vote and ban discrimination in employment," said Susan Moore, from down at the end of the table.

"Among other things," said Natalie. "We've been collecting donations to buy transportation for people to travel to Washington and march."

"And that's not all," Jenny said. "We've been organizing here on campus as well."

"Are you planning to go to Washington?" Julius asked.

"Of course not," Natalie said.

"Maybe," Jenny said.

The girls eyed each other.

"We don't think it's safe," Natalie said.

"Speak for yourself," said Jenny.

This set off a round of bickering, with the men weighing in. Cal wiped his mouth with his napkin and caught Jack's eye. He slid his foot until it bumped against Jack's and Jack smiled.

The conversation on civil rights continued through the next course, and as Cal ate his beef bourgignon, he couldn't help but wonder: would there ever be a time when people would organize to support people like him? Would the world ever accept a man who loved a man?

He hoped so…but he simply couldn't imagine it.

They stayed late, drinking scotch and playing charades. Cal and Jack were on the same team, and points began to rack up.

"It's a movie," Cal said, and Jack touched his nose.

He held up four fingers.

"Four words," said Jenny, who was also on their team. Jack nodded.

He then thought for a second, flapped his arms twice, and then made a stabbing motion.

"To Kill a Mockingbird," said Cal triumphantly. Jack clapped his hands.

"Yes! Is that a new record?" he laughed.

"Impossible," said George Webber.

"How did you do that?" asked Margaret.

Cal glanced at Jack. "I thought it was obvious," he said. "A really good clue."

"That's the fourth in a row that took you two seconds," Natalie said. "You're a dream team."

She picked up her brand new Polaroid camera, which she'd been using to take photos all night. "Dream Team, say cheese."

Jack slung his arm around Cal's neck and tilted his head. Cal felt an immediate wave of panic, but realized no one would think it odd...Natalie had just asked them to pose, after all.

He draped an arm on Jack's shoulders and grinned.

Natalie snapped the photo, the flash popping and leaving stars in their eyes. She pulled the soft plastic out of the dispenser and handed it to Cal.

"Let's see it," Jack said after a few minutes, leaning on his shoulder.

Cal carefully peeled the negative from the print and they peered at it, Cal's heart speeding up. He could feel the way Jack's curls had felt crushed against his temple, hear the breathy laugh he had let out just after the flash popped.

It was so much *them*, the way they'd been since meeting in June, captured in a single moment.

"Will you take another one, Nat?" Jack asked suddenly. "So we can each have one to mark the occasion of our sure victory?"

They all laughed, and that set off a round of posing for photos before the games resumed.

By the time they left, they were both a little drunk. Jack weaved in loops on the sidewalk in even crazier patterns than usual, and Cal simply watched him with a contented grin.

He loved seeing Jack here, in his place. Even thinking about the fact that it would soon be a memory didn't dampen his spirits, because...he'd *have* the memories. He patted his front breast pocket, where his Polaroid of them was secure. He was seized by a desire to make as many memories as possible in the time they had left.

As they passed by the entrance to Harvard Yard, Cal suddenly grabbed Jack's hand and dragged him through the gates at a run.

"What are we doing here?" Jack asked, as Cal pulled him across the quad, moving in and out of the deep shadows created by the moonless night.

"Shhh," said Cal. "Just follow me."

"To the ends of the earth," Jack said.

Cal grinned. Ignoring the thunder rumbling in the not really distance, he ran across the brick and up the steps to the Sever Hall entrance.

"Isn't this closed?" Jack asked. "Hang on, are we going to fuck in a classroom or something? Because—"

"I said *shhhhh*," Cal said. He pushed Jack into a corner of the stone archway at the entrance, then turned him around to face the wall.

"This is weird. You're being weird, Cal."

"Quiet, for fuck's sake," Cal said, laughing softly. "Stand there, don't talk, and don't move."

Jack shot him a skeptical look over his shoulder, but obediently turned to face the wall once more. "The things I do for you…"

Still chuckling, Cal crossed to the opposite side of the arch, twelve feet away. He leaned into the corner, and whispered softly.

"Hey, Jack."

"What the fuck?" Jack jumped back from his corner and whirled around. "Hang on—"

"Go back," Cal commanded.

Jack went back to his corner. A whispered voice echoed around Cal.

"Can you hear me?"

"Yes," Cal whispered back. "Welcome to the Whispering Arch."

"Far out," Jack said. "So how does it work? Magic?"

"Sound waves…something. I don't know. Say something."

"Like what?" Jack asked.

"Whatever you want."

There was a long pause, and then the whisper came again, a gentle utterance, almost like a prayer.

"I love you."

Cal swallowed hard.

"Me too," he whispered. "I love you, too."

Thunder crashed again, and they both turned around in unison. Cal looked at Jack, half in a silvery streetlight and half in shadow. His lips were slightly parted, and his eyes were shining.

Another rumble of thunder, louder, followed by a flash of lightning that lit Jack up from head to toe. Several fat droplets landed on the stone at Cal's feet.

"Let's go home," Jack said. "Now."

He grabbed Cal and they ran, just as the skies opened up. They were drenched in seconds, the rain coming down in steamy sheets. Cal splashed through puddles and gripped Jack's hand, laughing. It wasn't funny, but he didn't know where else his emotions should land.

As his clothes got soggier and soggier and clung to his skin, he was transported back to that day on the beach, when Jack had invited him out to walk in the rain. He'd been amazed when Jack had gripped the edge of his sleeve, wondering what it meant and barely daring to hope. Now, here they were, hand in hand.

Not all of the wetness on his face was from the rain.

He fumbled with the key to the dorm, and then they were stumbling up the stairs, alternating between laughing and telling each other to hush. The suite was empty; Harrison had snuck into Natalie's room before they'd left and planned to sneak out in the morning.

Once the door was closed and locked, their lips met immediately. Cal placed his palms on Jack's cheeks, slid them up into his soaked curls, and moaned.

"Wait — mmph — wait," Jack managed. He yanked his jacket off and fumbled for the light. Cal watched as he pulled the Polaroid out of the inside pocket. "It's okay," he said with relief, setting it aside and reaching for Cal once more.

Cal's breath caught, and he located his own photo. It was damp at the bottom edge but still intact. He set it beside Jack's. He flipped the light back off, and then let the man grab him.

The journey to the bedroom was a scramble to remove the wet clothing. Cal wrestled with his shirt and Jack's pants, dropping them to the floor and then kicking them along as he walked, not wanting to leave evidence in case Harrison came back before they were awake.

Jack shoved the bedroom door closed behind them and leapt at Cal. His skin was slick and slippery, and Cal held on as best he could. Jack's mouth was everywhere — his neck, his chest, his jaw — and he concentrated on breathing under the assault.

They fell onto Cal's bed, and Jack rolled to the side, pulling Cal with him.

"Don't wait," he said. "I want you inside me."

The bed was too small. Cal's knee crashed into the wall as he tried to reposition them.

"Ow. Fuck," he yelped.

Jack laughed. "Are you okay?"

"No," said Cal, but he was already moving again.

The next curse came from Jack as he attempted to scoot up the bed and jammed his elbow.

"We need more room," he said.

"I'm sorry I'm so huge," said Cal.

"I'm not." Jack giggled. "Come on, let's get the other bed."

Laughing uncontrollably now, they shoved the heavy wooden frame across the room so that the narrow beds were aligned. Jack scrambled onto the newly made space, crooked his finger with a smirk.

Cal crawled over him. "Now?" he asked.

"Now," Jack said.

The mood shifted immediately. Cal feasted on Jack's mouth and neck while he moved into place, then swallowed the man's gasp as he slid home.

Sweat mingled with rain on skin, giving Jack a mildly salty, dewy taste that had Cal groaning. As the storm continued, lightning created a series of still images that burned into Cal's mind.

Memory. Curls rioting around Jack's face as he gazed at Cal with pupils blown.

Memory. Jack's hands clenching the sheets, Cal's hands on his wrists.

Memory. Jack's head thrown back, the column of his throat exposed.

Memory. Love, in blue and silver.

In the morning, Cal woke first. Jack was tangled around him, face tucked into Cal's neck and snoring lightly. His breath and the soft vibrations of his snoring tickled Cal's skin, and he sighed, feeling happier than he remembered feeling...ever. He tightened his grip around Jack and basked in it for as long as he could.

After a while, Jack stirred. He inhaled deeply, then exhaled on a hum.

"Morning," he said, his voice blurry and rough.

"Morning," Cal replied. He kissed the top of Jack's head and stroked a palm along his back.

There was a long beat of silence, and then Jack sighed. "Thank you for bringing me here," he said.

"You're welcome," said Cal. "I'm glad you're having fun."

"I wanted to...see you here," Jack murmured. "So later, I can picture you, where you are. When you aren't with me."

Cal's heart thudded once, a second time. "You think you will? Imagine me here?"

"Every day," Jack said.

"I won't have that," said Cal. "For you. When you're back in Los Angeles, I've never been. So I can't…"

Another long pause. The sound of breathing, hearts beating. A whoosh of a car driving by outside.

"Well," said Jack, "you could visit."

Cal froze.

"Unless…I mean, that's only if you wanted to." Jack cleared his throat. "You probably—"

"Okay," said Cal.

"Okay? You'll visit?" Jack pushed himself up, looked down at Cal. "You'd want to?"

"Yeah," said Cal. "What would we…be?"

Jack blinked. "I don't know. I guess we'd have to figure that out. But friends, at least."

He settled back into place, and Cal tried to get his emotions under control. Jack wanted him to visit.

"Sure," said Cal. "At least that."

As the sun rose, he found himself, for the first time, wondering if maybe this is what he'd been feeling at the edge of. Being able to imagine something *else*, something other than the life that had been planned for him since birth.

It was probably nothing but a dream, but if he could visit…it would have to be enough.

CHAPTER 15

One morning, a week after the excursion to Harvard, Cal descended the stairs from his lawn to the beach. The August sunshine glittered off the gentle waves, the sky was a vibrant azure, and the gulls that soared overhead crooned their soothing calls.

Cal took in a deep lungful of the salty air, and grinned.

He and Jack had almost the whole day ahead of them. He'd left the man's embrace at dawn as usual to sneak back into his house, had an uneventful breakfast with his mother — his father was in New York for the week, which was a nice break — and now he had no obligations.

Maybe they'd spend hours on the beach. Maybe they'd rent bikes, take a picnic, and hit the trails at Woody Hill. Maybe they'd go to the movies. It didn't really matter. What was important was getting to spend the time together.

He climbed the stairs to Jack's lawn and bounded up to the house. The back door was unlocked, and he headed straight for the second floor. Chances were, Jack had rolled over and gone right back to sleep after their groggy good morning kiss.

But when Cal reached Jack's room and swung the door open, he wasn't greeted by the sight of his boyfriend burrowed under the sheets. Instead, suitcases were flung open on the rumpled bed, and the man was crossing the room with an armful of clothing.

"What are you doing?" Cal asked, hesitating in the doorway.

Jack whirled around, eyes wide, looking like he'd just been caught stealing. "Cal. I—"

"You're packing. Are you — are you leaving?" Cal's brain tried desperately to wrap itself around what seemed to be happening. This wasn't right. This couldn't be right.

"I'm sorry," Jack said, a pleading note in his voice. "I'm so sorry—"

"But you aren't leaving until after my birthday. We have two weeks left."

They had plans, Cal thought. Plans for their last two weeks. He didn't have to think about the end yet. It wasn't *yet*.

Jack tossed the clothes on the bed and turned back to Cal. His fingers twisted in the edge of his t-shirt and he suddenly looked…small.

"I got the call an hour ago. A film I had tried for last spring, the guy they hired dropped out and they want me. But I have to go today. I'm due on set in the morning. They're already filming."

No. Cal felt the protest bubble up in his throat, but swallowed it back down.

"So you're going to go," he said, trying to keep his voice as even as possible. *Buchanans don't show weakness.*

"I have to. It's not — this was a role I'm pretty sure I lost because of the bullshit that happened. But if they want me, that means that I'm forgiven. I have to take it, it's an opportunity I can't —"

"Right. I get it."

Jack's eyes begged Cal to understand. Cal looked away.

"Were you going to tell me, or were you just going to leave?"

Jack gaped at him. "Of course I was going to tell you. I was trying to pack, before you got back, and then I was going to…." He spread his hands wide. "I hadn't figured that part out yet, but I wasn't going to leave without saying goodbye."

In the silence that followed, Cal took several controlled breaths. He took all the pieces inside him that felt like they were shattering apart and wrapped them into a tight bundle, shoving them as deep as they would go.

He hadn't expected it to end now, but he'd always known it was going to end, after all. Jack had been clear about that… and so had Cal.

"Okay," he said.

"Okay?" Jack asked.

"Okay." Cal shrugged, schooling his features. "It's fine. Summer was going to end soon anyway. Might as well be now. You were always going to go back to Los Angeles and your life there."

Jack's eyes narrowed slightly. His eyebrow twitched.

"And you were always going to go back to Harvard, and your people," he said, "and the life that's all set up and ready for you to walk into it. I don't fit in there."

"Neither do I," Cal muttered. Jack seized on the comment.

"No, you don't. Or, you could, but you don't want to, and that's what's important. I've been trying to get you to see that all summer."

Cal flinched at the tone of Jack's voice, and immediately felt the prickle of defensiveness in his shoulder blades.

"What does it matter what I want? It's not like there's an alternative," he snapped.

"Maybe there is." Jack folded his arms across his chest. "Maybe there is, if you were brave enough to find it."

Cal hesitated, unsure what Jack was suggesting. If he was suggesting anything, and this wasn't just something he was saying to get the upper hand.

"So what is this alternative? What am I supposed to do?" Cal asked. "Just leave everything and move out to Los Angeles? For you?"

Jack's chin raised slightly, his Adam's apple bobbing as he swallowed. "That's such a bad idea?"

"Yes." Cal let out a short, humorless laugh. "It is."

"Why?"

Cal shook his head. "Ginny said it...you'll get distracted by someone else eventually. Forgive me if it's not appealing to me to ditch my entire life when you'll just get bored of me."

Jack's mouth fell open. "You think I'm going to get bored of you? Cal, that's the fucking most ridiculous thing I've ever heard."

"Is it?"

"What about you?" Jack asked. "You're going to marry Katherine. Which is a great deal for you. But am I supposed to be the person who hides on the side? I'm not...that's not for me."

They stared at each other for a long moment, and then Cal deflated, all the fight leaking out of him. He sighed, and said what he knew to be true.

"It sounds like this is for the best, then."

Jack pressed his fists against his eyes. "Fuck," he said. "This is why I don't get attached. But you..." He sighed, then dropped his hands to his sides and shook them out.

"But I...what?" Cal asked.

"Nothing," Jack said. "It's like you said. We always had an expiration date."

There were three feet between them, but it may as well have been a mile. Cal wanted to reach out, hold Jack one last time, feel his cheeks and his eyelashes and the soft planes of his neck. He wanted one last kiss, one last taste.

Instead, he took a step backwards.

"Good luck," he said. "I'm glad that — that you got the role you wanted."

"Cal—"

"I'll go see your movies." Cal smiled, realizing that he meant it. "You'll be great."

"You will be too," Jack said, his shoulders slumping. "In whatever you decide to do."

"Yeah." Cal took another step back, and Jack didn't follow. "Have a good flight."

When Jack didn't move, didn't say anything else, his features blank and shuttered, Cal swallowed hard. Then he turned and numbly walked out the door.

He made it all the way down to the first floor, out the back door, and halfway across the lawn before he heard the door bang open behind him and running footsteps, followed by a voice.

"Cal, wait."

Cal halted, but didn't turn around. If he did, he was afraid he'd crumble. And he couldn't afford to do that. *Buchanans are strong.*

Suddenly, Jack was in front of him, peering up at him through long, damp lashes.

"Here," he said. He thrust something into Cal's hand.

Cal reluctantly glanced down at it. A postcard, one of those hand-painted watercolors they sold in the souvenir shop on Main Street, the kind with "Westerly, Rhode Island" in a banner across the top. He turned it over, and saw an address and a telephone number scrawled in Jack's wild handwriting.

"In case you change your mind," Jack said. "That's where I am. In L.A."

Warily, Cal looked up, met Jack's gaze. The guy was watching him, green eyes luminous.

"You're always welcome," Jack said. "If you ever need to get away. Or something. You don't have to call first, you can just…anyway."

He chewed on his bottom lip, and Cal lost his grip on his control. He surged forward and took Jack's lips in a fierce, desperate kiss. Jack's muffled grunt of surprise quickly gave way to a deep moan. Cal felt Jack's fingers on his neck and in his hair, and tried to memorize every sensation.

He was dimly aware that anyone from his yard, or looking out his back windows, would be able to see them, but realized he didn't care.

He almost hoped someone would see. See this, see them, see *him*.

Though he wished the kiss would never end, it eventually did. They separated, lips pulling apart but hands still clutching.

Jack pressed his forehead against Cal's. "Thank you for the summer," he said, with a rasp in his voice that set off an ache deep in Cal's chest. "I had a marvelous time."

He let out a long breath, then carefully pressed a kiss to each of Cal's cheeks in turn. He took a giant step backwards and shook his head slightly, curls bouncing in zigzags around his face, then darted around Cal and into the house.

Cal turned to watch him go, and then stood staring at the closed door for a full minute before he turned and strode across the lawn and down the wooden stairs.

His feet hit the beach and he made it seven steps before his legs gave out. He stumbled onto his knees, then fell forward onto his palms. His fingers dug into the sand, grains scratching at his skin, as he pulled in a series of harsh, burning breaths, his heart pounding in his ears.

It was long minutes before he was able to stand.

Once on his feet again, he looked around, at the beach he'd always taken comfort in. Gentle waves lapped at the shore, the sun still sparkled on the water, gulls sailed overhead with soothing caws.

He couldn't stand to look at it. Not now, not when it held so many memories of Jack, and what he couldn't have.

Resolutely, he turned and marched up the stairs to his own backyard, across the grass and into the house, where he began to pack.

CAMBRIDGE in late summer was still quiet. It would be buzzing with life in a few weeks when the majority of university students descended on the city, but until then, Cal sought the peace he could no longer find on the beach in Westerly.

He took long runs along the Charles River and the Freedom Trail up into the North End of Boston. He sat in his library carrel, taking in the smell of musty books and the sounds of silence, staring at a crack in the cinder block wall. He went to the movies, where he could hide in the dark, surrounded by a haze of cigarette smoke and the flickering projector.

He carefully avoided the Whispering Arch, and slept in the other bed, and as the days passed, he pulled a numbness around him like a cloak and pushed thoughts of Jack as far back in his mind as he could. It worked, sort of.

When he could manage, he began to prepare for fall classes. He studied the course catalog, he visited the bookstore to peruse the textbooks, he made appointments to meet his professors, he set up his study spaces.

On the afternoon he was scheduled to meet with the Chair of the Economics Department, he put on a suit and a tie, polished his shoes, and looked at himself in the mirror. It was like putting on a costume — or rather, not a costume, a skin.

It was a familiar skin, one he'd easily slipped in and out of his entire life but that had never felt completely comfortable. Donning it now felt final in a way it never had before. As if the summer in shorts and sandals, with ever-present sand in his hair and the lingering scent of coconut suntan lotion was officially packed away, maybe for good this time.

Maybe it was because it was his senior year. Maybe it was because he was finally accepting what he'd known was looming all along: his future.

He knocked on Professor Jürgen's door at half past two. The sun coming in the window at the end of the hall illuminated panes of dust motes that circled lazily through the air. The floor under his feet creaked as he shifted his weight, and he took a moment to brush off his suit and clear his throat before he heard the call to come in.

"Mr. Buchanan," Professor Jürgen said, rising from his chair behind the heavy wooden desk that dominated the office. He stretched out a hand, and Cal took it in a firm handshake.

"Professor," Cal said. "Thank you for seeing me. How was your summer?"

"I was doing research with a small team," said Jürgen. "Public investment and taxation. Interesting findings, in light of the current social movements." He waved a hand. "You can likely read about it soon enough. Have a seat."

He gestured at the two visitor chairs, and Cal unbuttoned

his suit jacket and settled into one, crossing his left leg over his right.

"I assume you're here to discuss a course of study for your final terms?" Jürgen asked. "And perhaps post-graduation plans?"

"Yes," Cal confirmed. "Primarily the former. After graduation I'll be joining my father's firm."

"Hm, of course, that's the most logical path," Jürgen said. He picked up a pencil and twirled it between his fingers, peering at Cal from beneath bushy salt-and-pepper eyebrows. "Have you considered alternatives?"

Cal blinked, momentarily off balance. *It's not like there's an alternative,* he'd said to Jack. He cleared his throat.

"Alternatives?" he asked.

"Yes. I'd be interested in having you on my graduate team, if that would suit," Jürgen said. "You've got the background, and the mind, as well as a fresh perspective about some things and no hesitation in challenging old ideas. You'd be an excellent addition."

"Oh." Cal straightened up, surprised at the compliment. Is that how he acted? Challenging old ideas? "I appreciate the offer. I'm not sure my father would, I know he's anxious to have me working with him."

"Consider it, at least," Jürgen said. "The School of Business Administration is another alternative. That could open up other options for you, as well."

"I'll certainly think about both options," Cal said. "Thank you for having confidence in me."

"It's well deserved. Now, let's talk about your courses for the year."

When Cal walked out into the sunshine thirty minutes later, he was armed with a piece of paper with his course plan neatly sketched out. He stopped under one of the elms and eyed the paper. The schedule he planned to register for in a few weeks was his future, in stark lines of ink:

Economics 125 - Inflation, Growth and Stability - Professor Forster

Economics 144 - Government Policy Toward Business - Professor Van Louen

Economics 166 - International Trade and Economic Policy - Professor Brink

Statistics 139 - Regression and Analysis of Variance - Professor Morris

It was the culmination of his studies. Economics, Business, Math. The things the heir to the Buchanan fortune should study, so he could continue the family legacy. The education — as well as the prestigious degree — would serve him well as he moved up into his father's world.

He should be proud of himself. He was on the Dean's List, top of his class. The Chair of the Economics Department, a celebrated national scholar and expert, wanted him to pursue graduate studies, thought he was a shoe-in for the School of Business Administration. He had spent his time at Harvard forging important relationships with men who came from powerful families and who would be powerful of their own right before long. He was practically engaged to a woman who would be an asset to his career and his future. He should absolutely be proud.

Instead, he felt empty.

He walked back to Eliot house and up to his room without paying conscious attention to where he was going. Once his suit was hanging in his closet, he sat down at his desk and examined the paper with his impending schedule again.

It's not like there's an alternative.

Professor Jürgen had offered alternatives to the path laid

out for him. Had thought Cal had a choice about his future. Was there a possibility he was right?

He picked up the course catalog and flipped past Economics to English. He began to read. He flipped back to the beginning of the catalog, and then to the very end. After a while, he turned over his paper schedule and wrote a new one on the back.

Humanities 7 - Uses of the Comic Spirit - Professor Hocksley

English P - Dramatic Interpretation and Background of Theater - Professor Packer

English Ka - English Composition (Prose fiction) - Professor Lewis

Visual Studies 145 - Light and Communication (Cinema) - Mr. Harris

He let out a breath. His heart was beating fast, and he wiped a palm across his clammy forehead.

Of course this was just fantasy. He couldn't register for these classes...could he?

He'd already completed all the requirements for a major in Economics and a minor in Statistics the previous year. Technically, he didn't need any of the courses Professor Jürgen had told him to take.

If he planned to apply to the graduate school or the business program, it would matter. But if he was just going to go to work for his father, it really didn't. At all. So...maybe he could.

Jack had said maybe there was an alternative, if he was *brave enough to find it.*

He shoved the paper inside the course catalog, shoved the course catalog into the back of his desk drawer, and shoved Jack out of his mind. It worked, sort of.

∽

KATHERINE ARRIVED in town the day before his birthday. He had told her not to come early, that he wasn't in the mood to celebrate, but she had insisted.

"Don't be daft, Calloway," she'd said over the telephone when she'd called with the news. "I'm bored and anxious to get back...and you must be bored as well, with Jack gone back to—"

"I'm busy," Cal said. "Not bored."

"Busy with what?" Katherine asked. "Natalie told me that Harrison told her you never want to go out with them or have any fun. Please tell me you aren't wallowing. That's so dramatic."

"Come if you want to come," he'd said, before hanging up on her.

She insisted on taking him out for a "pre-birthday dinner," even though he told her again he wasn't in the mood to celebrate. In the end, it was easier just to go along than to put up a fight.

They went to the Ritz, which Cal found stuffy and uncomfortable. Since this clearly wasn't about him, however, he kept his mouth shut.

He followed Katherine — who was following the maître d — through the dining room to their table, and pulled out her chair. She smiled up at him, elegant as always in a narrow yellow dress with a white stole and white shoes, and he smiled back.

Maybe this had been a good idea after all, he thought, taking his seat. It was practice for the future.

They chatted lightly about their friends and their parents. Katherine asked him what he'd been up to, and how he'd been spending the end of the summer. He gave vague answers and turned the questions back on her, preferring to keep her talking about herself.

He remembered that being with her was easy, and comfortable, and began to relax.

When she asked about his course schedule, however, he tensed up again. He recited the classes Professor Jürgen had laid out for him, each one feeling like acid on his tongue.

"What's wrong?" Katherine asked. She reached across the table and touched his sleeve. "Are you sick? You look like you're going to be sick."

He laughed softly. "I'm not sick," he said.

"Are you sure?" she asked, squinting at him.

"I'm just…I might decide to go another route," he said.

Once it was out there, his stomach untwisted and he knew it was true. He might make that choice. He could make that choice, if he wanted to.

"What do you mean?" she asked.

"There are some other classes I'm considering," he said. He named them, and they rolled off his tongue easily. He was smiling by the time he was done.

She burst out laughing, and he stared at her until she dabbed at the corners of her eyes with her napkin. "Calloway," she said, catching her breath. "You're a comedian."

"I'm serious," he said. "I think I might — I think I'm going to take those classes instead."

"Don't be ridiculous," she said.

"Why is it ridiculous? I've completed all the content requirements for my degree. I just need credits. I thought I might take some things that interested me." He shrugged. "Doesn't seem so far-fetched."

"What will people think?" she asked.

She looked almost scandalized. Because he was planning on taking some English classes. He suddenly felt a laugh bubbling up himself, and forced it back down.

"Who cares?" Cal said. "I'm going to work for my father. I already have the job. No one is going to care what I took my senior terms at Harvard, they'll just care that I have the piece of paper to frame and hang on the wall."

"Your father might care," Katherine said, taking a sip of her water. "What if he refuses to support you because of it?"

"He won't know, but that won't matter either," Cal said, realizing it was true. "I'm going down to Providence tomorrow to take control of my trust. I'll be able to support myself."

She shook her head. "Well, I think it's a ridiculous plan. But if you need to get it out of your system, I suppose...we can say that you're looking to make contacts outside of your circles of Economics and Statistics. Broaden your reach. People will be impressed with your cleverness."

Cal bristled. It was a good plan, but it wasn't true. He didn't care about making contacts. He cared about learning some things that actually interested him while he was at this school. Wisely, he once again kept his mouth shut, and she seemed satisfied.

They talked a bit about the March on Washington, but disagreed about whether it would make a difference.

"What needs to happen," she said, "is that people need to use the political system to make change."

"That is what's happening, isn't it?" Cal asked. "Protests and demonstrations to show what the people want?"

"It just seems so uncivilized," she said, wiggling her fingers distastefully.

"Uncivilized? Protesting?" Cal stared at her. "Are you... you're joking around, right?"

"Look, I'm not saying that they shouldn't have equal rights, I'm not a philistine," Katherine said, rolling her eyes. "I'm just saying, instead of doing something so disruptive, write about it. Run for office. Use the court system."

"I think that has all gone on and continues to go on," Cal said. "But it's difficult to use the system to make change when the system is built by people who benefit from the status quo. It's too easy for them to rig the deck."

He realized he'd raised his voice, and cleared his throat softly. He reached up and tugged at his collar, shifting uncomfortably in his seat. Katherine blinked at him, then glanced around and squared her shoulders.

"Well. You don't have to get upset with me about it," she sniffed. "It doesn't really involve us, anyhow. I just hope it gets resolved before June."

"June?" Cal frowned. "Why June?"

"Well, I have a surprise for you," Katherine said, leaning forward, her eyes sparkling. "Daddy was able to get us the Plaza for the wedding reception. He had to call in some favors — of course it was booked — but it's ours."

"For the...wedding," Cal muttered. He tugged at his collar again, this time because it suddenly felt too tight.

"Yes. Are you pleased?" She looked so hopeful, he simply nodded. "Oh, good."

"So you told your father we're engaged?" Cal asked.

"Not exactly. I just hinted that it was likely to happen soon. He's thrilled, by the way."

"I'd imagine," Cal said. "My parents will be too."

She started chattering about the wedding then: colors, flowers, cake designers. Apparently he was meant to be in white tie. She also began to rattle off a guest list, and he winced at all the powerful names of people he didn't know personally.

It felt so real. He'd known it was going to happen, had decided he would go through with it, but sitting here now, with Katherine, talking about having a fucking string quartet for the ceremony? It was too much.

"Wait a second. Stop," he said, after a while.

"What?" she asked.

"Before, you said that you hoped the protests were resolved before June. What does that have to do with our wedding?" he asked.

"Oh." She waved her hand. "Just because these things are such an inconvenience. Imagine if we'd had a wedding planned in Washington this week. I'd be beside myself."

He stared at her. "I think," he said carefully, "that people fighting for rights and equality, and to not be treated as a subclass of citizens, is a little more important than a party."

"A wedding is not a party," she said. "It's a sacred ceremony."

"A wedding is a party," he countered. "We can have the sacred ceremony at the courthouse any day at all. The wedding is just a party."

"Even so," she said. "It's an important one."

"Not more important than what people are fighting for." Cal sat back in his chair and folded his arms across his chest. "You said that this 'doesn't really involve us.' But what if it did?"

"What do you mean?" she asked.

"What if it involved you? What if it involved women's rights? Women are starting to fight for more equality, or so I've heard."

"And they're doing it the right way," Katherine said, frowning. "They are organizing politically, and lobbying."

"Fine. What if …" He steeled himself before saying the thing that was running through his head. "What if it involved me?"

"Why would it involve you?" she asked, her brow wrinkling in confusion.

"What if people like me decided to fight for rights. To be able to love whoever we wanted to love."

Her eyes widened, and she looked around to be sure no one had heard. "Lower your voice," she said, urgently.

"Relax. No one knows what I'm talking about," Cal said. "So? What if? Would it be an inconvenience then?"

"You mean people would be…open about it?" she asked

incredulously.

"Is it such a strange idea?" he asked, knowing that, in essence, it was a strange idea. He tried to imagine marching in the street, letting everyone know, demanding the right to just be who he was, without judgment or danger of being arrested. To maybe marry the person he was in love with, instead of...

He looked across the table at Katherine. She was looking at him oddly. After a moment, she spoke.

"Even if that happened," she said quietly, "it's not like you could join them."

"Why not?" Cal asked.

"Because, in the eyes of the public, you'll be the heir to the Buchanan legacy, the leader of an important company, who is very much married to your dutiful and loving society wife." Her eyes grew sharp and alert. "It wouldn't make any sense for you to petition for rights that apparently don't affect you. And you know your family wouldn't approve."

She was right. She was absolutely right, on every point. If he married Katherine, if he went to work for his father, if he took that path...that was it. There was no way he could ever do what people were doing with the March on Washington. No way he could ever be anything — in the open, anyhow — other than what he was told.

Bands of tightness wrapped themselves around his chest, squeezing and squeezing until he couldn't breathe. He could see it. A lifetime of working beside his father, never being good enough, being bored to tears with work that didn't excite him. Decades of living with Katherine, accompanying her to events he didn't care about, associating with people he found shallow and false. An eternity in a cage he couldn't break out of, because he'd put himself in it.

And why? Because he wasn't brave enough to consider an alternative? Because he thought he didn't have a choice?

Something snapped inside his chest, and he was able to breathe again.

"Unless," he said, "I wasn't."

"What?" She frowned.

"Unless I wasn't the heir to the legacy. Unless I wasn't the leader of the company. Unless I wasn't married to you." He gripped the edge of the table for stability, as he made his decision and said it out loud. "I'm sorry, Katherine. I can't do this."

"Calloway," she said, caution in her tone. "What are you saying?"

"I can't marry you. It would be a lie. It's not what I want." He blew out a breath, feeling lightheaded.

There was a beat, and then she laughed nervously. "Stop it. This isn't funny."

"No, it isn't," he said. "It isn't funny at all."

"You can't be serious," she said. "It was all worked out. It benefits us both. I promise you, I'll help you have what you want."

"You can't possibly help me have what I want," Cal said. "If I marry you, I'll be walking right into an entire life I don't want."

"I won't just look the other way, I'll...I'll actively cover for you," she said. "You can have what you want."

"Katherine. I don't just want...it's not just about that. It's about everything. The job, my family, the position in society...I want none of it. I want other things."

"You want him," she said. "You think you can just go and—"

"No," Cal leaned forward. "Listen to me. It's not about him. He helped open my eyes to possibilities I'd never let myself consider. But this is about me. Who I am. I don't want to work for my father. I don't even want to be in business. I don't want to summer in a stuffy community with people I can't stand. I don't want to worry about society and rankings and what people think."

"What do you want, then?" Katherine asked. "Maybe I can help you get it."

He shook his head in disbelief. "You can't. And I don't exactly know, because I've always been too afraid to entertain the notion that I might have a choice. But I do have a choice — lots of them — and my first choice is that I'm not going to marry you."

He got to his feet, tossing his napkin on top of his half-eaten dinner. He pulled some bills out of his wallet and dropped them on the table.

"I have to go. That should cover the meal, and there's extra there for you to hire a car to take you back."

"Calloway," she said, reaching out to clutch at his wrist. "Cal. Listen to me. You don't have to decide this right now. You're in a vulnerable place. Take some time, think it over—"

"I have," Cal said. "I really am sorry, for getting your hopes up. But I can't do it."

Her fingernails dug into his skin. "You're ruining everything," she hissed.

He pulled away. "Maybe. Or maybe I'm fixing it. Goodnight, Katherine."

The air outside was cool, and he stopped and took several lungfuls and grinned. Then he turned and walked up the street towards the subway, his steps lighter than they'd ever been.

CHAPTER 16

*T*he morning after his dinner with Katherine, on his twenty-first birthday, Cal drove down to Providence to meet with his father and the trustee.

Normally, he'd be dreading a meeting like this. To be stuck in a room with people who would no doubt be judging him, to know that his father was expecting him to perform in a particular fashion and to also know he'd never be able to measure up to those expectations, these were some of the things he hated most about his life.

That day, however, the dread was mysteriously absent. Instead of feeling sick to his stomach, he felt...nothing. Just a calm acceptance, a detached knowledge that he was about to cause more disappointment, and a realization none of it actually mattered, not in a way that was important.

He met his father in the lobby of the trustee's office in one of the looming downtown skyscrapers. As he crossed the plush carpeted space, surrounded by floor-to-ceiling windows that looked out over the city, his steps were sure and confident.

Normally, he'd hesitate, his steps faltering as he saw the immediate disapproval on his father's face. But today...he didn't. It felt good. It felt right.

Theodore frowned as he rose from his chair, of course.

"What are you wearing?" he hissed, when Cal got close enough to shake his father's hand.

Cal glanced down at his khaki trousers, blue striped Lacoste polo, and brown leather loafers.

"Clothes," he said.

"That's hardly proper attire for this meeting," Theodore said. "Look around you. You know better than that."

Normally, he'd quietly assent, apologize, and feel shame wash over him. The near-automatic *yes, sir* was on the tip of his tongue, but instead, he shrugged, and said something else.

"I doubt anyone will really care. This meeting is about me, after all, so shouldn't I be setting the tone? Shouldn't everyone be worried about what I think, and not the other way around?"

Theodore blinked at him, and made a huffing sound, but said nothing further.

Cal smiled. He wasn't sure where that had come from, but an image of a grinning Jack flashed in his mind. He flinched and pushed it aside.

Within a few minutes, a young woman beckoned for them to follow her down the hall to a conference room, ending the threat of any additional conversation. He followed his father silently, sat in the proffered wing-back chair silently, folded his hands on the polished wooden table silently, and waited.

Howard Morgan, the lead trustee, arrived with a brown accordion folder and a large grin beneath his bushy mustache. Cal and Theodore stood to greet him.

"Theodore, Calloway, good to see you." He shook their

hands, and gestured for them to be seated once more. He pulled out a stack of papers and began to shuffle them into piles on the table. He pushed one pile towards Cal, another towards Theodore, and kept one for himself.

Cal flipped through the papers quickly. He'd seen this before; it was the terms of the trust. He realized he had some questions, ones that had never occurred to him in the past.

"Howard, could I trouble you for some paper and a pen?" he asked.

The older man nodded, unearthed a yellow legal pad and a blue Bic ballpoint from a sideboard, and handed them to Cal before taking his own seat.

"Will that do?" he asked.

"Perfect. *Writes the first time, every time,*" Cal said, parroting the pen's popular slogan. Theodore gave him a severe look, but Morgan laughed.

"Now," Morgan said, "it's an exciting day. I don't expect there to be anything terribly complicated to go over. The significant shift taking place is that, as he has reached the age of twenty-one — happy birthday, by the way — Calloway now has the right to withdraw certain funds from the trust at will, and he will begin to receive a monthly set allowance from the rest of the assets. He also takes over the oversight of the trustees, in that he may re-appoint trustees and has a say in the management of the assets, replacing Theodore in that capacity."

Cal listened as Morgan explained the allowance, the funds he had immediate access to, and those he'd gain access to in nine years. He took notes about the current valuation of the assets and the investment strategy. He asked questions about the stock and bond portfolio, and the lack of diversification that he saw.

Theodore jumped in at that point. "Calloway, Howard has

been managing these assets for nearly two decades. He's doing a fine job."

The *yes, sir*, was on the tip of his tongue again, but he swallowed it back.

"Of course he is," Cal said calmly. "I'm just trying to acquaint myself with the strategy. I might be comfortable with a more aggressive approach than we have now, as long as we aren't putting all our eggs in the same basket."

"You have a good eye," Morgan said. "And if you have the stomach for a more aggressive approach, I'll certainly have my team re-examine the spread. If you have any ideas, you're more than welcome to send them my way."

"I might want to be more hands on," Cal said. "Could we arrange a quarterly meeting?"

"Absolutely," Morgan replied. "I'm glad to see you taking an interest."

When the meeting was over and the paperwork was signed, they bid farewell to Morgan and exited the offices. The elevator took them down to the building lobby in silence.

Theodore waited until they were out on the street before he turned to Cal.

"What was that?" he asked, poking Cal in the chest.

"What was what?" Cal asked, rubbing at the spot.

"Your attitude in there. I didn't appreciate it."

Cal laughed. "You didn't appreciate that I was interested in the details, and had opinions on the management of my own assets?"

"Don't be smart," Theodore said. "You were acting like you knew more than Howard Morgan. It was disrespectful."

Cal watched him for a moment. "I don't agree," he said. "I was simply doing what I've spent my life training to do. Pay attention to the financials. Thanks to that training, I know what I'm talking about, and since it's my money, I've a right to ask questions. Howard didn't seem offended."

"Well, you will not repeat it this afternoon," Theodore said.

Cal frowned. "What's this afternoon?"

"We're having lunch with the firm who will be managing the assets you'll be drawing out," Theodore said. "I mean it, don't embarrass me."

Cal stared at his father, and something snapped inside him. Much like the night before, he suddenly saw clearly the choices before him, and he knew which path he was going to take. He might as well say so, rather than beat around the bush.

"That's easy enough," Cal said. "I won't be going."

"You what?" Theodore's mouth dropped open. "Calloway—"

"You didn't ask me if I was available, and I'm not. I'm headed straight back to school. I have things to do," Cal said. "Also, I plan to choose my own investment managers, and until then, or until I need them, I'll leave the funds where they are. Howard Morgan is doing a fine job. As you said."

Cal could barely believe the words that were coming out of his mouth, but hearing them, in a confident voice, felt good. From the look on Theodore's face, he couldn't believe them either.

"Nonsense," he sputtered. "We have reservations, and they're expecting us."

"You're free to meet them," Cal said. "Go ahead and break the news that you've spoken out of turn, and I'll be going my own way on this."

"Calloway," Theodore said, "I know what's going on here."

"You do?" Cal chuckled. "Please, enlighten me."

"You've let that boy—" he spit out the word as if it were

bitter, "—influence you. I should have put a stop to it when he showed his colors on Independence Day."

"Who?" Cal asked. He swallowed, and forced himself to speak the name aloud. "Jack?"

"He's got a smart mouth, too. Speaking up when he should keep his silence. I should have listened to your mother."

Cal's thoughts whirled. His first instinct was denial, to protect Jack, to protect himself, to sever a link between them so no one would suspect what had really gone on.

But Theodore was right. Cal had been influenced by Jack. It was because of Jack, and their time together, that he'd finally begun to let himself want something specific, something else, and stopped being resigned to his fate.

It was because of Jack that he'd broken things off with Katherine, decided he no longer wanted to trap himself into the appearance of a life he knew he'd hate.

Theodore shook his head. "Get it out of your system now," he said. "When you come to work for me, I'll expect you to fall in line. You'll be representing me and the entire family."

It was because of Jack that Cal was even considering doing what he was about to do. He cleared his throat, took a deep breath, and tried to ignore his somersaulting stomach.

What do you really want to do? Jack had asked.

I don't know. Not that, he'd replied, referring to the entire life his parents had planned out for him.

It was time to admit that to more than just Jack, and himself.

"I won't be coming to work for you," he said.

There was a long beat of silence, before Theodore threw his head back and laughed.

"Be serious, Calloway," he said.

"I am serious," Cal said. "I don't want to work for you. I'm sorry, I should have said something sooner. But the company, and what you do...it's not what I want to spend my life doing."

Theodore wasn't laughing anymore. He reached out and gripped Cal's shoulder hard. "That's nonsense."

"It's not nonsense," Cal said, shaking his father off. "It's my decision to make, and I'm making it."

"Listen to me," Theodore said, dropping his voice. "If you decide to walk away—"

"I don't need your money," Cal said. "Weren't you paying attention up there? I have the trust."

"It's not just the money," Theodore said. "If you make this choice...we won't protect you."

Cal was brought up short by Theodore's tone. There was a warning in it that sent chills down Cal's spine.

"Protect me?" he asked.

"You think I don't know?" Theodore asked, his lips curling into a bitter smile. "About you?"

"I don't know what you're talking about," Cal said, taking a step back. Every cell in his body was screaming at him to run.

"Of course you do," Theodore said. "And we can protect you. Make sure that no one else talks, make sure that your reputation is secure. But if you walk away? That ends."

For a moment, the fear took over. He couldn't walk away. He needed the protection. If people found out about him, it would ruin everything. He thought wildly about how to fix it all, get Katherine back, make his father happy, forget all these ideas—

A truck roared by on the street, and the exhaust fumes billowed around them. He coughed, blinked against the irritant, and then, as the smoke cleared, so did his fear.

What was he doing?

The entire reason he needed his reputation protected,

needed to make sure no one knew about him, was because it would ruin him…but only if he was working for his father, maintaining the family name. If he left, if he chose his own life? It mattered less, because there was nothing to ruin.

He smiled. "I appreciate the offer," he said calmly. "But it doesn't change my mind. I'm not interested in the company. If you still want to be involved in my life, I'd like that. But if not? I still need to follow my own path."

Theodore looked like he was about to argue, but then he sighed. "I can see you're not going to change your mind today," he said. "I propose you take some time to think about this, and we can revisit the subject on a later date."

"I've done plenty of thinking," Cal said, "but you're welcome to try to persuade me in ways that don't involve threats. Tell mother I said hello."

Then he turned, and, without a look back, walked away from his father and the comfort of knowing exactly what was next.

THE SEMESTER BEGAN, and Cal registered for his alternative list of courses. His suitemate thought he'd gone crazy.

"Why are you ruining your future?" Harrison asked, when he saw Cal's registration card. "I don't understand."

"I'm not ruining anything," Cal said. "People keep saying that, but that's not the case at all. I'm still graduating with a degree in economics. I still have all the knowledge and training I've gained. I'm just diversifying."

Harrison laughed at his use of the term. "Whatever you say. If anyone asks, I'll tell them you're doing it to meet freshman coeds, now that you and Katherine are quits."

Normally, Cal would have second thoughts, worry

about what everyone would think, overcompensate in about twelve ways. Instead, he let Harrison's comment slide.

His other friends were equally curious, but he shrugged off their questions. Being around Katherine was awkward, so he avoided it as much as possible, though to her credit, she was civil and didn't show any signs of being vindictive with the information she had.

Instead of Katherine and her closest friends, Cal found himself gravitating toward Jenny and her new crowd, drawn in by their commitment to the civil rights cause. He found their passion inspiring, and it was she who suggested he write for the *Crimson*.

"You want to write, Calloway, then you have to write," she said firmly one night over beer at the Underground. "Don't wait. Do it now, while you can."

She got him a meeting with the president of the editorial board, who'd gone with her to the March on Washington in August. Cal prepared some sample pieces — a news item about an upcoming NAACP-sponsored March on Roxbury in support of desegregation, and an opinion piece about de facto segregation in Boston's public schools — and hoped for the best.

A week later, Cal entered the Harvard *Crimson* building on Plympton Street, palms sweating and heart racing. He patted the leather briefcase that hung from his shoulder, hoping its contents would be impressive enough.

He walked out an hour later with a set of new assignments and a place on the staff.

When his first article was published, under the byline *Cal Buchanan*, he cut it out, removed Jack's postcard from the bottom of his desk drawer, carefully copied out the address onto a manila envelope, placed the article in the envelope, and walked it to the post office. He walked out seeing stars at the edge of his vision, and once again pushed Jack to the corners of his mind.

He never heard back. He didn't expect to, but he was disappointed nonetheless.

Over the course of the school year, he began to find his place and his voice. He worked with the Harvard-Radcliffe Civil Rights Alliance, he wrote for the *Crimson,* he studied the arts, and he completely shed the skin he'd been wearing his entire life.

Throughout everything, despite his attempts otherwise, Jack was never far from his mind. He saw two new movies and read every article written about him, even though it made his chest ache. He heard the man's voice in his ear as he made each decision, imagined how proud Jack would be of the changes he'd made.

He continued to mail his articles to California, even though there was no indication the recipient was receiving them or desiring them. It was enough to send them, and fantasize about Jack reading each one with a smile on his face.

As graduation approached, Theodore asked to meet him for lunch. He agreed, and mentally prepared for another attempt to persuade him to come to work at the company in June. He'd weathered all the previous attempts, holding firm, but he knew his father wasn't likely to give up.

They met at the Harvard Club in Back Bay. Cal wore a suit, in deference to the Club's dress code, and he smirked, remembering Theodore's issue with his clothing choice on his birthday. When he arrived, the maitre'd showed him to a table with his father and a man he'd never met. Both men stood as he approached.

"Calloway," Theodore said, in greeting. "This is Wallace Denton, a friend of mine from Harvard."

Cal shook the man's hand, offered pleasantries, and they

sat down. He was puzzled by the man's presence until after they'd placed their orders.

Theodore turned to him. "Wallace is an editor at the *Sun-Times* in Chicago," he said, raising an eyebrow significantly.

Cal immediately got the message, and tried to mask his surprise. "Really," he said. "I've been writing for the *Crimson* this year."

It was clear from Denton's reaction that Theodore hadn't yet mentioned that to him, which also surprised Cal.

"What do you write?" Denton asked.

"Mostly political news," Cal replied. "Some op-eds, and I've recently been writing a financial column."

"Are you enjoying it?" Denton asked.

"Very much," Cal said. He hesitated, and then plowed forward. "I've actually been considering journalism for after graduation," he said.

Denton hummed. "Are you any good?"

"I suppose that's not for me to say," Cal said. "I could send you some of my pieces."

"Let the work speak for itself," Denton said with a nod of approval. "Send them along. If they're up to par, I might have a spot for you. Would you consider relocating to Chicago?"

"I would," Cal said, although this was the first time he was even letting himself think about where he'd end up. "If the right position was available."

Theodore sat back in his chair, a smug smile on his face.

After lunch, they bid farewell to Denton, and Cal shook his head.

"I didn't expect this," he said to his father. "Thank you."

"I didn't do anything," Theodore said. "All I did was invite you for lunch."

"Still, it means a lot," Cal said.

Theodore shrugged. "If you're going to continue to be bullheaded about choosing something other than my company, I might as well do what I can to help. You're still my son."

Cal was still in shock as he gathered up samples of his work to send to Denton.

Chicago. It wasn't the thing he secretly dreamed about, but since he knew what he dreamed about was just a dream…it was something.

Graduation was anticlimactic. He stood with his classmates, moved his tassel, drank toasts to their future successes. He expected to feel something more than he did, some gravity, but instead it was just another step, another moment, one among many that would fade into dim memory just like everything else.

Everything but last summer, that is. He remembered every second of his summer with Jack. Every smile, every laugh, every scent, every sensation. It all stood out in vivid technicolor, and all else paled in comparison. He wondered if it would be like that forever.

He packed up his car, bid his friends farewell, and headed out into the next chapter of his life.

But when he reached Chicago…he just kept going. His foot wouldn't leave the gas, his hands wouldn't turn the steering wheel towards the exit ramp. He just drove, and drove, and drove, barely stopping to sleep a few hours a night on the side of the road and grab a meal a day, until he got all the way to California.

Once he hit the outskirts of Los Angeles, he stopped at a motel. He took a shower, tried a nap, and then gave up. Being this close to Jack, after all this time, there was no way he was going to be able to sleep. So he got back in the car, stopped at a gas station, bought a map, and thirty minutes later he was pulling up to a sprawling single-level ranch house in the Hollywood Hills, Jack's postcard clutched tightly in his hand.

He sat in the car for ten minutes after the engine stopped

humming, talking himself through what he was about to do. Would Jack be happy to see him? Would he already have someone new? Was Cal walking right into disaster, or something else?

Finally, he screwed up the courage to get out of the car and make his way up the walk to the front door. He rang the bell, and stepped back to wait.

The door swung open, and J.C. stood on the other side. When she saw him, her face lit up.

"Cals!" she cried. "I knew it. I knew it," she said again, louder, over her shoulder.

She reached out and punched him in the chest.

"Ow," he said, rubbing at the spot with his palm. "J.C.—".

"Hey, Ginny," she called out, "I win. You owe me."

"You...you win?" Cal asked. His head was spinning.

"I had a bet with Ginny when you'd show up here. You just got me a cool hundred because it's been less than a year. Hey, answer me a question, will you? If you answer right it'll be double the bread."

"Uh...okay," he agreed.

"Did you tell your old man to take his job and kiss off?" She grinned up at him. "Please say you did."

"I..." He laughed. "I didn't use those words, but basically, yeah."

"Cal." Now she jumped across the threshold and hugged him, hard. "What a guy. I knew you had it in you."

"Thanks. I think," Cal said. "Is...is he here?"

His heart pounded until she shook her head. Disappointment and relief mixed in his gut.

"He's on set," she said. "Won't be back until later."

"Oh. Okay. Then I'll just...you can tell him I came by, I can leave a number?"

"Don't you dare," she said, reaching out and grabbing his wrist. She tugged him into the house. "Jack'll never let me hear the end of it if I let you walk away. You can have dinner with us and wait."

As she said the words, he realized that the smells of garlic and onion permeated the house.

"Are you sure?" he asked. "I don't want to be in the way."

She rolled her eyes. "You're not. And there's plenty of food. Ginny is making meatballs and she always makes too much. Come on."

In the kitchen, Ginny was indeed elbow-deep in mixing ground meat, but was equally enthusiastic to see him, kissing him on the cheek when he approached. "I don't even mind that I just lost money," she said. "I'm so glad you're here."

Within minutes, the girls had put him to work chopping vegetables for a salad while they chattered around him. He began to relax, remembering how comfortable he'd become around these people over the summer. He'd missed the ease of it, how they just accepted him without expecting him to be anything or get them anything. He grinned down at the tomatoes.

Greg wandered in as Ginny was transferring the meatballs from the frying pan to the sauce and J.C. was setting water on to boil for the pasta.

"Cal!" he cried. He crossed the room and slapped Cal on the back. "Good to see you, man."

"You too," Cal said, grinning.

Greg went to the fridge and swung the door open. "You want a beer?" he asked.

"Sure," Cal agreed. Then he stopped shredding lettuce and leaned forward, squinting at the refrigerator door. His breath caught in his throat.

Pinned to the center of the door with a tacky plastic lobster magnet, half buried by the flotsam and jetsam of life — postcards, business cards, scraps of paper with phone numbers and grocery lists — was the Polaroid he and Jack had taken together at the dinner party at Radcliffe.

He turned back to the vegetables and tried to focus. It was the only photo on the refrigerator. What did it mean? Had Jack just stuck it up there when he returned, then got used to the sight of it and forgot about it? Or did the fact that it was still there mean Jack still thought of him sometimes?

He spent dinner filling everyone in on his senior year, and hearing what they'd been up to. Ginny had just finished filming a project she was sure was going to be her big break, Greg had landed a job at a music studio, and J.C. was planning to attend UCLA in the fall.

"You inspired me," she said, patting Cal's shoulder. "I can't be arm candy all my life, can I?"

The dinner was cleared away and they were laughing at J.C.'s latest escapades in the dating world when the sound of the door opening made Cal sit up straight.

A voice rang out. The sound of it, earthy and animated, brought Cal right back to the sunny days and secret nights in Westerly. His pulse began to race.

"Hey guys, whose car is that out front? In the dark, it almost looked like...."

Jack came around the corner into the dining room and stopped short.

"Cal," Jack whispered, eyes wide.

Everyone was still for a moment. Cal drank in the sight of the man he had loved — still loved, who was he kidding — and felt all the hollow places inside him fill up all over again. Jack looked the same. His hair was a little longer, but otherwise...

...he was Jack.

Cal got to his feet. "Hi," he said.

"Hi," Jack said. "You...what are you doing here?"

"I'm sorry. I should have called," Cal said. "I didn't know I was coming, and then I was here, and—"

"You don't ever have to call," Jack said. "You're always welcome. Remember?"

"Yeah."

Cal became aware that the others were quietly retreating into other parts of the house. He cleared his throat.

"So...how have you been?" Jack asked.

"Good. I graduated last week. From school," he said, unsure of what else to say.

"Congratulations," Jack said. "Do you...I'm going to get a drink. You want one?"

"Sure," Cal said.

He followed Jack into the kitchen, waited while Jack retrieved two bottles of beer from the fridge and opened them, and then took one. They both took a drink, and then they sat at the small kitchen table. Jack looked at Cal for a moment and smiled.

"You look good," he said.

"You too," said Cal. There was a beat of awkward silence. "How is filming going?"

"It's good," Jack said. "This one is a challenge. The character is a real psycho."

"Sounds interesting." Cal tapped his thumb on his beer bottle. "I saw your last two."

"You did? What did you think?" Jack asked, leaning slightly forward.

"You were great," Cal said. "No surprise there."

Another long beat of silence, and then Jack coughed.

"What brings you to California?" he asked.

"You," Cal said. "I was on my way to Chicago — I have a job there starting in a couple of weeks — but when I got there I just kept going until I was here. I guess I wanted to see you."

Jack set his beer down. "Tell me something. Are you seeing anyone?"

"No," Cal said, shaking his head. "I haven't...there's not anyone. And I broke up with Katherine, back in August."

"Good," Jack said.

Then he stood so fast the chair legs scraped loudly against the floor, and he was across the table and in Cal's lap. Their mouths met immediately, and Cal made an inhuman sound, a groan that came from deep in his chest. He grabbed at Jack, his hands wrapping around the man's biceps and then cupping his neck and chin.

They broke apart gasping.

"Fuck," Jack said. "Please tell me you don't have to leave right away."

"No, I can stay," Cal said. He moved in for another kiss.

"Wait," Jack said. He stood and took Cal's hand. "Come with me."

Cal followed Jack through the house to a bedroom at the back.

"This is me," Jack said, flicking on a lamp to reveal a large, messy room with sleek modern furnishings. He closed the door behind them.

Cal scanned the room, noting all the stuff of *Jack*, and his eyes landed on something familiar. He crossed to the bedside table and picked up an open folder filled with newspaper clippings. His clippings.

"You kept them," he said, a trace of wonder in his voice. "All of them."

"Well...of course," Jack said. "Thank you for sending them to me. They're great, you're good at this."

"You read them?"

"Yeah. I actually...never mind."

Cal set the folder down and peered at Jack. "You what? Tell me."

Jack rubbed a hand on the back of his neck and winced. "I read them at night. Before I go to sleep."

"Because they're boring?" Cal asked. The balloon of disappointment hovered over his head, but Jack's next words stunned him.

"Because they're you. Your voice is so clear, when I read them, I can hear it. Like the one you wrote about Kennedy? And what LBJ should do? After the assassination? Reading it is like having you in the room, and you're just talking to me, about civil rights and leadership and progress. So...I read them before I go to sleep."

Cal stared at Jack, something exploding into life deep in his core.

"So you aren't seeing anyone either?" he asked.

"No," Jack said, laughing. "There's been no one."

"Really?"

"Really."

"Good," Cal said, and this time he launched himself at Jack.

They fell onto the bed kissing, and rolled until Jack was straddling Cal. He pushed himself up, his palms splayed on Cal's chest.

"I missed you," he said softly. "I missed you a ton."

"Me too," Cal said. He tugged at the hem of Jack's t-shirt. "Can I..."

"Yes." Jack wriggled free of his shirt, tossed it aside, and then went to work on the buttons of Cal's Oxford. "You're still wearing these," he murmured.

"Sometimes," Cal said. "I wanted to look nice."

"For me?" Jack asked, looking delighted. "You were worried I would...what? Suddenly not find you the most gorgeous man on earth? Have I gone blind?"

He spread Cal's shirt apart and, with a hum of satisfaction, set to work driving him mad with lips, teeth, and tongue. Cal thought he'd vividly remembered what being with Jack was like, and he did…but it was also so much better in reality than it could ever be in memory.

With a growl, he rolled them over to reverse positions and spent what seemed like forever reacquainting himself with the taste and scent of Jack's skin, the sounds he made, the way he felt.

They didn't rush. Cal would have guessed — if he'd let himself imagine it — that they'd be frantic, but that didn't happen. Instead, they took their time, removing articles of clothing bit by bit, taking turns enjoying each other, until finally, when the house was fully quiet and the moon was high overhead, Cal slid into Jack with a grateful sigh.

They moved together as if no time had passed at all, falling into familiar rhythms and patterns without missing a step. Cal knew what catches of breath to listen for, how Jack's muscles would tense and bunch underneath his fingers, the way his motions would stutter just so as he got close to losing it, and he reveled in all of it.

Afterwards, they lay tangled together, skin slick and hearts racing in a duet of post-exertion percussion. Cal ran his fingers along Jack's arm, up and down, and Jack sighed.

"I'm glad you came," he murmured. "I hoped you would."

"I wasn't sure," Cal said. "I wasn't sure if you'd still want me to. You never…I didn't hear from you at all."

"I know," Jack said. "I thought about calling, but I knew you'd be busy, and I didn't want to interfere. With your life. Any more than I already had."

"Maybe it was better that way," Cal said quietly. "Getting over you was the hardest thing I ever tried to do, and it would have been even harder if you'd…you know."

"So did you? Get over me?" Jack asked, holding himself very still.

Cal buried his face in Jack's curls. "Not even a little bit."

Jack let out a breath. "Good. Me either," he said, sounding relieved. He tipped his head up and caught Cal's lips. "What now?" he asked, when they broke apart.

"I don't know," Cal said.

"You said you were starting a job in Chicago. Does that mean you told your father you didn't want to work for him?" Jack asked.

"I did," Cal said. He laughed. "I ended things with Katherine, got control of my trust, and broke the news to my father the next day. It was like shedding a thousand pounds of weight all at once."

They talked quietly for hours. Cal filled Jack in on his year, his work with the civil rights causes, his writing, taking control of his future. Jack talked about the movies he'd filmed, the books he'd read, the way he'd felt more focused and centered than he ever had before.

As the night wore on, Jack tightened his arms around Cal. "I'm so proud of you," he whispered. "And excited to hear what you've chosen for yourself. What's the job in Chicago?"

"Writing for the *Sun-Times*," Cal said.

"That's so boss," Jack said.

"So—" Cal searched for a way to ask what he desperately wanted to ask. "So I should go to Chicago?"

"Well, you have that lined up," Jack said. "And that's something you want. Right?"

"Where does that leave this? Us? Is there us?" Cal asked, his heart sinking. He'd let himself hope, for a moment, that he could have what he'd dreamed about all summer. But maybe that wasn't the case.

"I think there's us," Jack said. He nibbled on Cal's collarbone and then licked the spot soothingly. "If that's what you want. I can come out and visit. And you can come here. We can talk on the telephone."

"Do you think that will be enough?" Cal asked.

Jack sighed. "I don't know. I hope so? I've never been in love before, Cal. I don't know how to do it."

"You're still in love with me?" Cal asked.

"What do you think?" Jack reached up and kissed Cal soundly.

They were quiet for a while. Cal did his best to enjoy the feel of Jack in his arms, despite knowing that it might not be permanent. But maybe it could be. Jack certainly sounded like he wanted to be with Cal, even with the obstacle of long distance.

At long last, Cal spoke.

"What if I didn't go to Chicago?" he asked.

"No," Jack said. "Don't do that."

"Don't do what?"

"You've spent your whole life doing what other people wanted. I want you to be doing what you want now. I don't want you to change things for me."

Cal wanted to protest, but instead he turned that idea over in his mind. He'd spent the past year taking charge of his life, making sure that it was what he wanted, and not what someone else wanted. It had gotten him this far.

So. What did he want?

"I want you," Cal said. "And you're here. I can always find another job."

Jack pushed himself up so he could peer down at Cal. "Are you sure?" he asked. "I don't want you to be resentful when I fuck things up."

"Why would you fuck things up?" Cal asked.

"Because I'm me," Jack said. He rolled his eyes. "I'm going to make mistakes."

"I will too." Cal sighed. "Nothing is perfect. We'll still need to hide, for your career."

"Maybe," Jack said. "But maybe not forever. Maybe things will change. I changed because of last summer. So did you."

Cal considered that. It was true, with the civil rights movement having momentum, maybe things would change. Maybe one day, he'd be able to stand proudly by Jack's side, and not have to hide in the shadows.

Maybe he could be a part of bringing about that change. Maybe they could, together.

"I'm willing to try if you are," Cal said, kissing Jack gently.

"Stay with me," Jack said, kissing him back.

"Okay," said Cal. He grinned. "Whatever happens, we'll have a marvelous time."

AUTHOR'S NOTE

Cal and Jack's story takes place in 1963, a turbulent and crucial period in the Civil Rights history of the United States. At this time, in the shadow of the overt threats of the McCarthy Era, early gay rights demonstrations were just beginning and only Illinois had repealed its sodomy laws. Essentially, being gay was a felony in every other state in the country, and this fact changed slowly; it was only in the landmark case of Lawrence v. Texas in 2003 that the Supreme Court declared sodomy laws unconstitutional. Discrimination against LGBTQIA+ citizens was common and accepted, and Cal and Jack would have been unusual because of Cal's financial freedom, which gave him choices many others did not have.

I wrote this story because the celebration of queerness and queer love has never been more important than in a time when being queer and the right to loving as we see fit are under attack by powers that be. While we have made much progress since Cal and Jack's time, the current period in the nation's history is an unstable one for many people who rely on the rights they have fought so hard to protect. For a country that purports to subscribe to the holy grail of individual rights, there is frightening rhetoric and there are even more frightening actions that threaten the ability of people to live as their true selves with dignity, safety, and joy.

We can't go back.

~

To contribute to the defense of the LGBTQIA+ community and equal rights and dignity for all, please consider the following causes.

- Trevor Project - https://www.thetrevorproject.org/
- Lambda Legal - https://legacy.lambdalegal.org/
- American Civil Liberties Union - https://www.aclu.org/
- Out & Equal - https://outandequal.org/
- LGBTQ Freedom Fund - https://www.lgbtqfund.org/
- Center for Black Equity - https://centerforblackequity.org/
- National Center for Transgender Equality - https://glaad.org/tag/national-center-for-trans-equality/
- Matthew Shepard Foundation - https://www.matthewshepard.org/
- Transgender Law Center - https://transgenderlawcenter.org/
- The Equality Federation - https://www.equalityfederation.org/

To help fight the banning of books with LGBTQIA+ content, consider supporting these organizations:

- Lambda Literary Foundation - https://lambdaliterary.org/
- LGBT Books to Prisoners - https://lgbtbookstoprisoners.org/
- American Library Association's Unite Against Book Banning - https://uniteagainst bookbans.org/

And, if *you* need help and support:

- Trevor Project - https://www.thetrevorproject.org/get-help/ or call 1-866-488-7386 or text "START" to 678-678
- Trans Lifeline - https://translifeline.org/ or call 877-565-8860
- LGBT National Help Center - https://lgbthotline.org/ or call 888-843-4564
- Sage LGBT Elder Hotline - https://www.sageusa.org/hearme/
- National Suicide Prevention Lifeline - https://988lifeline.org/ or call 988
- Crisis Text Line - https://www.crisistextline.org/ or text "HOME" to 741741

An updated list of the above can be found at the author's website, stbellauthor.com.

ACKNOWLEDGMENTS

For as long as I've been able to talk, I've been telling stories. This book is the culmination of a lifetime of storytelling and the support of the greatest cheerleading squad, coaches, and teammates anyone could imagine.

Thank you to Mom and Dad, for encouraging my storytelling and writing from day one, and thanks for letting me read anything I wanted and not restricting me to the kids' section of the library after I'd read everything in there twice.

To my writing crew in Boston, you were the incubator I needed at the exact right time of my life and I miss you terribly. Carrie, Rebecca, Tara, Annie, Lauren, Julia, and Katie, you're all magicians with words and the kindest critique partners to exist and you deserve the world.

To my beta readers and editors, this would not have been possible without your honest feedback, eagle eyes, and excitement. To name a few: Joy, Speedy, Sheeri, Bonnie, Freya, Dr. Sin, Laurel, Kayla, Sophie, Ashley, and Cristobal. Your partnership has been invaluable and I hope you're in this for the long haul because there are many more stories to come.

To Adele, who is the best artist I could possibly have hoped for. You made my cover dreams come true and were a patient guide throughout this process.

To Avery, my tech guru who never hesitates to take time out of your day to help me fumble through the technical aspects of this adventure, you have saved my sanity on multiple occasions.

To my online community who welcomed me with open arms, screamed with joy over the things that emerged from my brain, and always said such nice things to me even when I didn't deserve it, this would definitely never have happened without your enthusiasm and support.

To Pete and Jenyon, thanks for decades of friendship and enthusiastic encouragement.

To Stephanie, Kelly, Jessica, Jami, and Benjamin, you kept me sane when our professional lives were definitely anything but, providing me with the emotional energy I needed to keep going.

To Rhode Island, for being the quirkiest little state in the nation.

To Samantha and Alice, who might one day read this and be proud of their Auntie; and to Erik and Robin, just because.

And to Linda, my partner-in-crime since childhood, you have always been my most vocal fan and greatest (but most loving) nag. I have this to say to you: I finally published something! I hope it was worth the wait.

ABOUT THE AUTHOR

 S.T. Bell lives in Austin, Texas, with two cats and a list of life ambitions that could fill an entire library. Writing is just one of these ambitions, but it's the one that has been around the longest.

When not writing, she can be found tripping over rocks on a hiking trail, ruining a bake in the kitchen, tangling up yarn while crocheting, forgetting what she came into the room for, or otherwise making good trouble.

stbellauthor.com

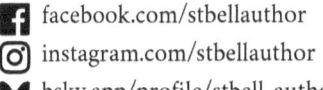 facebook.com/stbellauthor
instagram.com/stbellauthor
bsky.app/profile/stbell-author

www.ingramcontent.com/pod-product-compliance
Lightning Source LLC
Chambersburg PA
CBHW020123120726
47903CB00007B/2079